c o p p e r

graphix

AN IMPRINT OF

■SCHOLASTIC

New York   Toronto   London   Auckland   Sydney   Mexico City   New Delhi   Hong Kong

ISBN: 978-0-545-09892-2 (hardcover)
ISBN: 978-0-545-09893-9 (paperback)

10 9 8 7 6 5 4   12 13 14

First edition, January 2010
Edited by Sheila Keenan
Creative Director: David Saylor
Book design by Phil Falco
Printed in Singapore   46

CONTENTS

The *Copper* comics began life as a design for a sticker and a T-shirt. The design featured a scared little boy and his equally scared-looking dog; underneath this picture was the line "I live in a strange town."

This first *Copper* image and text was reflective of a time in my life when things weren't working out so well: My parents needed financial assistance; I lost my graphic design job; I was kicked out of my apartment; and I was attacked by a crazy guy in the street who told me to go back to my "home country," all in the span of two days. The saying "When it rains, it pours" never felt so apt.

A few months later, I snapped out of my funk and decided to pursue the career that I always felt best suited my abilities: cartooning. I had been drawing cartoons all my life, but had never committed to cartooning as a profession. All of a sudden, my cartoons mattered to me more than ever before.

I had a chance to contribute a comic to an Asian American magazine and thought back to that image of the scared boy and dog. I decided to give them names and draw a story about them. That story, "Rocket Pack Fantasy," which you can see on page 5, was the first published comic that I actually took very seriously, since I had produced mostly immature comic strips up to that point.

What had begun as a somewhat dark comic strip series quickly became more optimistic, more hopeful. The boy, Copper, was at first an observer, but by the third comic he became an active participant in his world, making choices based on his hopes and fears. Fred, the dog, was always there to question his best friend's optimism, but Copper walked ahead with his ideals, undeterred. In many ways the characters reflected my life at the time I wrote these strips, and as I look back at them I feel like I can see myself growing up. Drawing these comics gave me a sense of confidence in myself and helped me develop a sense of purpose in the work that I do. These are among the many reasons Copper and Fred hold a special place in my heart. I love these guys dearly, and I hope you enjoy their adventures as much as I have over the years.

Kazu

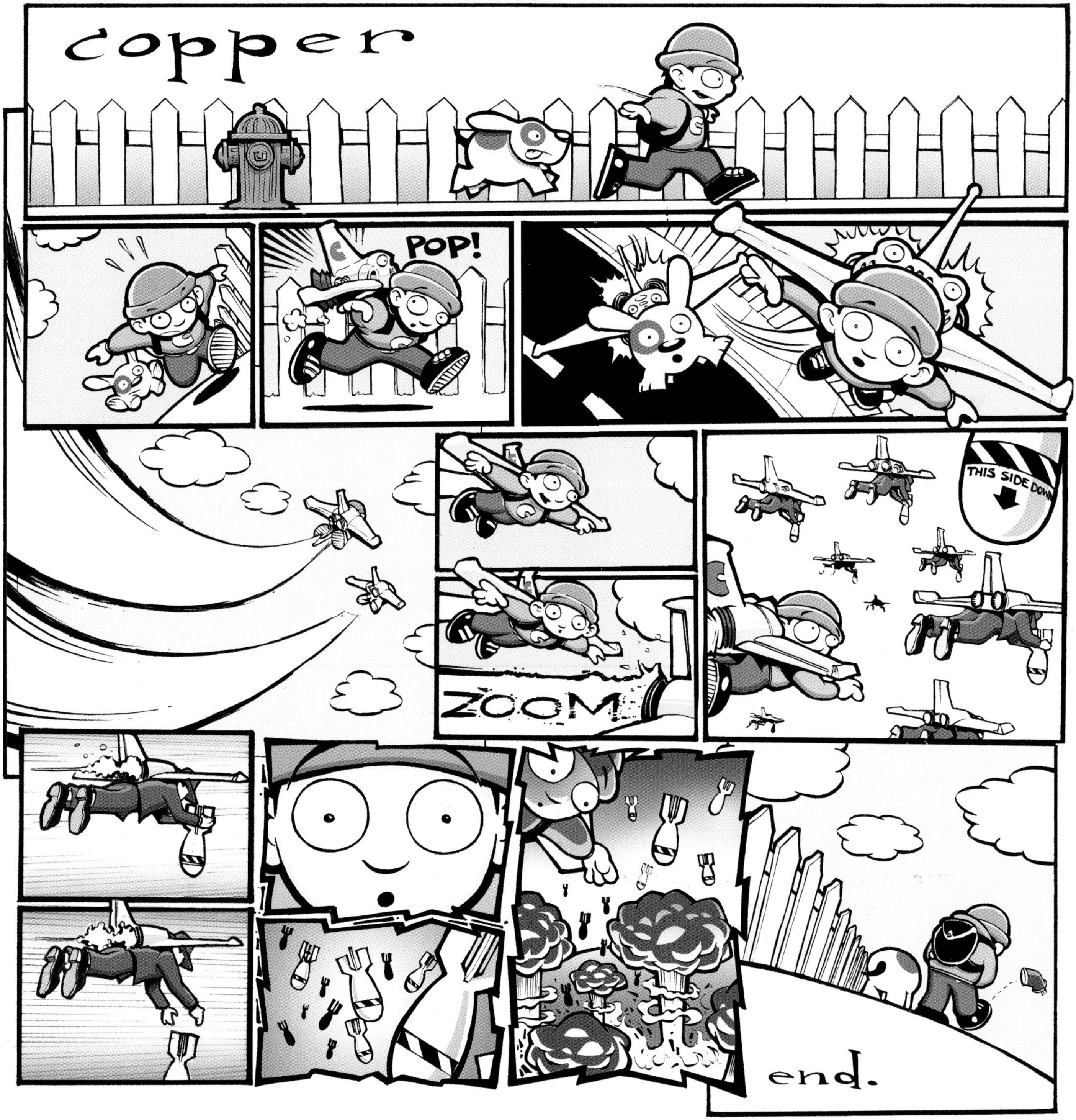
copper
POP!
THIS SIDE DOWN
ZOOM!
end.

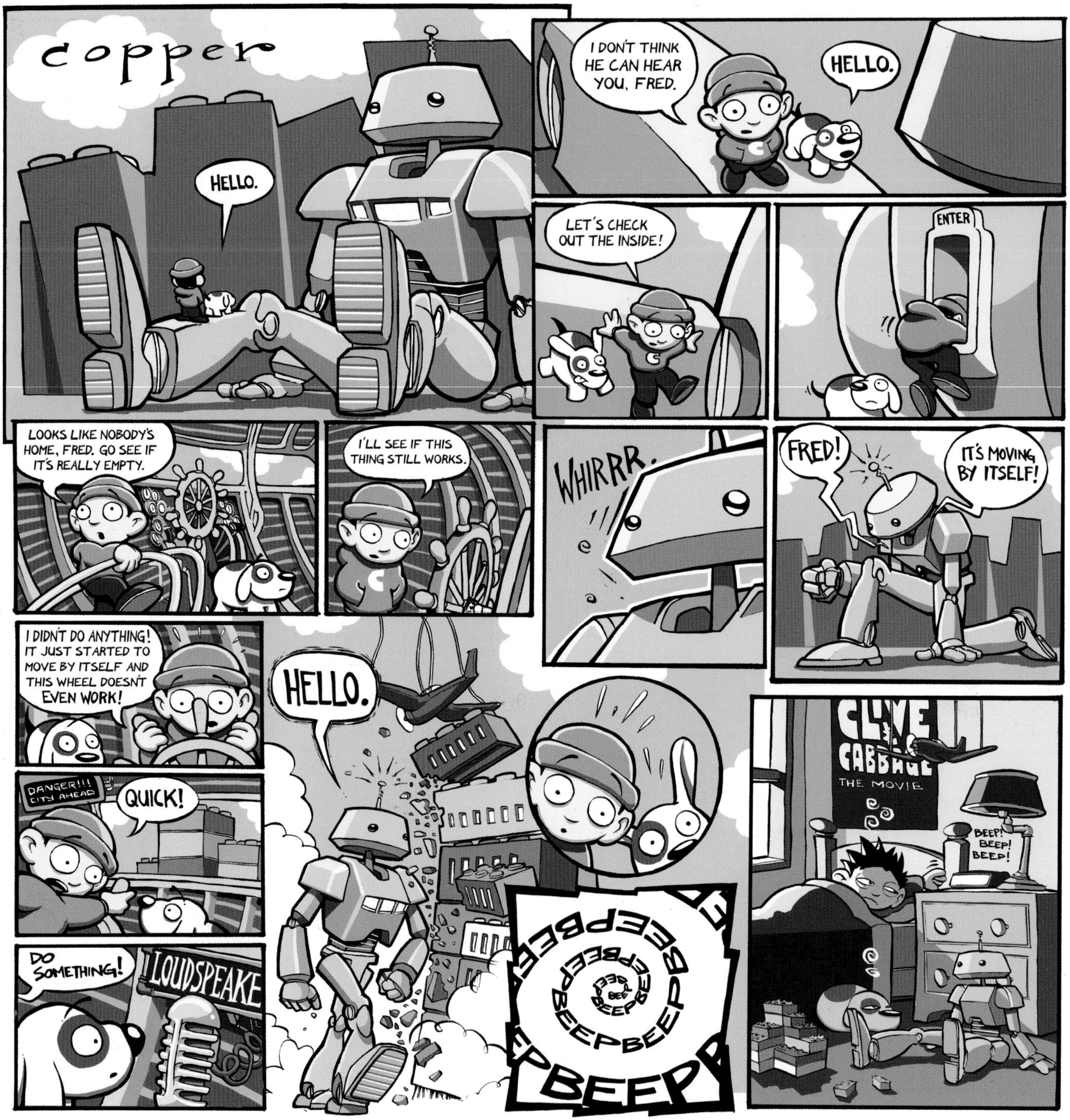
copper
HELLO.
I DON'T THINK HE CAN HEAR YOU, FRED.
HELLO.
LET'S CHECK OUT THE INSIDE!
ENTER
LOOKS LIKE NOBODY'S HOME, FRED. GO SEE IF IT'S REALLY EMPTY.
I'LL SEE IF THIS THING STILL WORKS.
WHIRRR.
FRED!
IT'S MOVING BY ITSELF!
I DIDN'T DO ANYTHING! IT JUST STARTED TO MOVE BY ITSELF AND THIS WHEEL DOESN'T EVEN WORK!
HELLO.
DANGER!!! CITY AHEAD
QUICK!
DO SOMETHING!
LOUDSPEAKE
BEEPBEEPBEEPBEEPBEEPBEEP
CLIVE & CABBAGE THE MOVIE
BEEP! BEEP! BEEP!

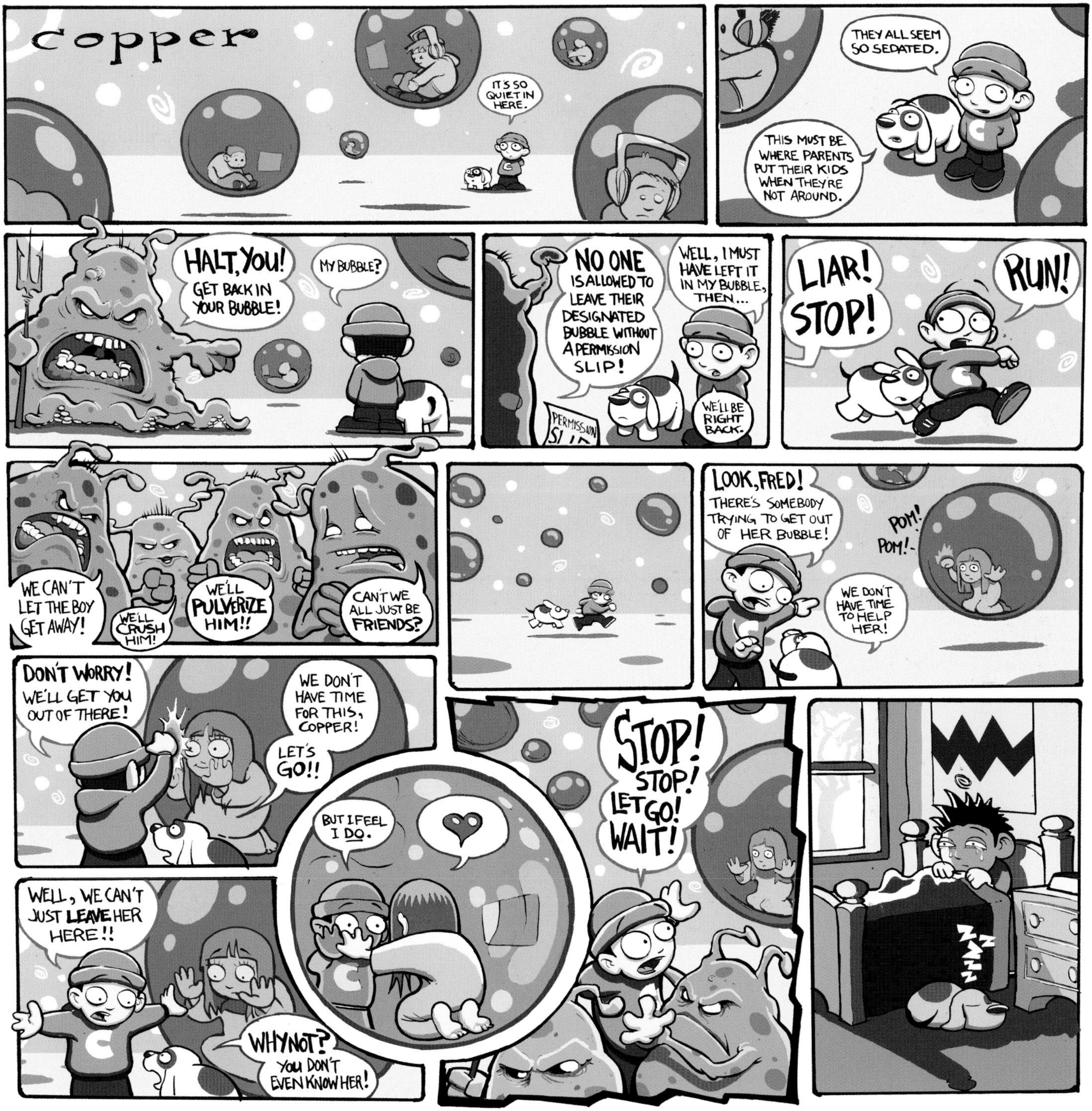
copper
IT'S SO QUIET IN HERE.
THEY ALL SEEM SO SEDATED.
THIS MUST BE WHERE PARENTS PUT THEIR KIDS WHEN THEY'RE NOT AROUND.
HALT, YOU! GET BACK IN YOUR BUBBLE!
MY BUBBLE?
NO ONE IS ALLOWED TO LEAVE THEIR DESIGNATED BUBBLE WITHOUT A PERMISSION SLIP!
WELL, I MUST HAVE LEFT IT IN MY BUBBLE, THEN...
WE'LL BE RIGHT BACK.
PERMISSION SLIP
LIAR! STOP!
RUN!
WE CAN'T LET THE BOY GET AWAY!
WE'LL CRUSH HIM!
WE'LL PULVERIZE HIM!!
CAN'T WE ALL JUST BE FRIENDS?
LOOK, FRED! THERE'S SOMEBODY TRYING TO GET OUT OF HER BUBBLE!
POM! POM!
WE DON'T HAVE TIME TO HELP HER!
DON'T WORRY! WE'LL GET YOU OUT OF THERE!
WE DON'T HAVE TIME FOR THIS, COPPER!
LET'S GO!!
WELL, WE CAN'T JUST LEAVE HER HERE!!
WHY NOT? YOU DON'T EVEN KNOW HER!
BUT I FEEL I DO.
STOP! STOP! LET GO! WAIT!
Z Z Z Z

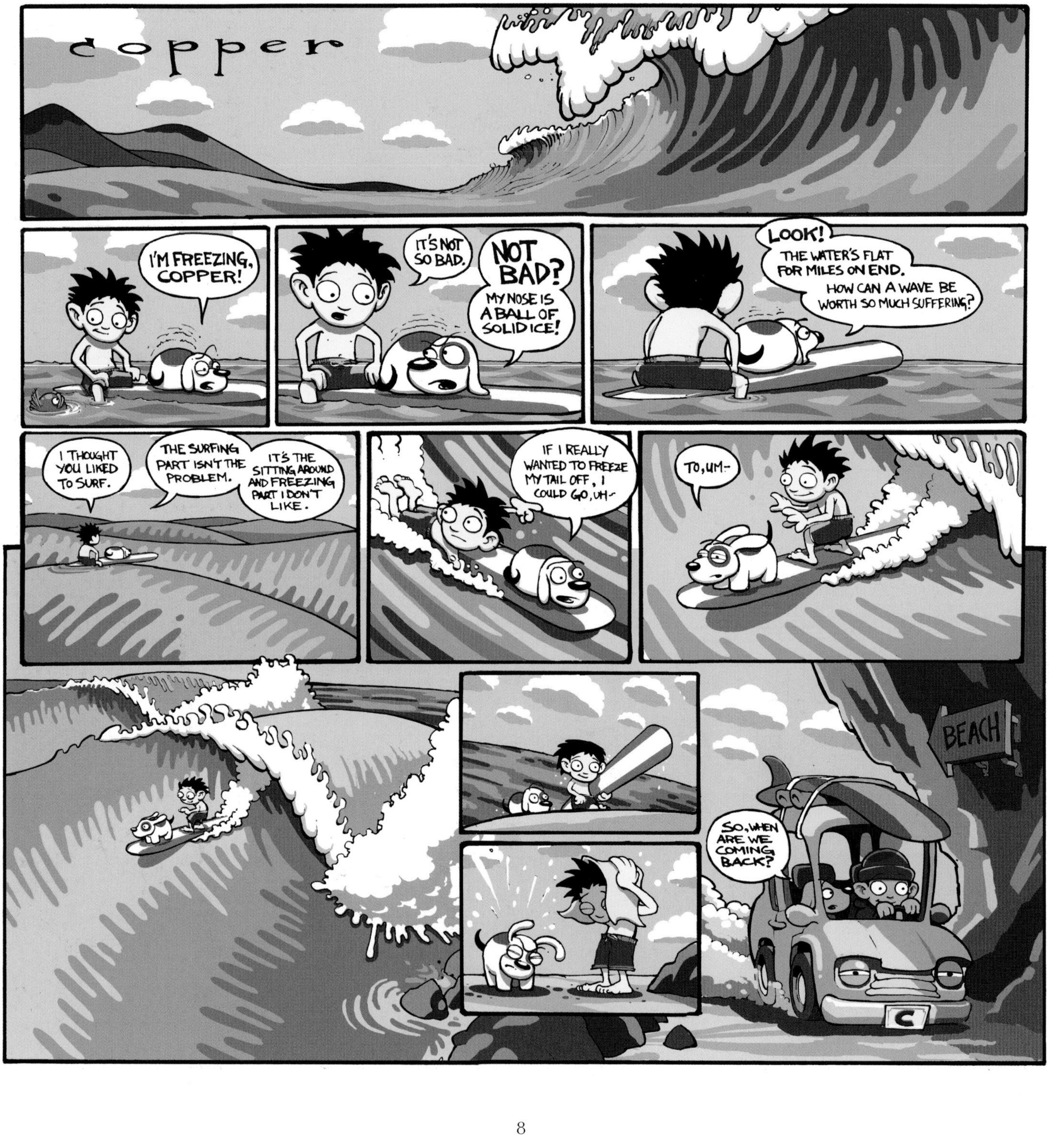
copper
I'M FREEZING, COPPER!
IT'S NOT SO BAD.
NOT BAD?
MY NOSE IS A BALL OF SOLID ICE!
LOOK!
THE WATER'S FLAT FOR MILES ON END.
HOW CAN A WAVE BE WORTH SO MUCH SUFFERING?
I THOUGHT YOU LIKED TO SURF.
THE SURFING PART ISN'T THE PROBLEM.
IT'S THE SITTING AROUND AND FREEZING PART I DON'T LIKE.
IF I REALLY WANTED TO FREEZE MY TAIL OFF, I COULD GO, UH-
TO, UM-
BEACH
SO, WHEN ARE WE COMING BACK?
C

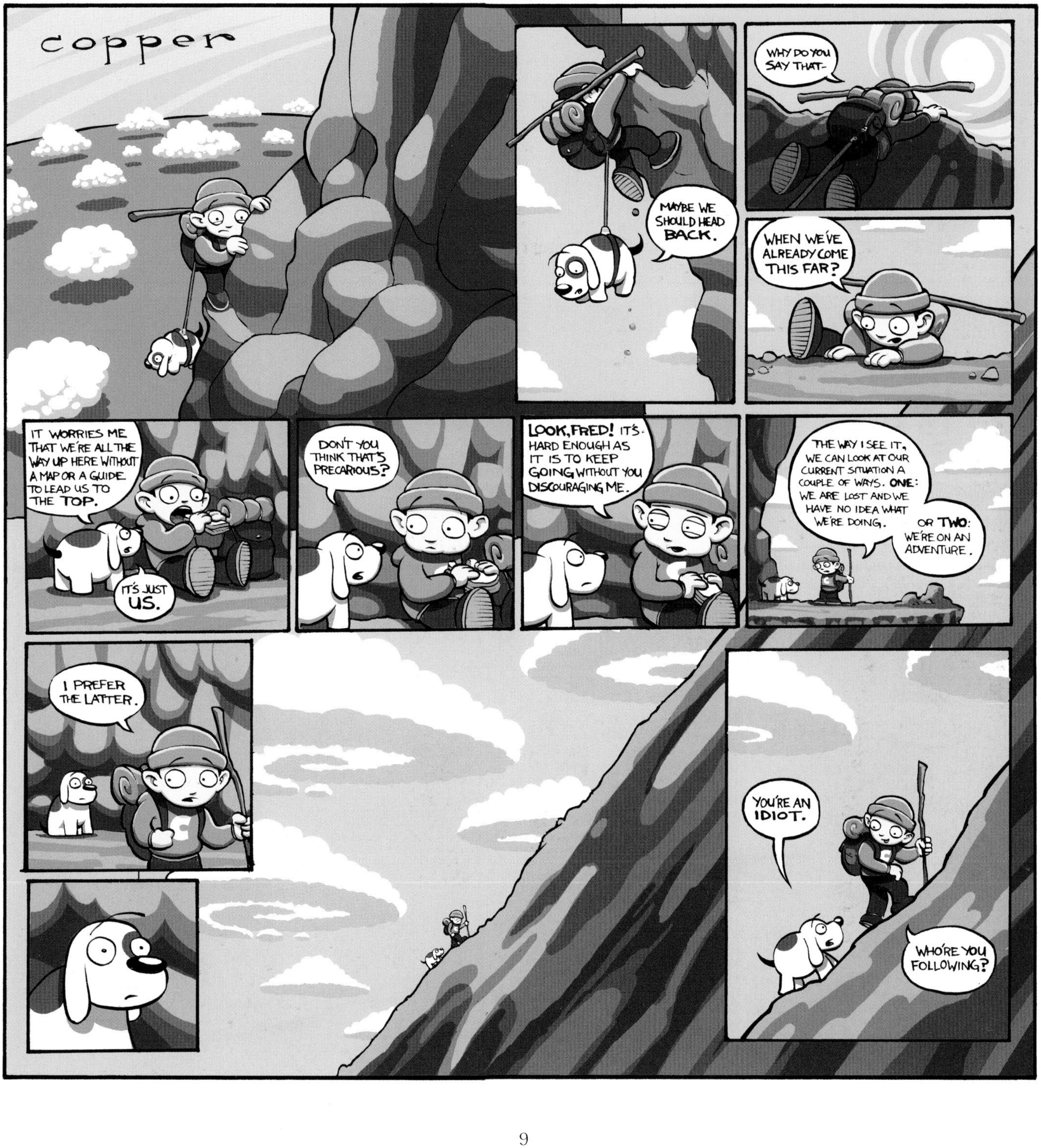
copper
MAYBE WE SHOULD HEAD BACK.
WHY DO YOU SAY THAT-
WHEN WE'VE ALREADY COME THIS FAR?
IT WORRIES ME THAT WE'RE ALL THE WAY UP HERE WITHOUT A MAP OR A GUIDE TO LEAD US TO THE TOP.
IT'S JUST US.
DON'T YOU THINK THAT'S PRECARIOUS?
LOOK, FRED! IT'S HARD ENOUGH AS IT IS TO KEEP GOING WITHOUT YOU DISCOURAGING ME.
THE WAY I SEE IT, WE CAN LOOK AT OUR CURRENT SITUATION A COUPLE OF WAYS. ONE: WE ARE LOST AND WE HAVE NO IDEA WHAT WE'RE DOING.
OR TWO: WE'RE ON AN ADVENTURE.
I PREFER THE LATTER.
YOU'RE AN IDIOT.
WHO'RE YOU FOLLOWING?

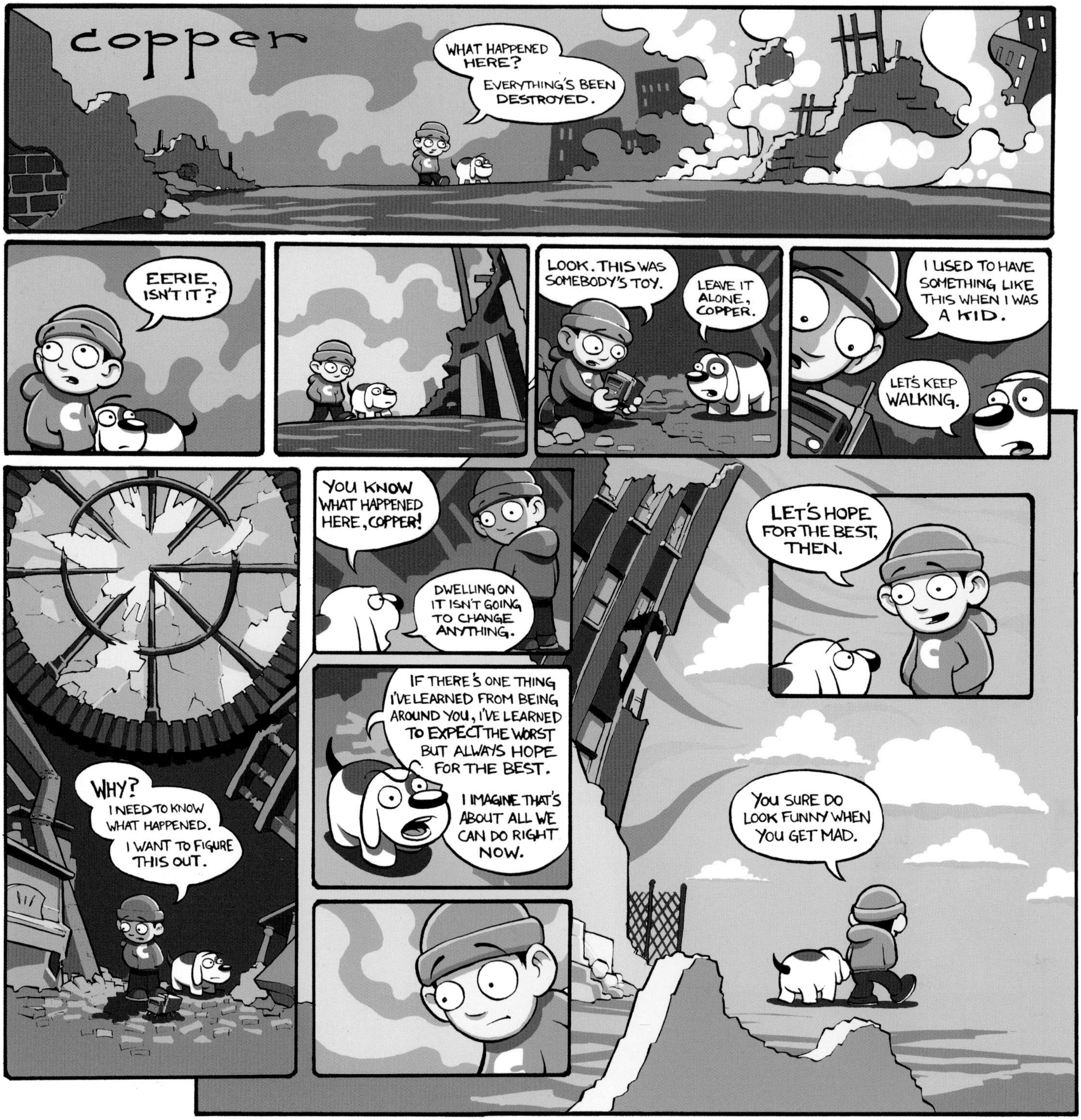
copper
WHAT HAPPENED HERE?
EVERYTHING'S BEEN DESTROYED.
EERIE, ISN'T IT?
LOOK. THIS WAS SOMEBODY'S TOY.
LEAVE IT ALONE, COPPER.
I USED TO HAVE SOMETHING LIKE THIS WHEN I WAS A KID.
LET'S KEEP WALKING.
WHY?
I NEED TO KNOW WHAT HAPPENED.
I WANT TO FIGURE THIS OUT.
YOU KNOW WHAT HAPPENED HERE, COPPER!
DWELLING ON IT ISN'T GOING TO CHANGE ANYTHING.
IF THERE'S ONE THING I'VE LEARNED FROM BEING AROUND YOU, I'VE LEARNED TO EXPECT THE WORST BUT ALWAYS HOPE FOR THE BEST.
I IMAGINE THAT'S ABOUT ALL WE CAN DO RIGHT NOW.
LET'S HOPE FOR THE BEST, THEN.
YOU SURE DO LOOK FUNNY WHEN YOU GET MAD.

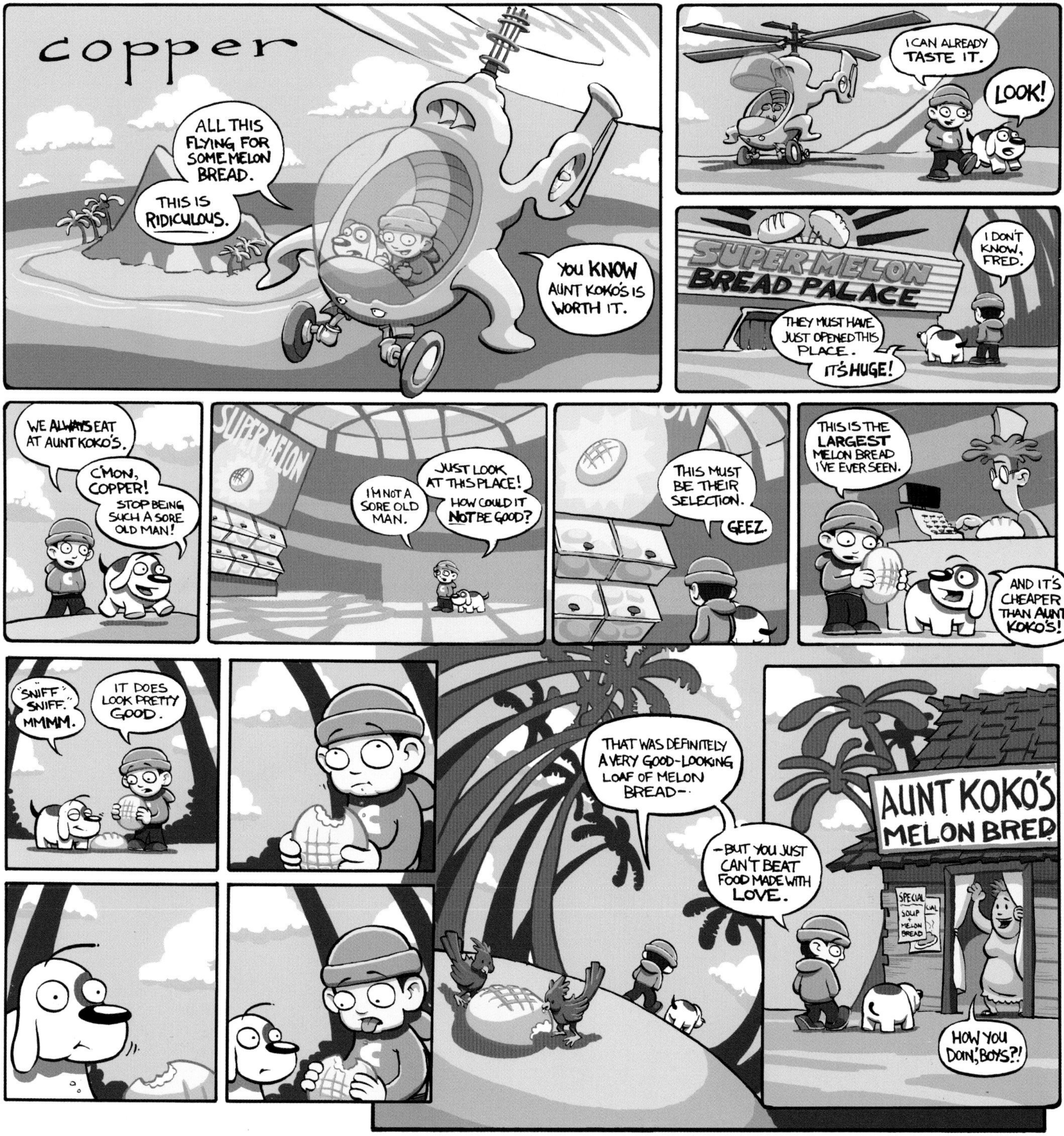
copper
ALL THIS FLYING FOR SOME MELON BREAD.
THIS IS RIDICULOUS.
YOU KNOW AUNT KOKO'S IS WORTH IT.
I CAN ALREADY TASTE IT.
LOOK!
SUPER MELON BREAD PALACE
THEY MUST HAVE JUST OPENED THIS PLACE.
IT'S HUGE!
I DON'T KNOW, FRED.
WE ALWAYS EAT AT AUNT KOKO'S.
C'MON, COPPER!
STOP BEING SUCH A SORE OLD MAN!
SUPER MELON
I'M NOT A SORE OLD MAN.
JUST LOOK AT THIS PLACE!
HOW COULD IT NOT BE GOOD?
THIS MUST BE THEIR SELECTION.
GEEZ.
THIS IS THE LARGEST MELON BREAD I'VE EVER SEEN.
AND IT'S CHEAPER THAN AUNT KOKO'S!
"SNIFF SNIFF." MMMM.
IT DOES LOOK PRETTY GOOD.
THAT WAS DEFINITELY A VERY GOOD-LOOKING LOAF OF MELON BREAD—
—BUT YOU JUST CAN'T BEAT FOOD MADE WITH LOVE.
AUNT KOKO'S MELON BRED
SPECIAL SOUP + MELON BREAD
HOW YOU DOIN', BOYS?!

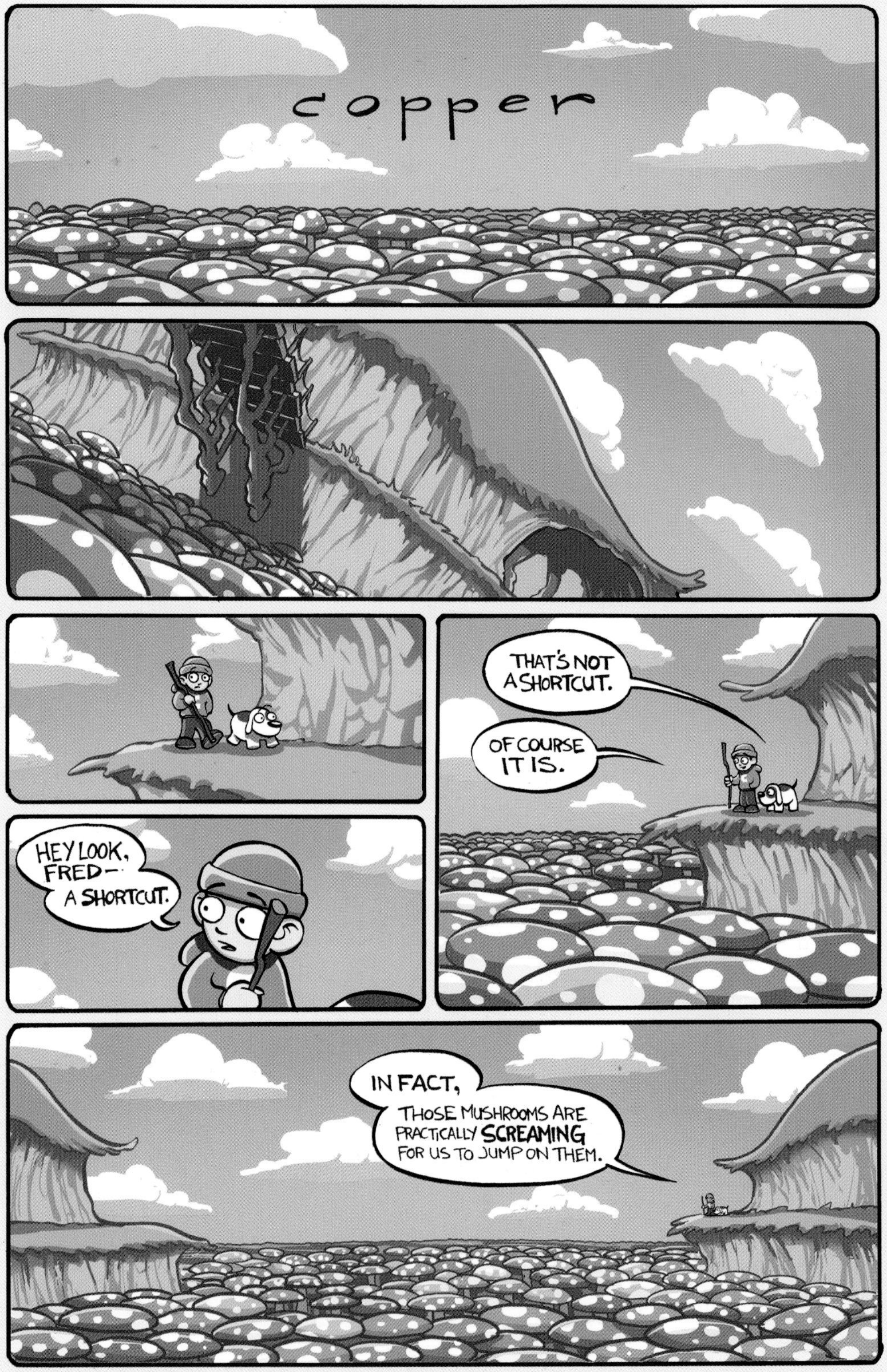
copper
HEY LOOK, FRED- A SHORTCUT.
THAT'S NOT A SHORTCUT.
OF COURSE IT IS.
IN FACT, THOSE MUSHROOMS ARE PRACTICALLY SCREAMING FOR US TO JUMP ON THEM.

M U S H R O O M C R O S S I N G

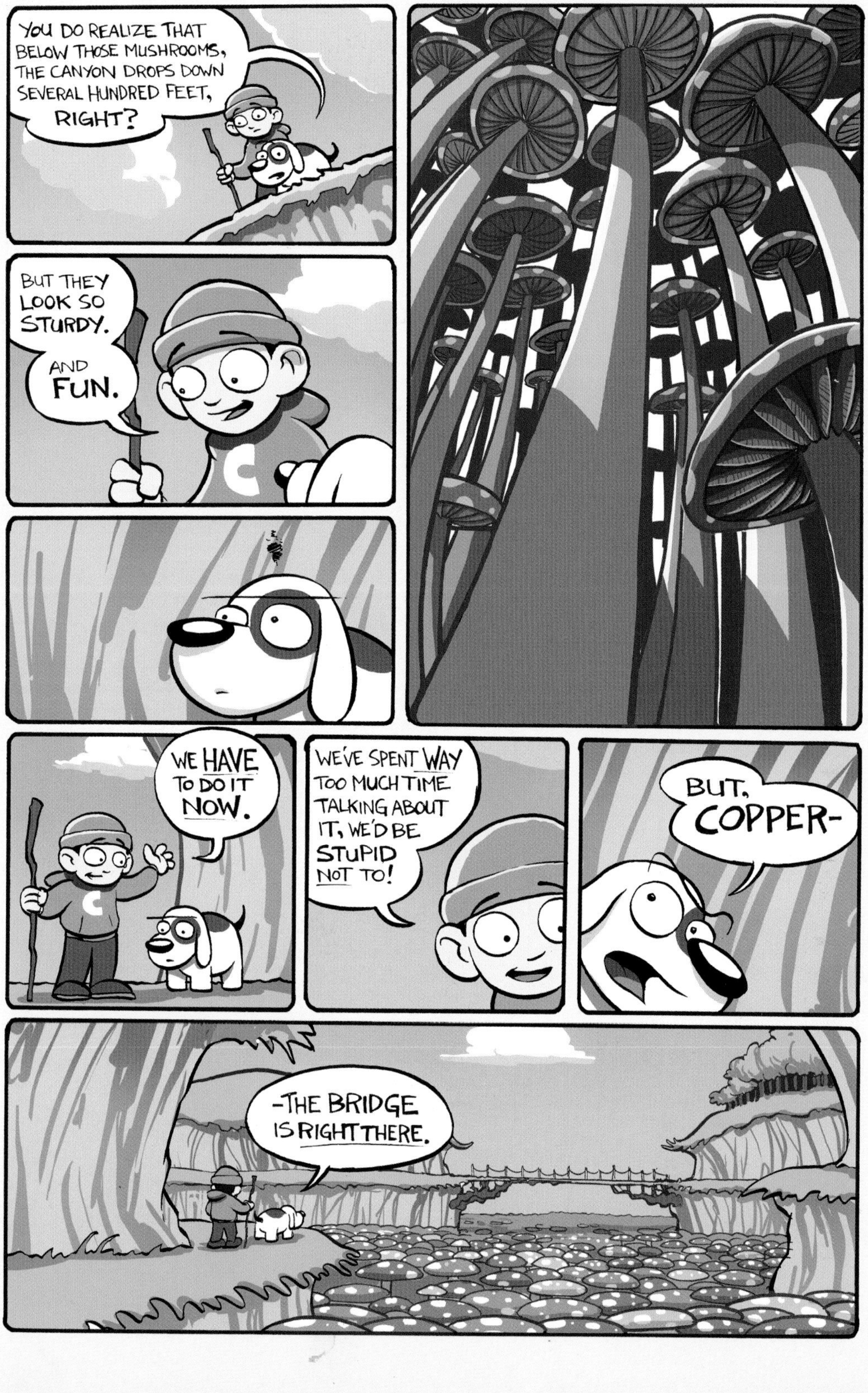
YOU DO REALIZE THAT BELOW THOSE MUSHROOMS, THE CANYON DROPS DOWN SEVERAL HUNDRED FEET, RIGHT?
BUT THEY LOOK SO STURDY.
AND FUN.
WE HAVE TO DO IT NOW.
WE'VE SPENT WAY TOO MUCH TIME TALKING ABOUT IT, WE'D BE STUPID NOT TO!
BUT, COPPER-
-THE BRIDGE IS RIGHT THERE.

M U S H R O O M   C R O S S I N G

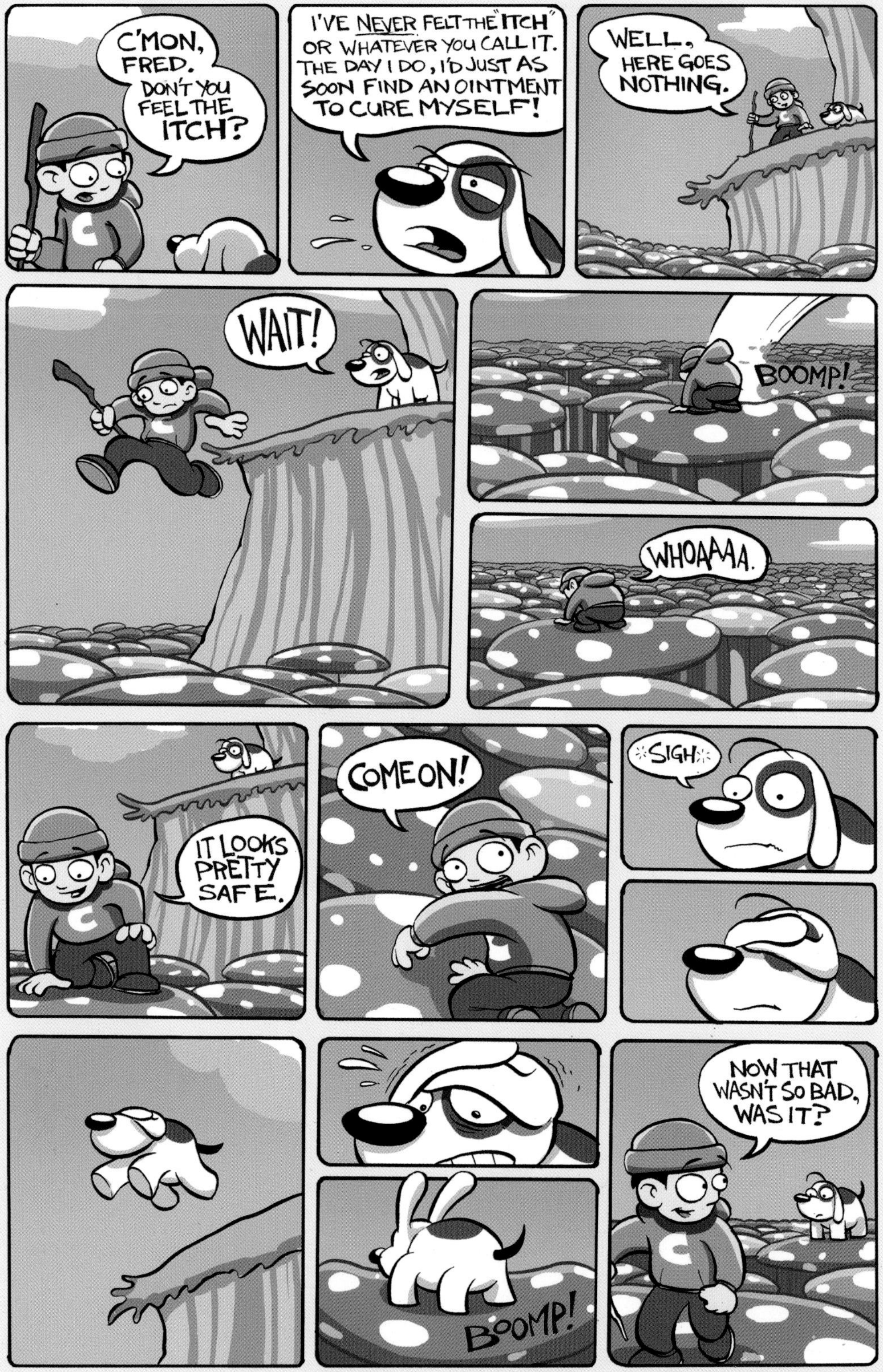

C'MON, FRED. DON'T YOU FEEL THE ITCH?
I'VE NEVER FELT THE "ITCH" OR WHATEVER YOU CALL IT. THE DAY I DO, I'D JUST AS SOON FIND AN OINTMENT TO CURE MYSELF!
WELL, HERE GOES NOTHING.
WAIT!
BOOMP!
WHOAAAA.
IT LOOKS PRETTY SAFE.
COME ON!
SIGH
BOOMP!
NOW THAT WASN'T SO BAD, WAS IT?

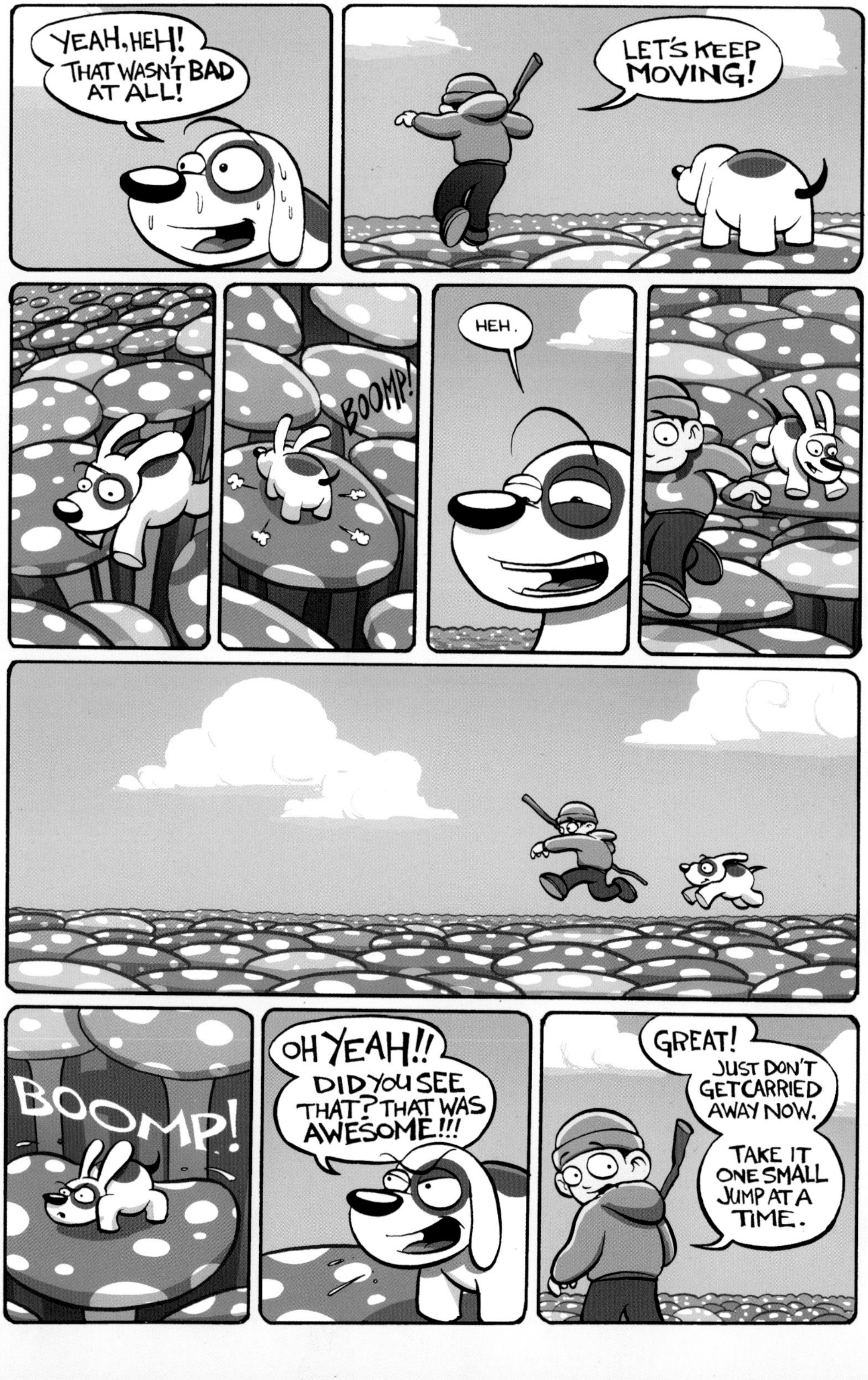
YEAH, HEH! THAT WASN'T BAD AT ALL!
LET'S KEEP MOVING!
BOOMP!
HEH.
OH YEAH!! DID YOU SEE THAT? THAT WAS AWESOME!!!
GREAT! JUST DON'T GET CARRIED AWAY NOW.
TAKE IT ONE SMALL JUMP AT A TIME.

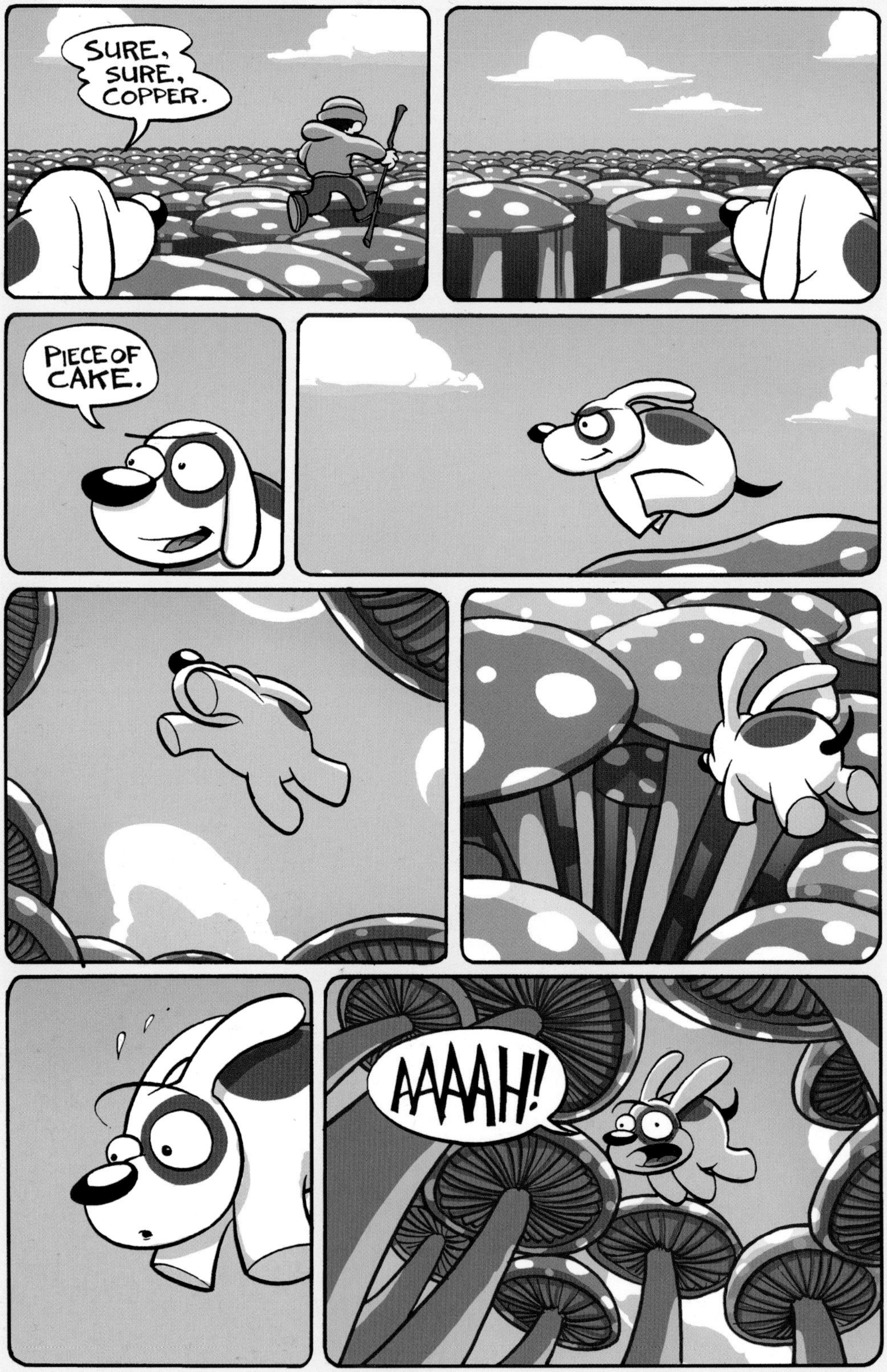
SURE, SURE, COPPER.
PIECE OF CAKE.
AAAAH!

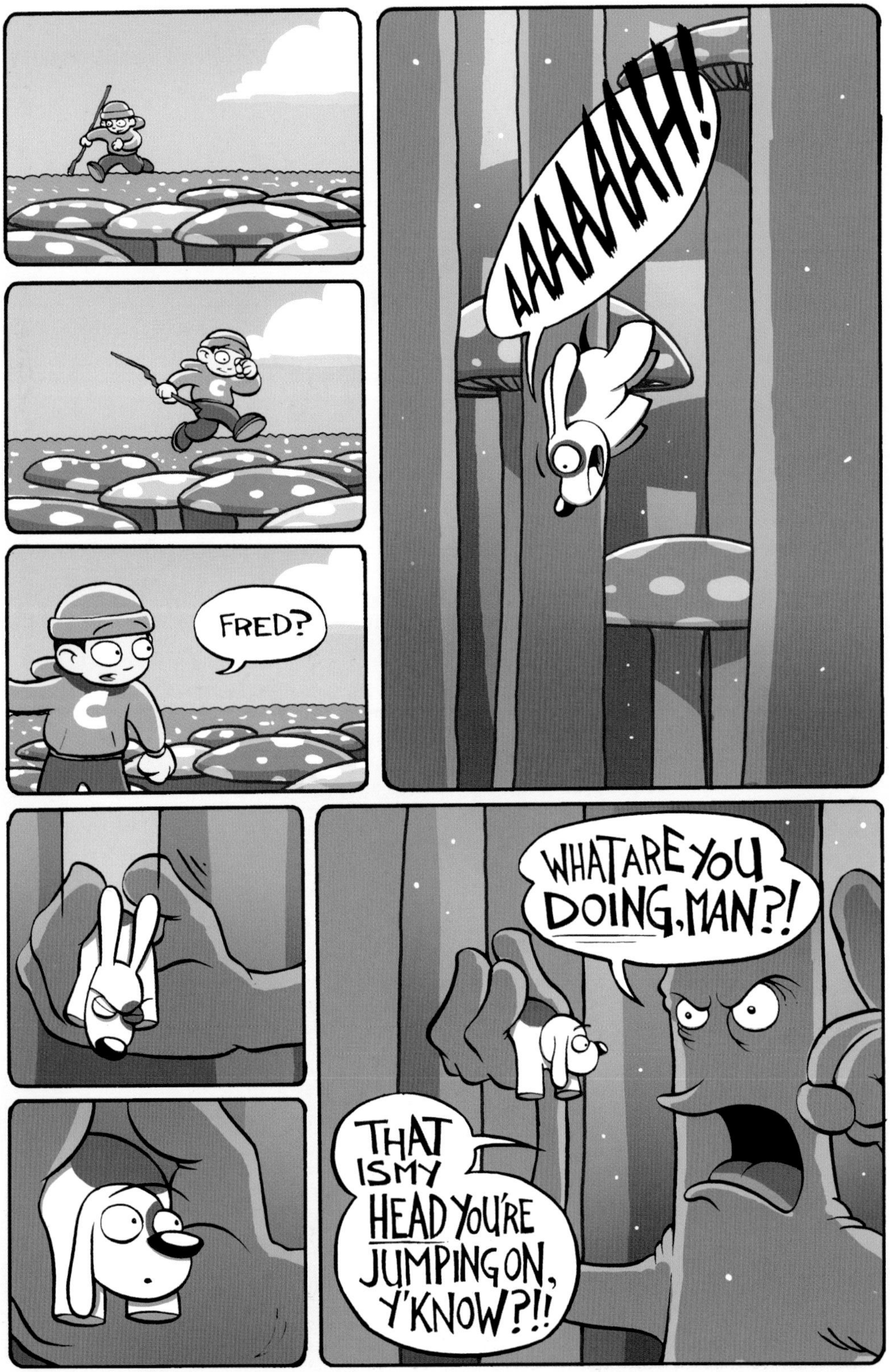
FRED?
AAAAAAH!
WHAT ARE YOU DOING, MAN?!
THAT IS MY HEAD YOU'RE JUMPING ON, Y'KNOW?!!

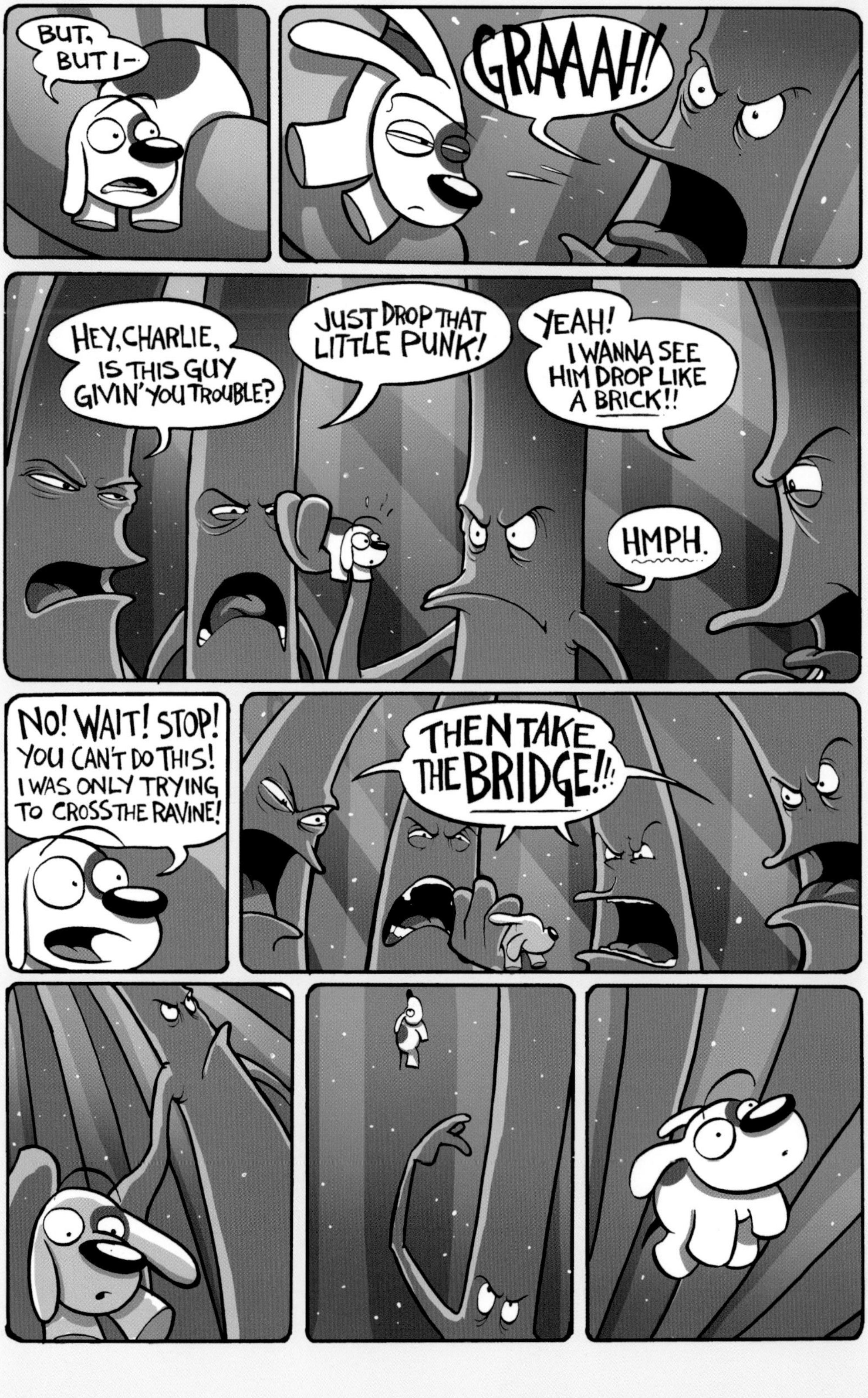
BUT, BUT I-
GRAAAH!
HEY, CHARLIE, IS THIS GUY GIVIN' YOU TROUBLE?
JUST DROP THAT LITTLE PUNK!
YEAH! I WANNA SEE HIM DROP LIKE A BRICK!!
HMPH.
NO! WAIT! STOP! YOU CAN'T DO THIS! I WAS ONLY TRYING TO CROSS THE RAVINE!
THEN TAKE THE BRIDGE!!!

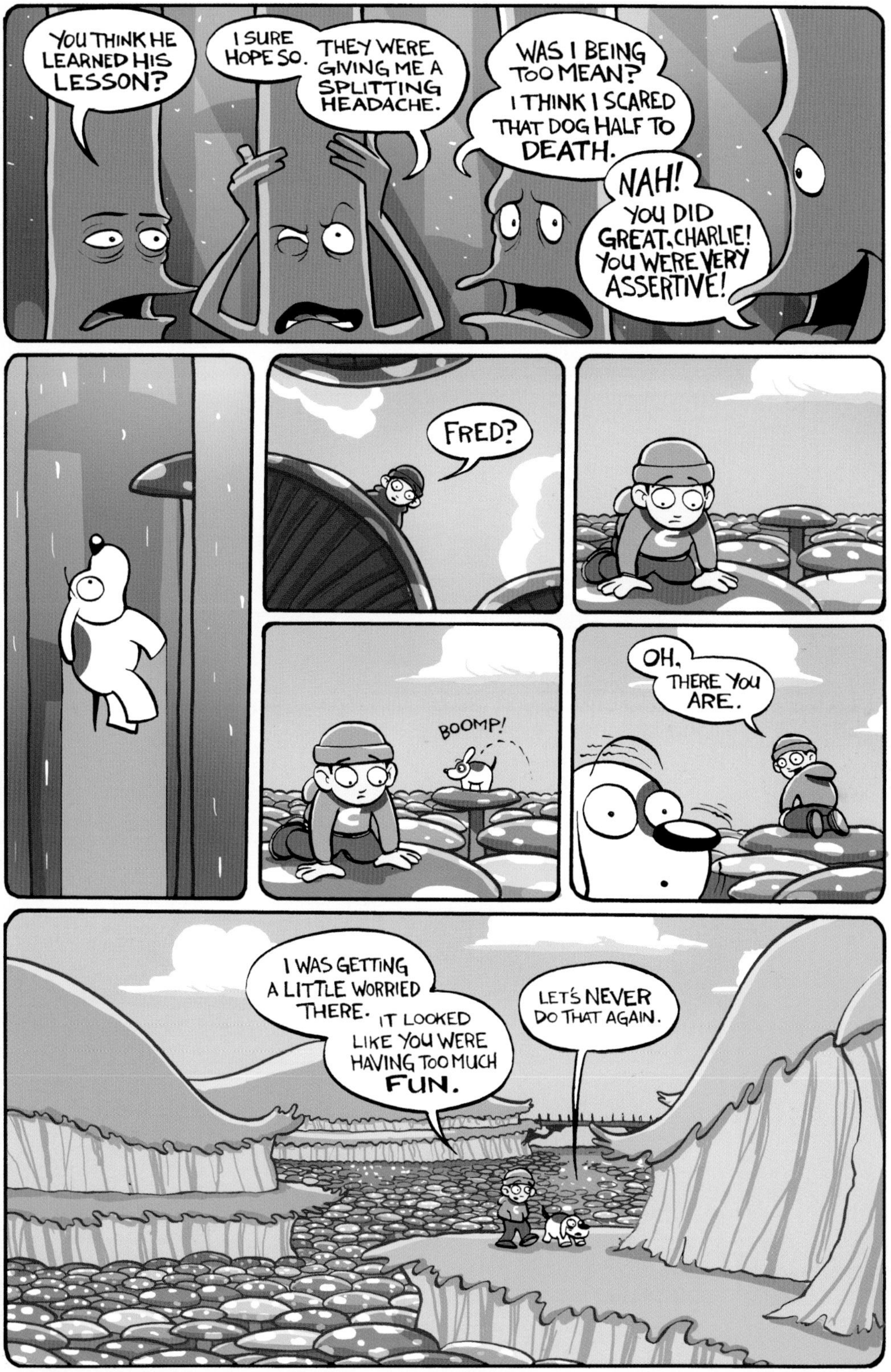
YOU THINK HE LEARNED HIS LESSON?
I SURE HOPE SO.
THEY WERE GIVING ME A SPLITTING HEADACHE.
WAS I BEING TOO MEAN?
I THINK I SCARED THAT DOG HALF TO DEATH.
NAH! YOU DID GREAT, CHARLIE! YOU WERE VERY ASSERTIVE!
FRED?
BOOMP!
OH, THERE YOU ARE.
I WAS GETTING A LITTLE WORRIED THERE.
IT LOOKED LIKE YOU WERE HAVING TOO MUCH FUN.
LET'S NEVER DO THAT AGAIN.

the end.

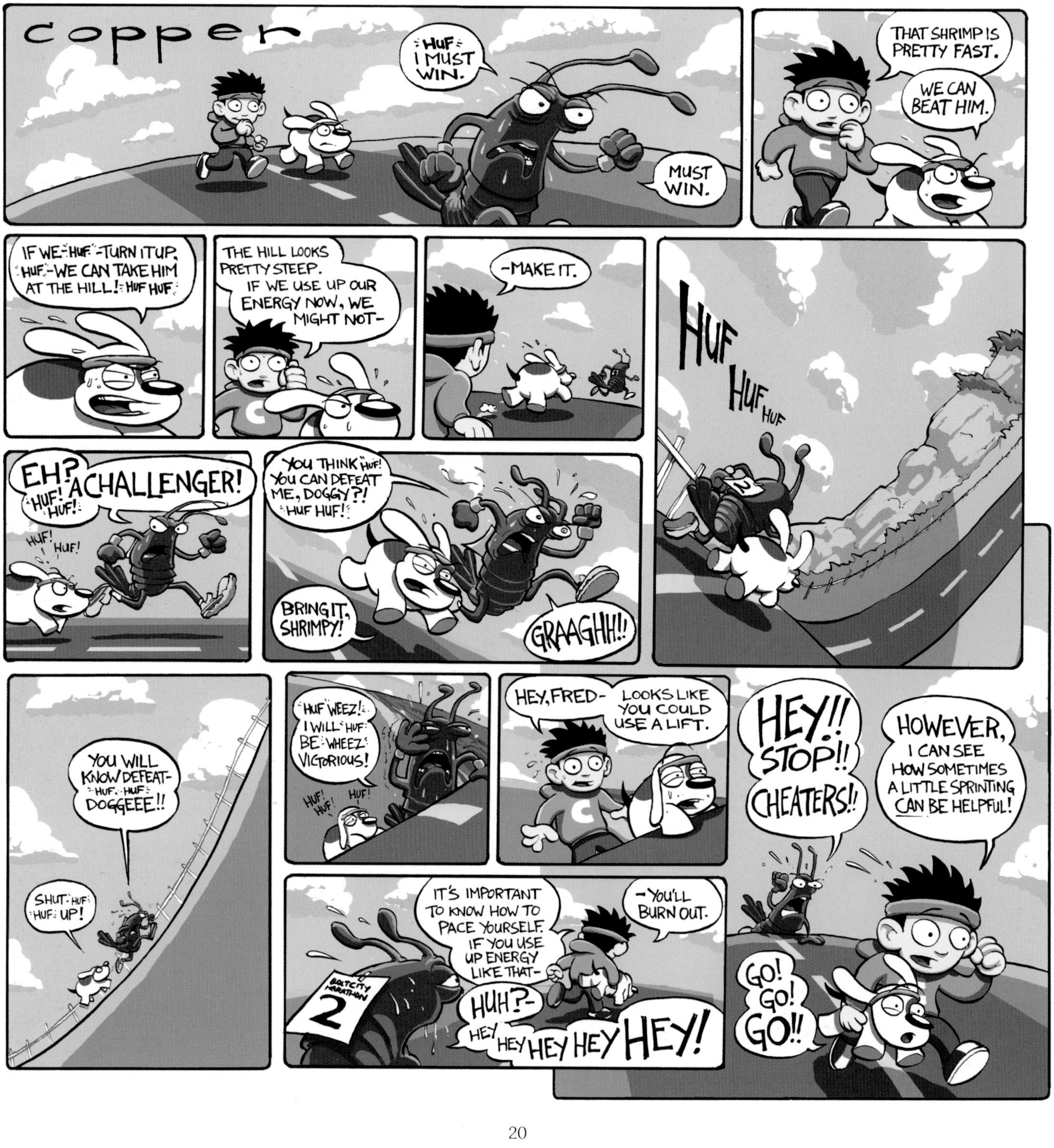
copper
HUF I MUST WIN.
MUST WIN.
THAT SHRIMP IS PRETTY FAST.
WE CAN BEAT HIM.
IF WE HUF -TURN IT UP, HUF -WE CAN TAKE HIM AT THE HILL! HUF HUF
THE HILL LOOKS PRETTY STEEP.
IF WE USE UP OUR ENERGY NOW, WE MIGHT NOT-
-MAKE IT.
HUF HUF HUF
EH? HUF! HUF! A CHALLENGER!
HUF! HUF!
YOU THINK HUF! YOU CAN DEFEAT ME, DOGGY?! HUF HUF!
BRING IT, SHRIMPY!
GRAAGHH!!
YOU WILL KNOW DEFEAT- HUF HUF DOGGEEE!!
SHUT HUF HUF UP!
HUF WEEZ! I WILL HUF BE WHEEZ VICTORIOUS!
HUF! HUF!
HUF!
HEY, FRED-
LOOKS LIKE YOU COULD USE A LIFT.
IT'S IMPORTANT TO KNOW HOW TO PACE YOURSELF. IF YOU USE UP ENERGY LIKE THAT-
-YOU'LL BURN OUT.
BOLT CITY MARATHON 2
HUH?-
HEY HEY HEY HEY HEY!
HEY!! STOP!! CHEATERS!!
HOWEVER, I CAN SEE HOW SOMETIMES A LITTLE SPRINTING CAN BE HELPFUL!
GO! GO! GO!!

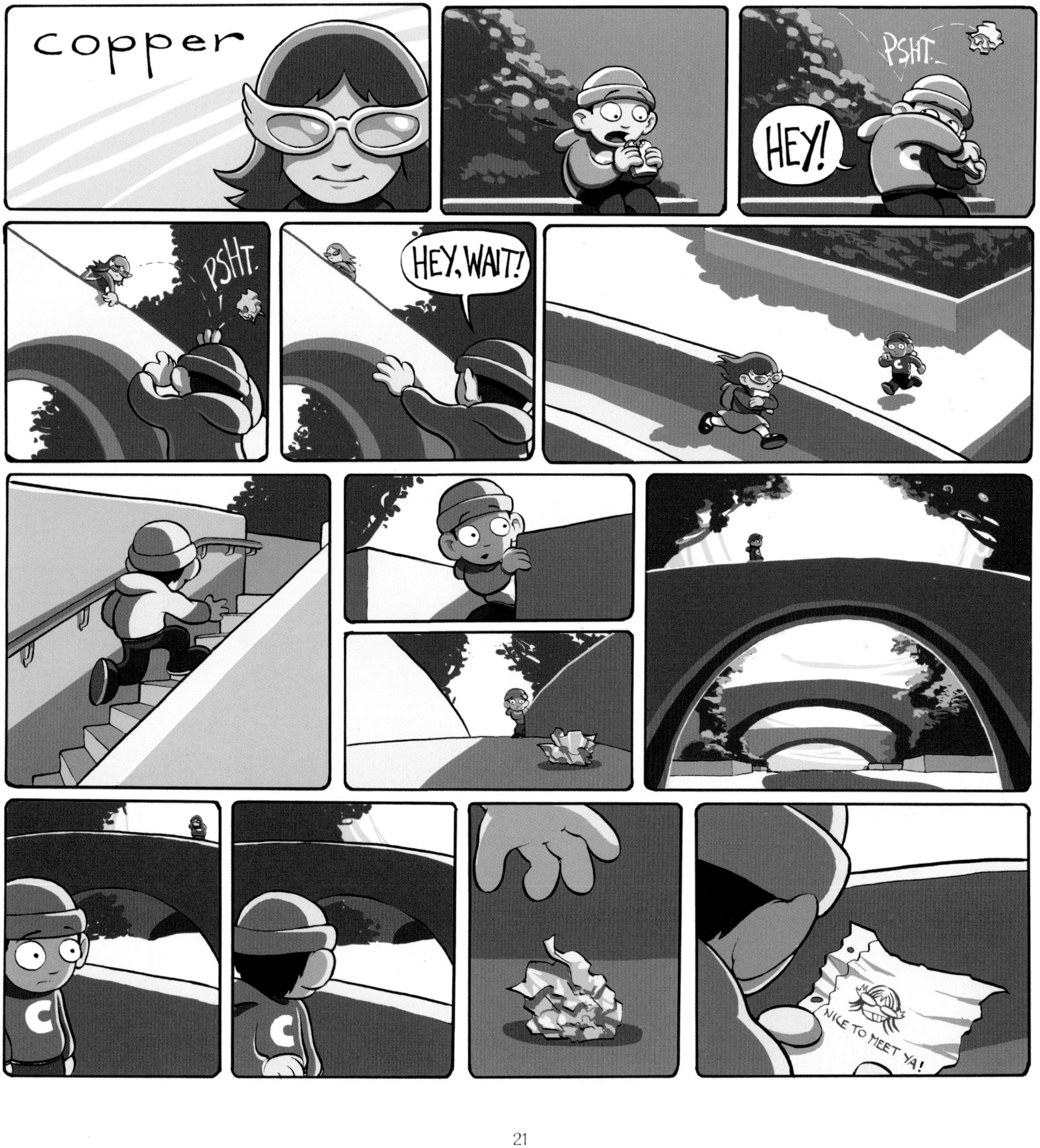
copper
PSHT.
HEY!
PSHT.
HEY, WAIT!
NICE TO MEET YA!

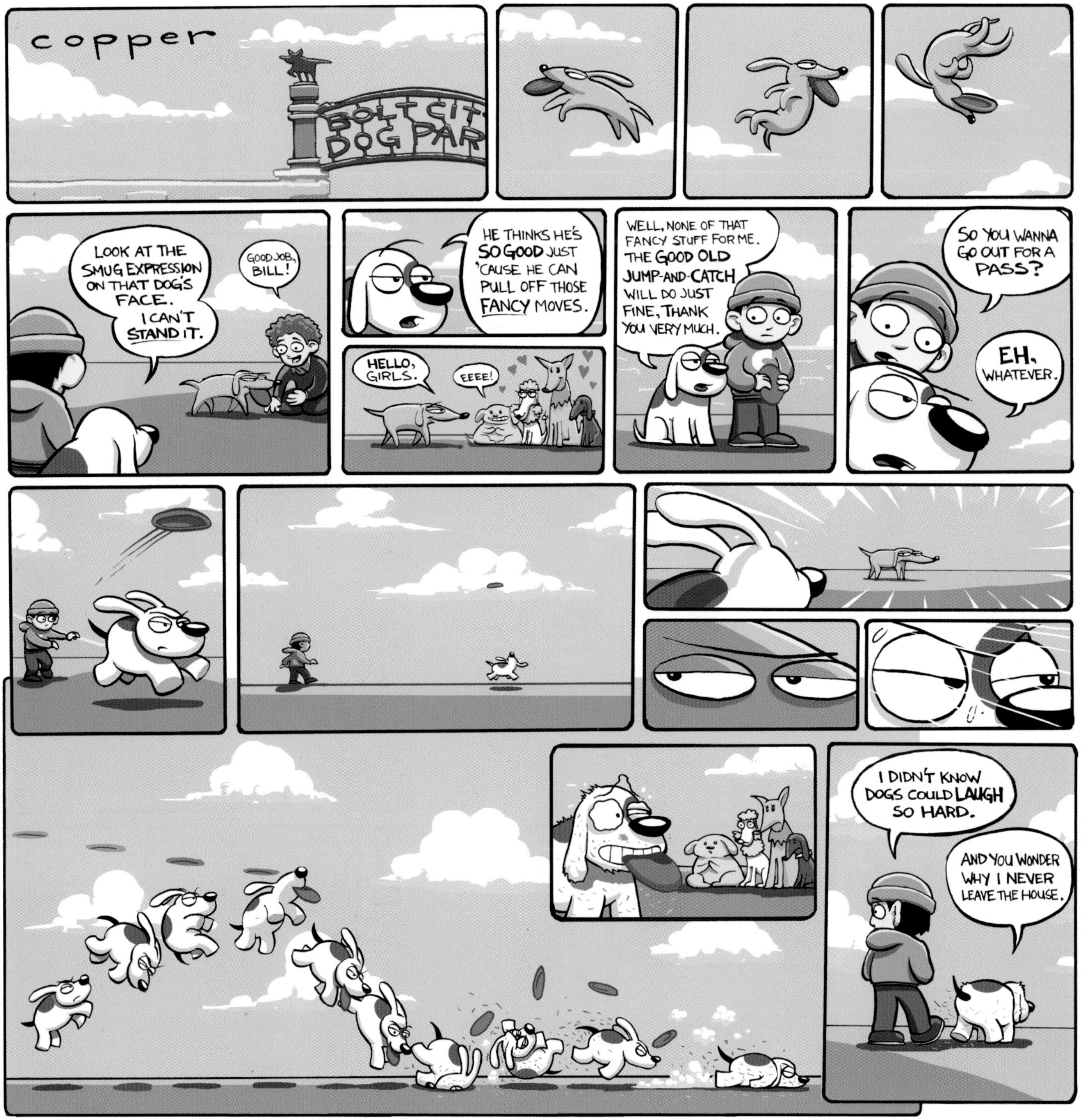
copper
BOLT CITY DOG PAR
LOOK AT THE SMUG EXPRESSION ON THAT DOG'S FACE. I CAN'T STAND IT.
GOOD JOB, BILL!
HE THINKS HE'S SO GOOD JUST 'CAUSE HE CAN PULL OFF THOSE FANCY MOVES.
HELLO, GIRLS.
EEEE!
WELL, NONE OF THAT FANCY STUFF FOR ME. THE GOOD OLD JUMP-AND-CATCH WILL DO JUST FINE, THANK YOU VERY MUCH.
SO YOU WANNA GO OUT FOR A PASS?
EH, WHATEVER.
I DIDN'T KNOW DOGS COULD LAUGH SO HARD.
AND YOU WONDER WHY I NEVER LEAVE THE HOUSE.

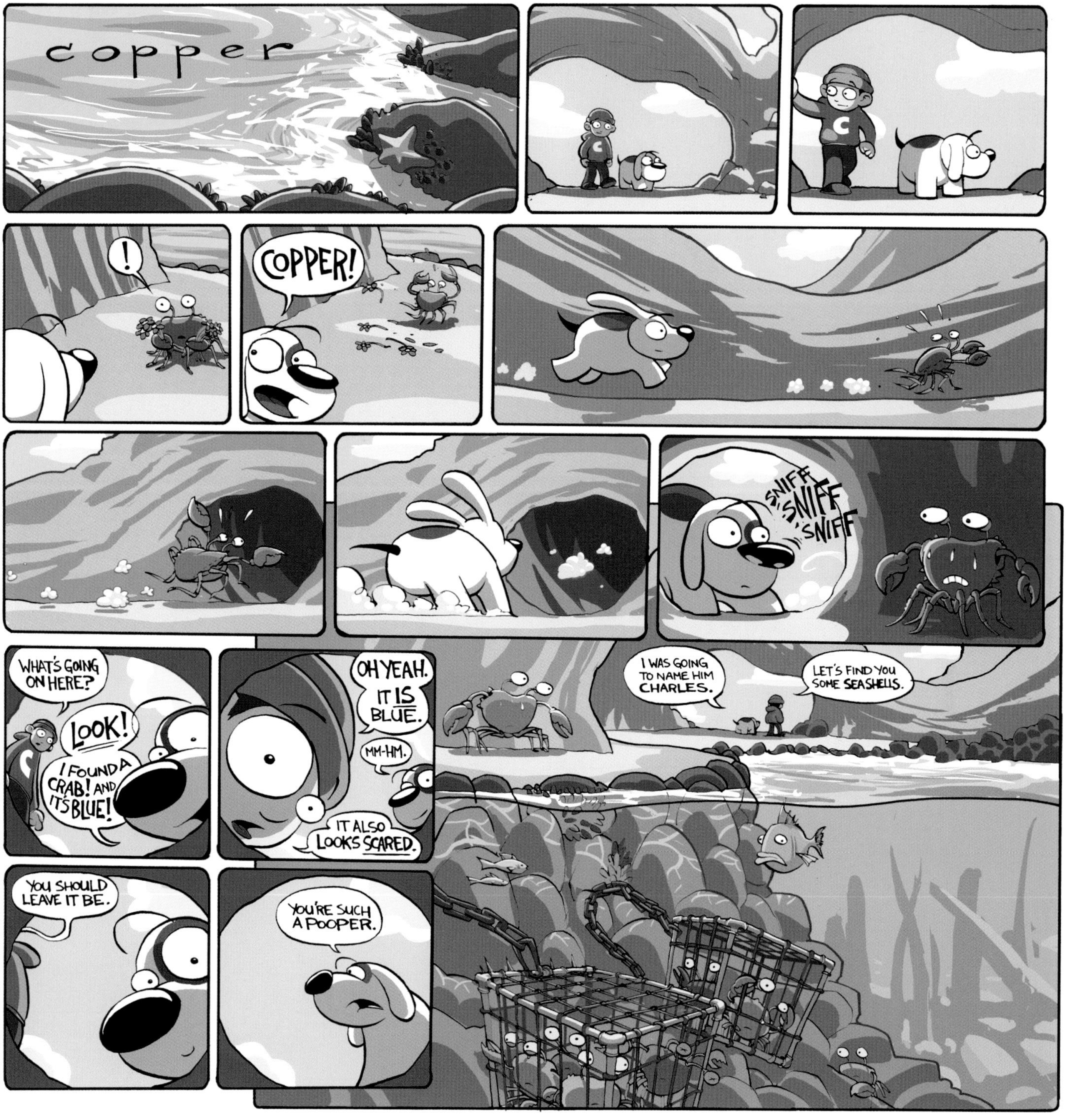
copper
!
COPPER!
SNIFF SNIFF SNIFF
WHAT'S GOING ON HERE?
LOOK!
I FOUND A CRAB! AND IT'S BLUE!
OH YEAH. IT IS BLUE.
MM-HM.
IT ALSO LOOKS SCARED.
I WAS GOING TO NAME HIM CHARLES.
LET'S FIND YOU SOME SEASHELLS.
YOU SHOULD LEAVE IT BE.
YOU'RE SUCH A POOPER.

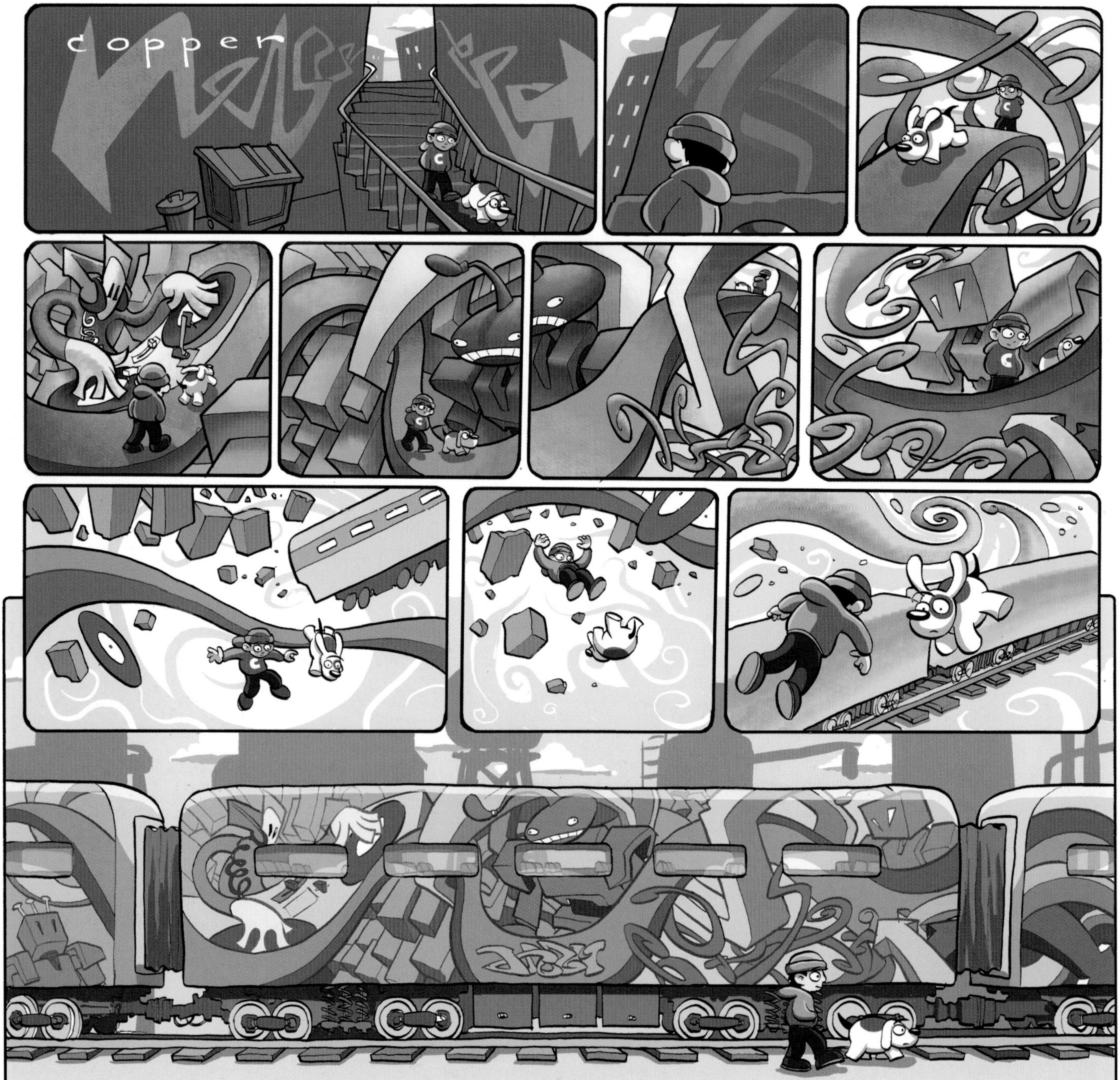
copper

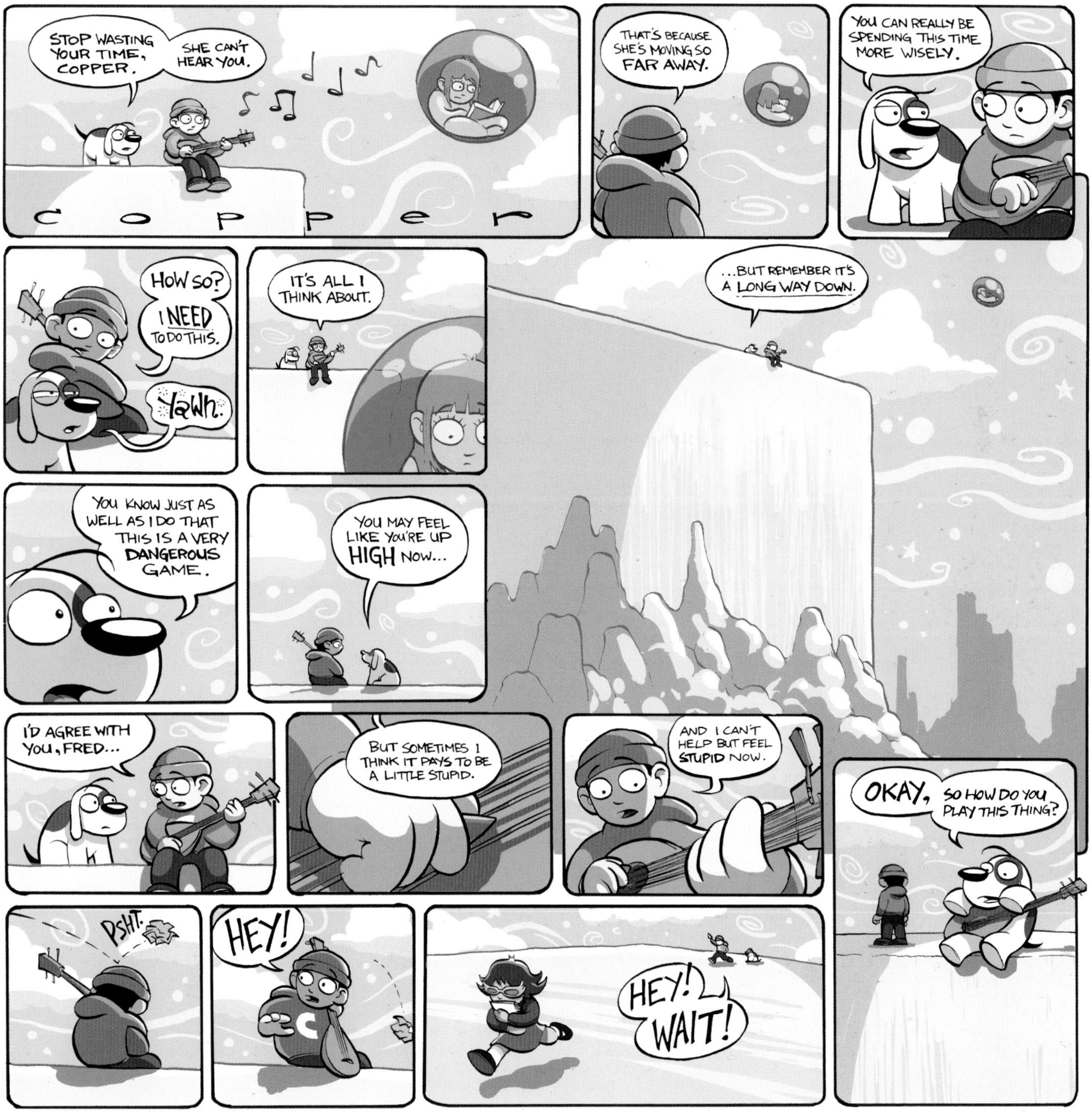
STOP WASTING YOUR TIME, COPPER.
SHE CAN'T HEAR YOU.
COPPER
THAT'S BECAUSE SHE'S MOVING SO FAR AWAY.
YOU CAN REALLY BE SPENDING THIS TIME MORE WISELY.
HOW SO?
I NEED TO DO THIS.
YAWN.
IT'S ALL I THINK ABOUT.
...BUT REMEMBER IT'S A LONG WAY DOWN.
YOU KNOW JUST AS WELL AS I DO THAT THIS IS A VERY DANGEROUS GAME.
YOU MAY FEEL LIKE YOU'RE UP HIGH NOW...
I'D AGREE WITH YOU, FRED...
BUT SOMETIMES I THINK IT PAYS TO BE A LITTLE STUPID.
AND I CAN'T HELP BUT FEEL STUPID NOW.
OKAY,
SO HOW DO YOU PLAY THIS THING?
PSHT.
HEY!
HEY! WAIT!

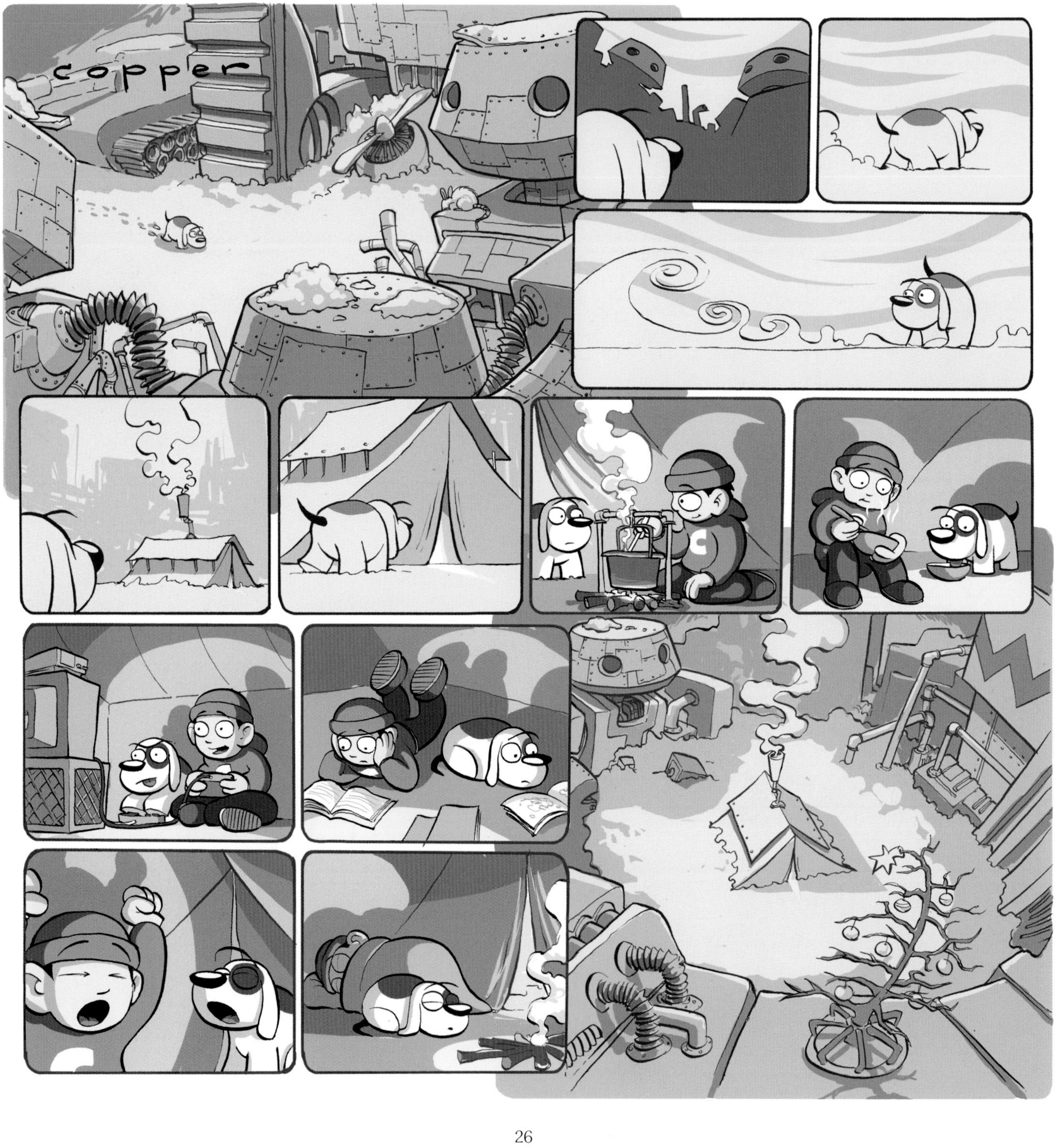
copper

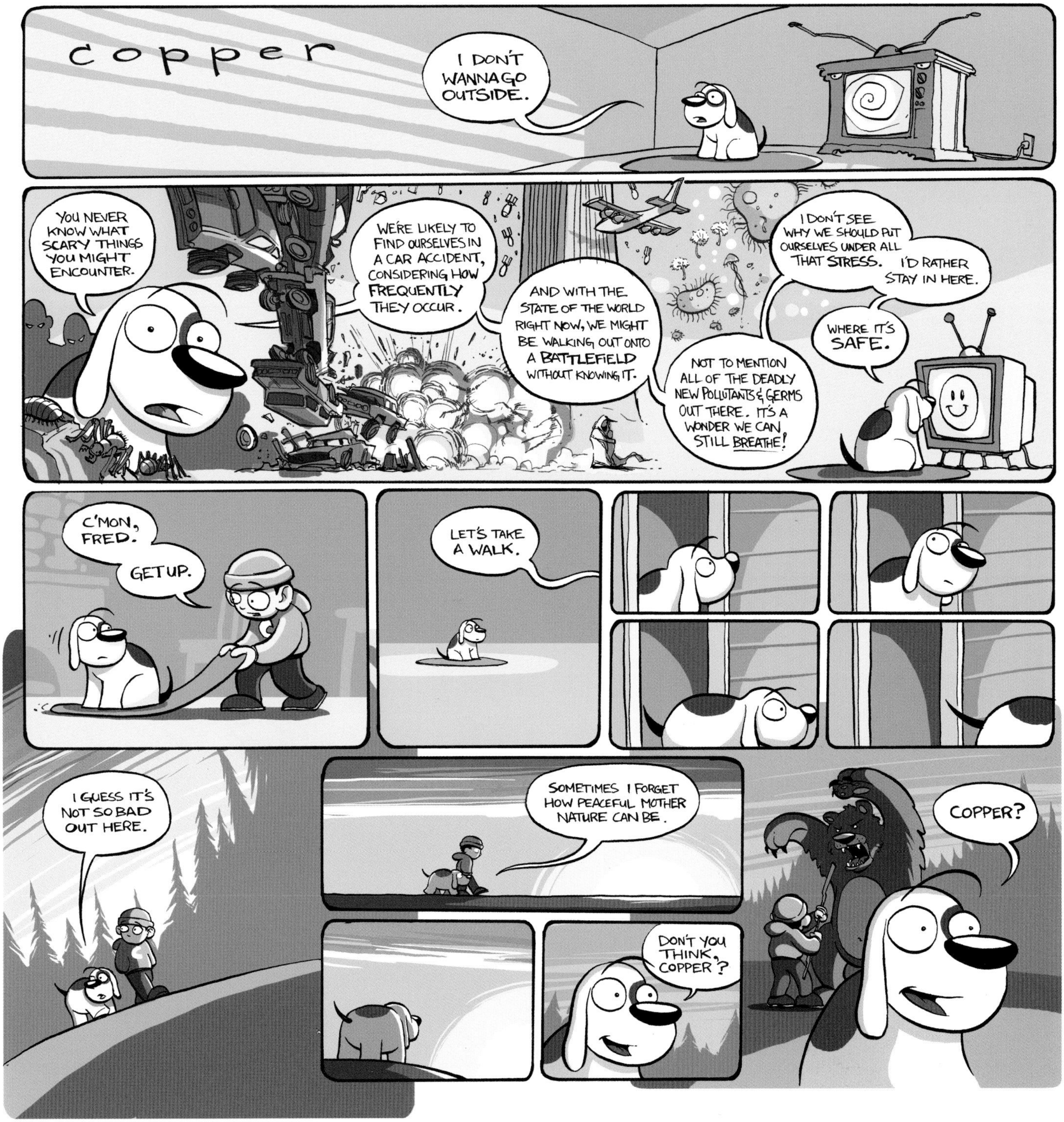
copper
I DON'T WANNA GO OUTSIDE.
YOU NEVER KNOW WHAT SCARY THINGS YOU MIGHT ENCOUNTER.
WE'RE LIKELY TO FIND OURSELVES IN A CAR ACCIDENT, CONSIDERING HOW FREQUENTLY THEY OCCUR.
AND WITH THE STATE OF THE WORLD RIGHT NOW, WE MIGHT BE WALKING OUT ONTO A BATTLEFIELD WITHOUT KNOWING IT.
NOT TO MENTION ALL OF THE DEADLY NEW POLLUTANTS & GERMS OUT THERE. IT'S A WONDER WE CAN STILL BREATHE!
I DON'T SEE WHY WE SHOULD PUT OURSELVES UNDER ALL THAT STRESS. I'D RATHER STAY IN HERE.
WHERE IT'S SAFE.
C'MON, FRED.
GET UP.
LET'S TAKE A WALK.
I GUESS IT'S NOT SO BAD OUT HERE.
SOMETIMES I FORGET HOW PEACEFUL MOTHER NATURE CAN BE.
DON'T YOU THINK, COPPER?
COPPER?

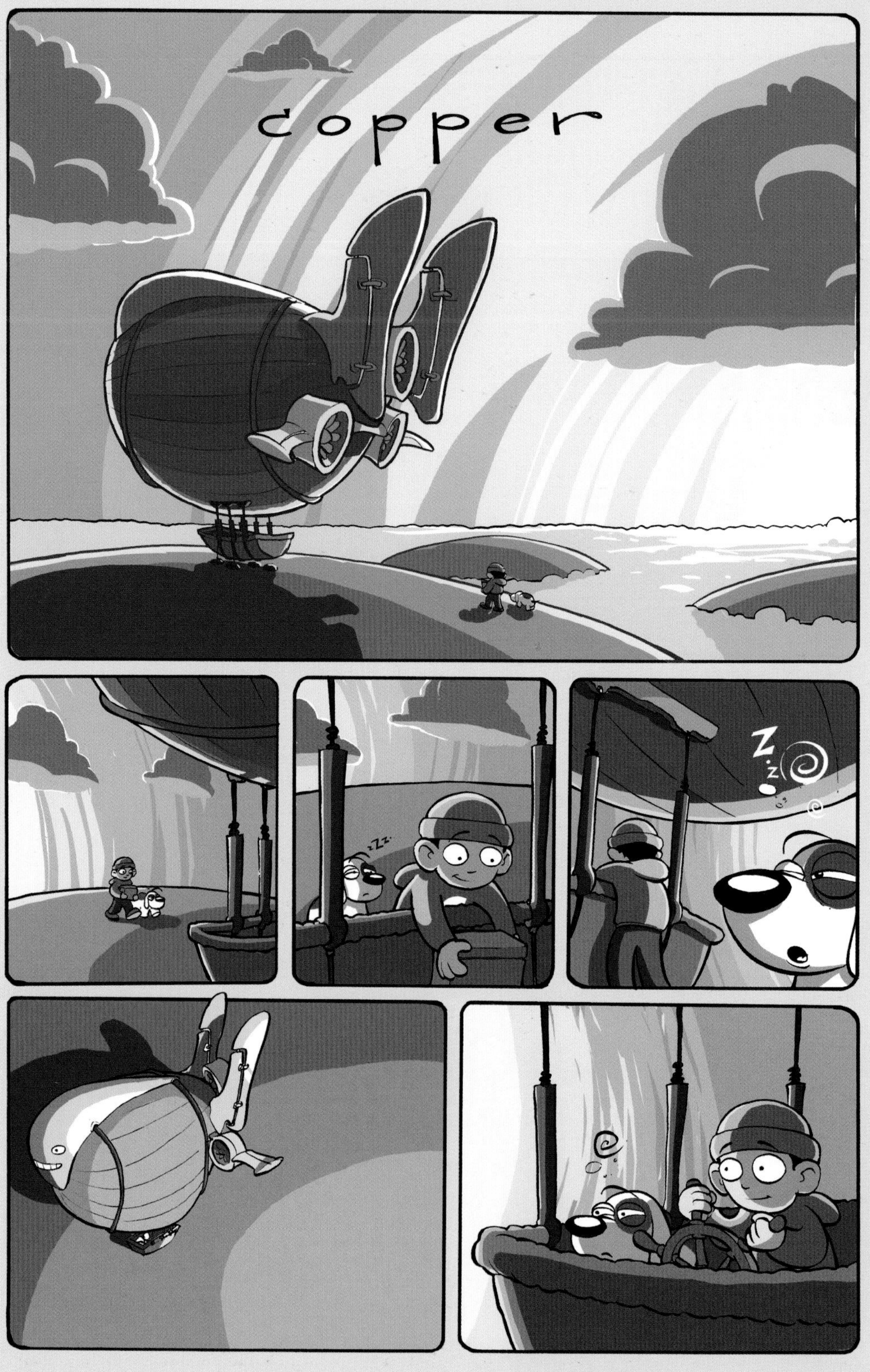
copper

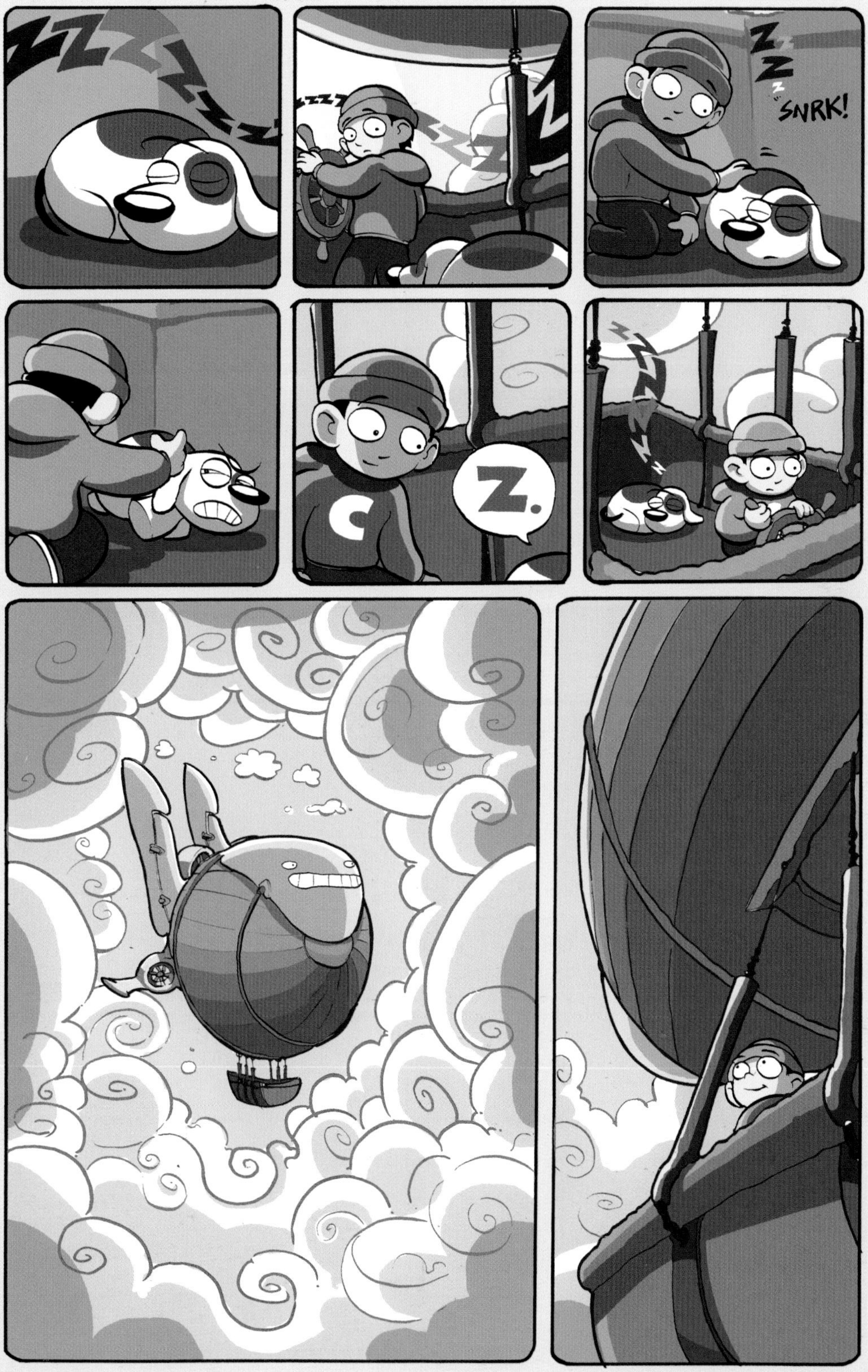
ZZZZ
SNRK!
Z.

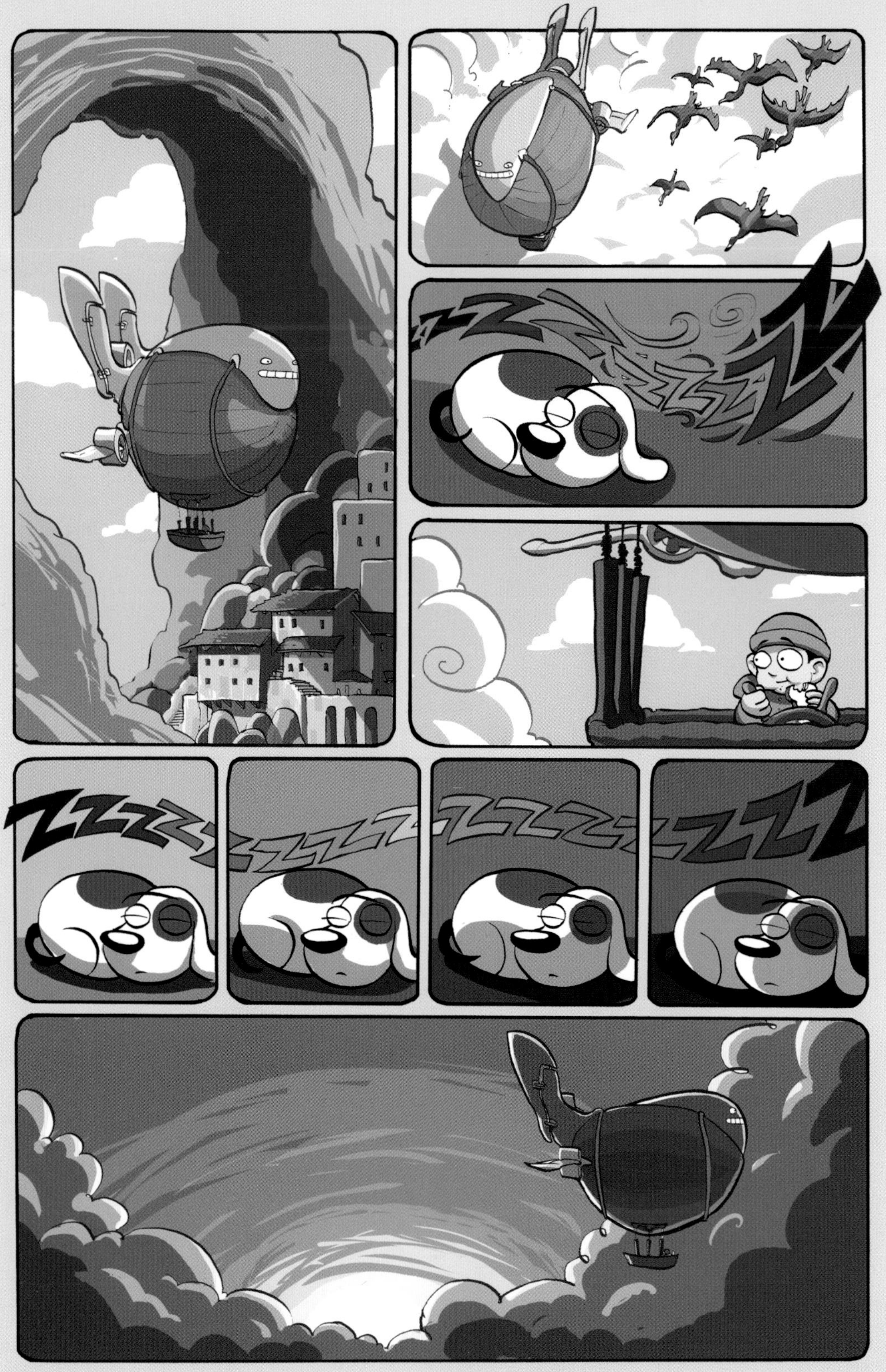

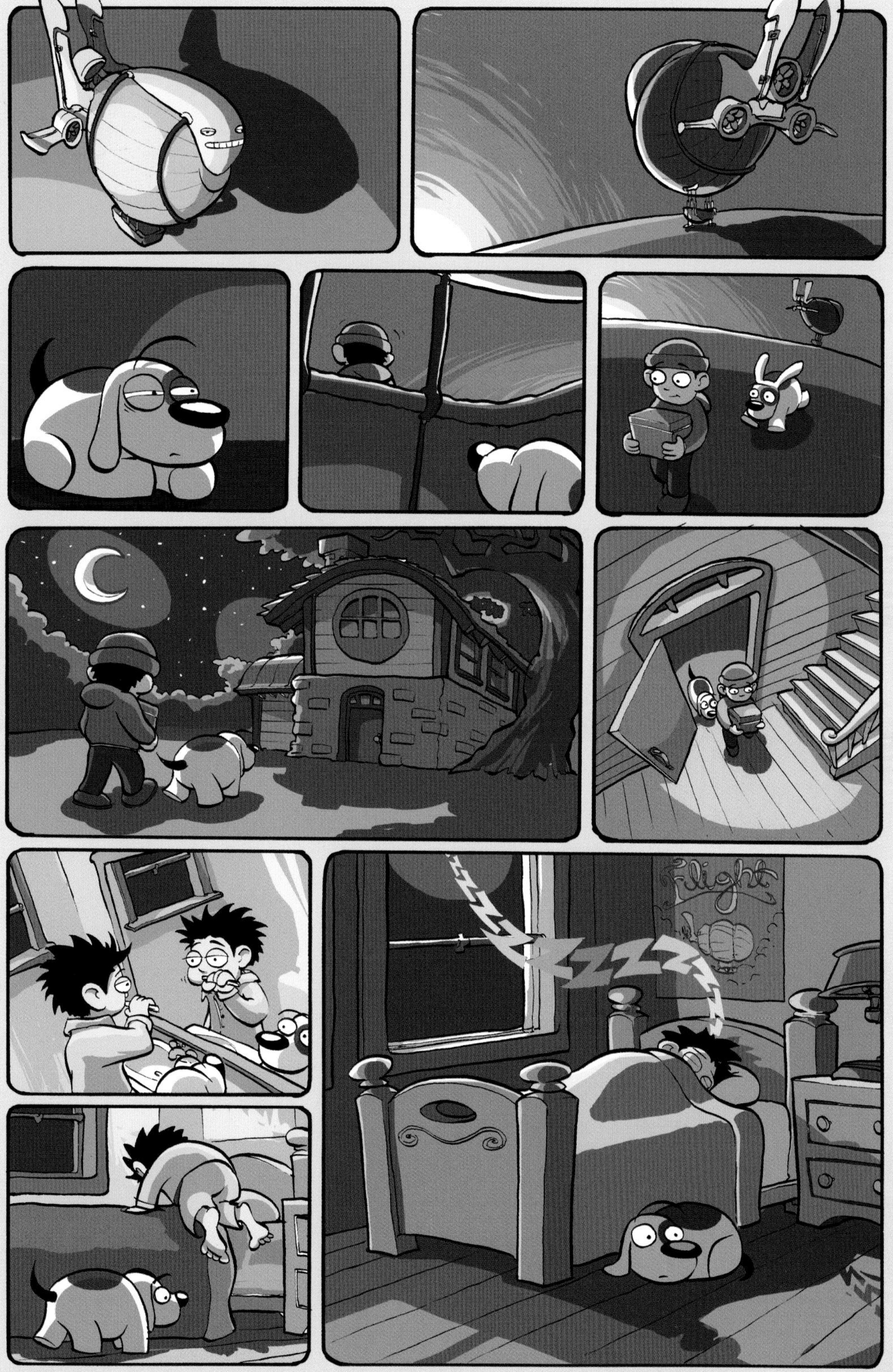
Flight

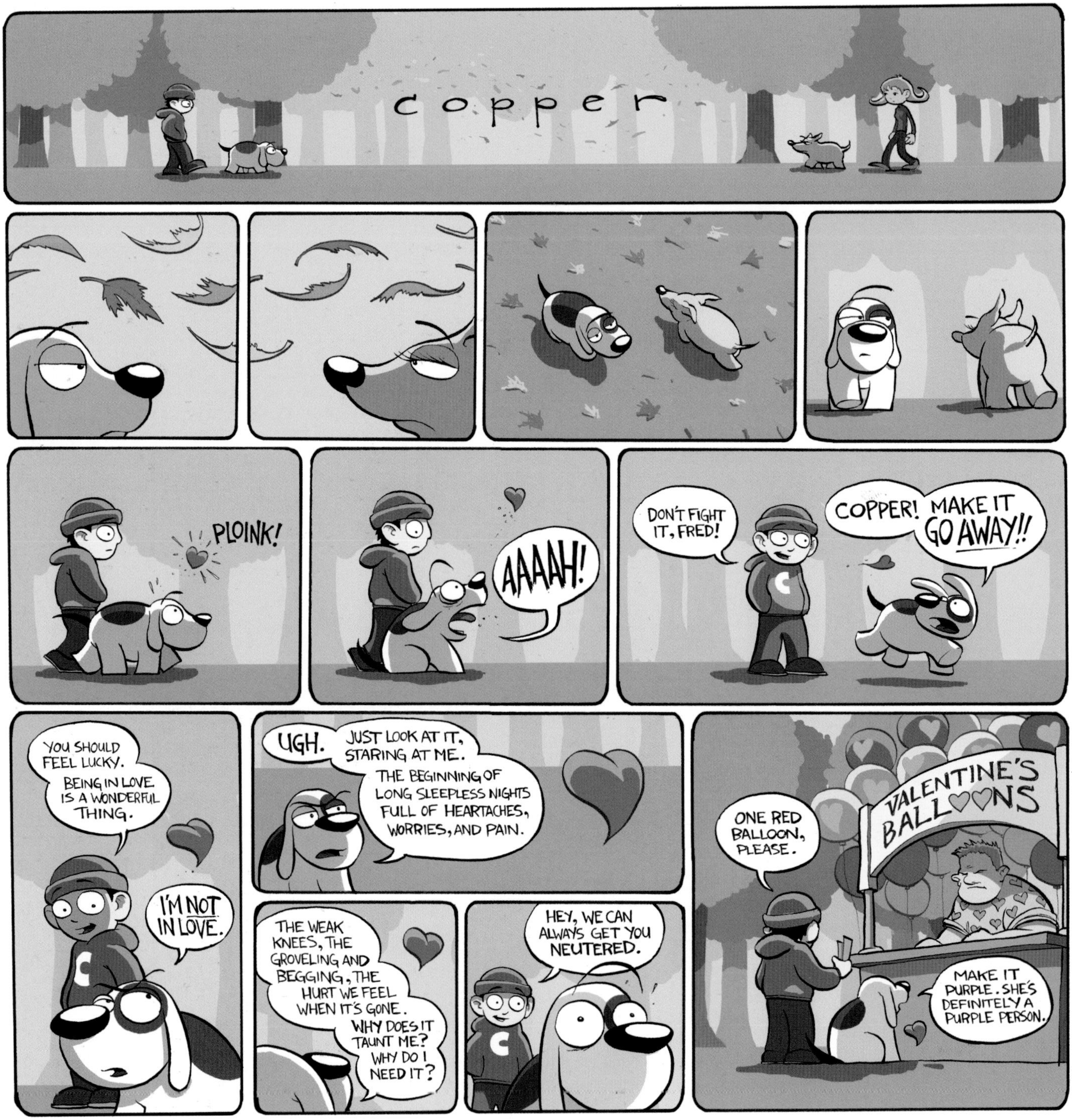
copper
PLOINK!
AAAAH!
DON'T FIGHT IT, FRED!
COPPER! MAKE IT GO AWAY!!
YOU SHOULD FEEL LUCKY.
BEING IN LOVE IS A WONDERFUL THING.
I'M NOT IN LOVE.
UGH.
JUST LOOK AT IT, STARING AT ME.
THE BEGINNING OF LONG SLEEPLESS NIGHTS FULL OF HEARTACHES, WORRIES, AND PAIN.
THE WEAK KNEES, THE GROVELING AND BEGGING, THE HURT WE FEEL WHEN IT'S GONE.
WHY DOES IT TAUNT ME? WHY DO I NEED IT?
HEY, WE CAN ALWAYS GET YOU NEUTERED.
VALENTINE'S BALLOONS
ONE RED BALLOON, PLEASE.
MAKE IT PURPLE. SHE'S DEFINITELY A PURPLE PERSON.

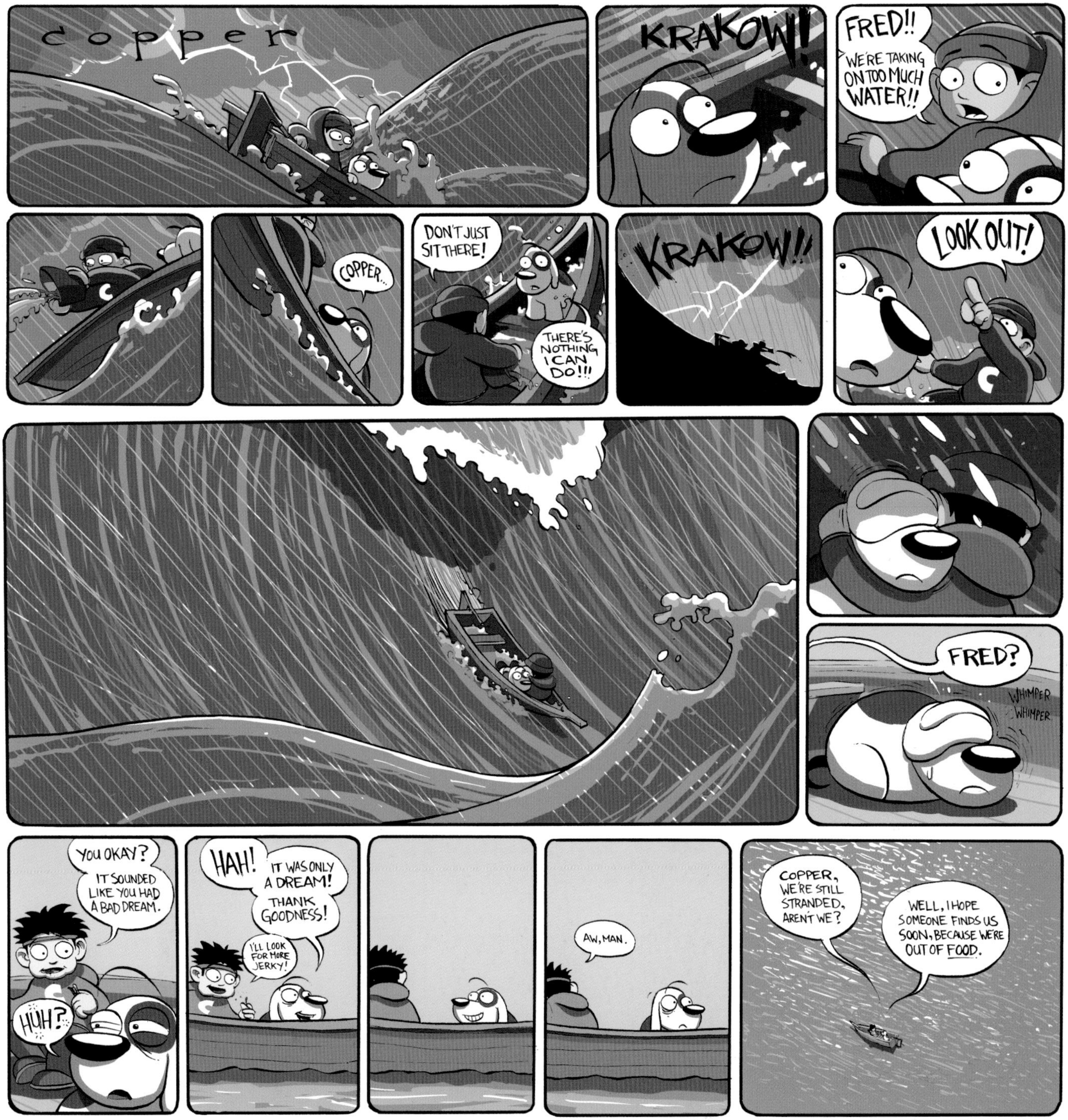
copper
KRAKOW!
FRED!!
WE'RE TAKING ON TOO MUCH WATER!!
COPPER...
DON'T JUST SIT THERE!
THERE'S NOTHING I CAN DO!!!
KRAKOW!!
LOOK OUT!
FRED?
WHIMPER WHIMPER
YOU OKAY?
IT SOUNDED LIKE YOU HAD A BAD DREAM.
HUH?
HAH!
IT WAS ONLY A DREAM!
THANK GOODNESS!
I'LL LOOK FOR MORE JERKY!
AW, MAN.
COPPER, WE'RE STILL STRANDED, AREN'T WE?
WELL, I HOPE SOMEONE FINDS US SOON, BECAUSE WE'RE OUT OF FOOD.

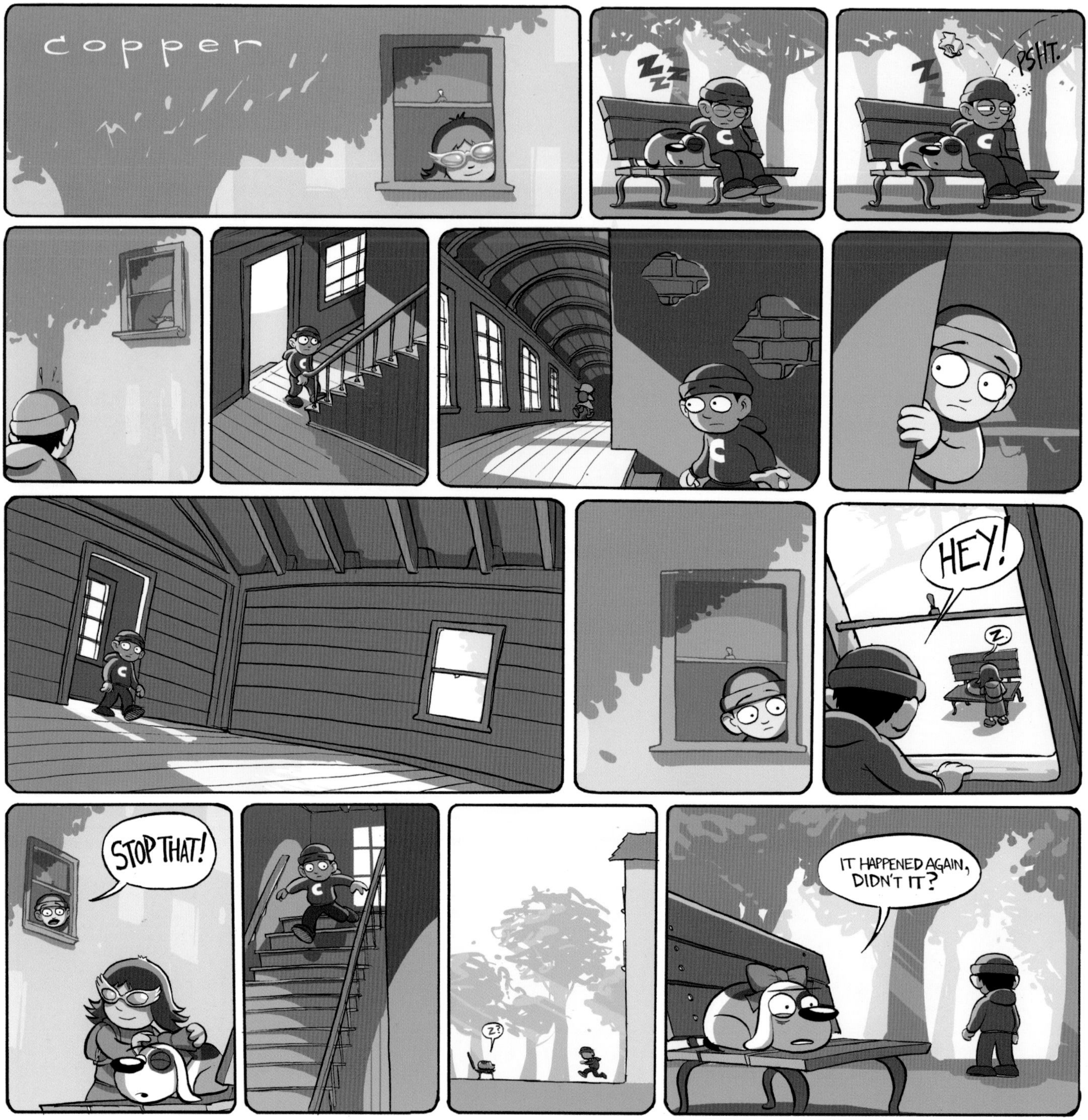
copper
PSHT.
HEY!
STOP THAT!
IT HAPPENED AGAIN, DIDN'T IT?

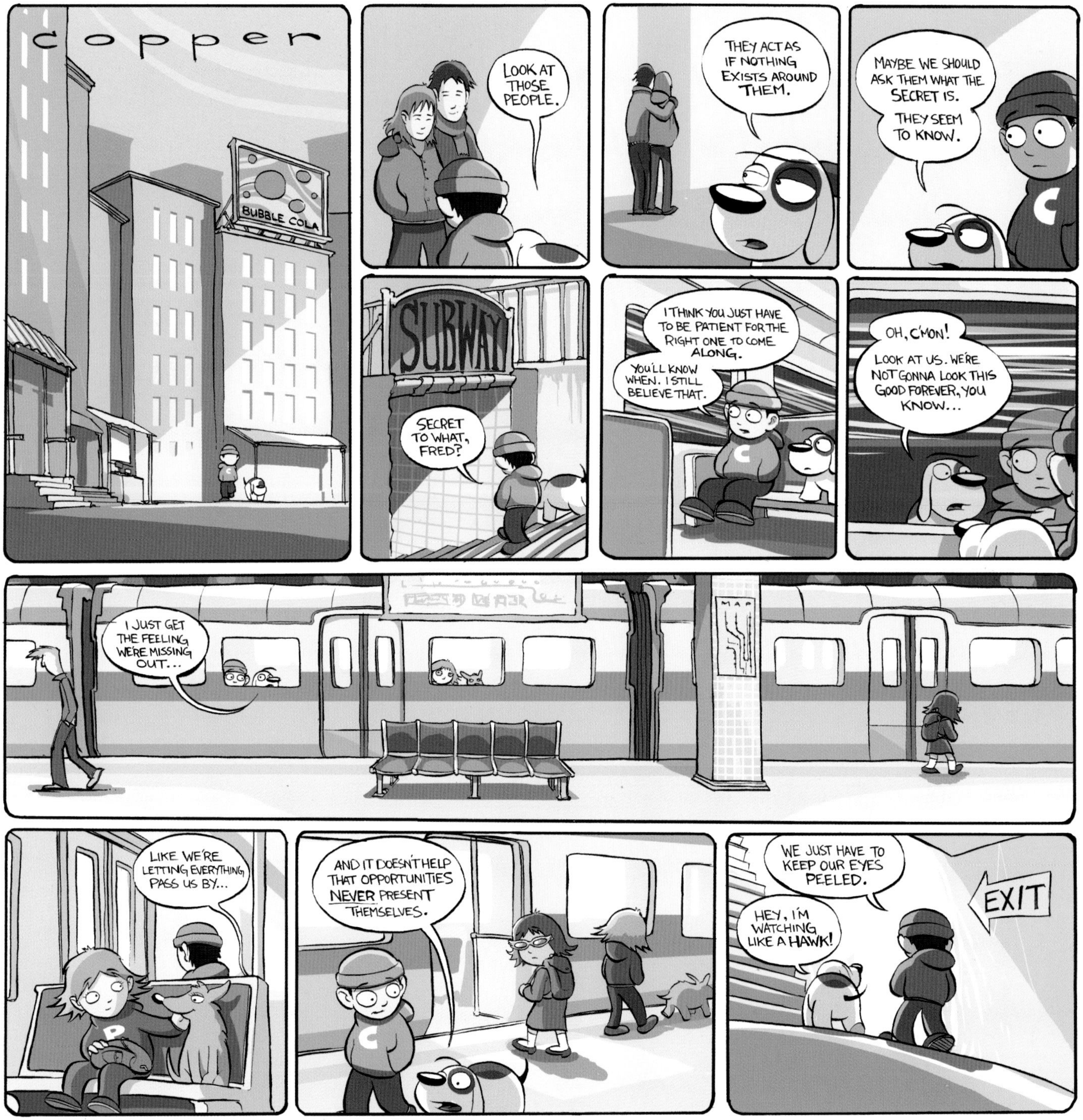
copper
BUBBLE COLA
LOOK AT THOSE PEOPLE.
THEY ACT AS IF NOTHING EXISTS AROUND THEM.
MAYBE WE SHOULD ASK THEM WHAT THE SECRET IS.
THEY SEEM TO KNOW.
SUBWAY
SECRET TO WHAT, FRED?
I THINK YOU JUST HAVE TO BE PATIENT FOR THE RIGHT ONE TO COME ALONG.
YOU'LL KNOW WHEN. I STILL BELIEVE THAT.
OH, C'MON!
LOOK AT US. WE'RE NOT GONNA LOOK THIS GOOD FOREVER, YOU KNOW...
I JUST GET THE FEELING WE'RE MISSING OUT...
MAP
LIKE WE'RE LETTING EVERYTHING PASS US BY...
AND IT DOESN'T HELP THAT OPPORTUNITIES NEVER PRESENT THEMSELVES.
WE JUST HAVE TO KEEP OUR EYES PEELED.
HEY, I'M WATCHING LIKE A HAWK!
EXIT

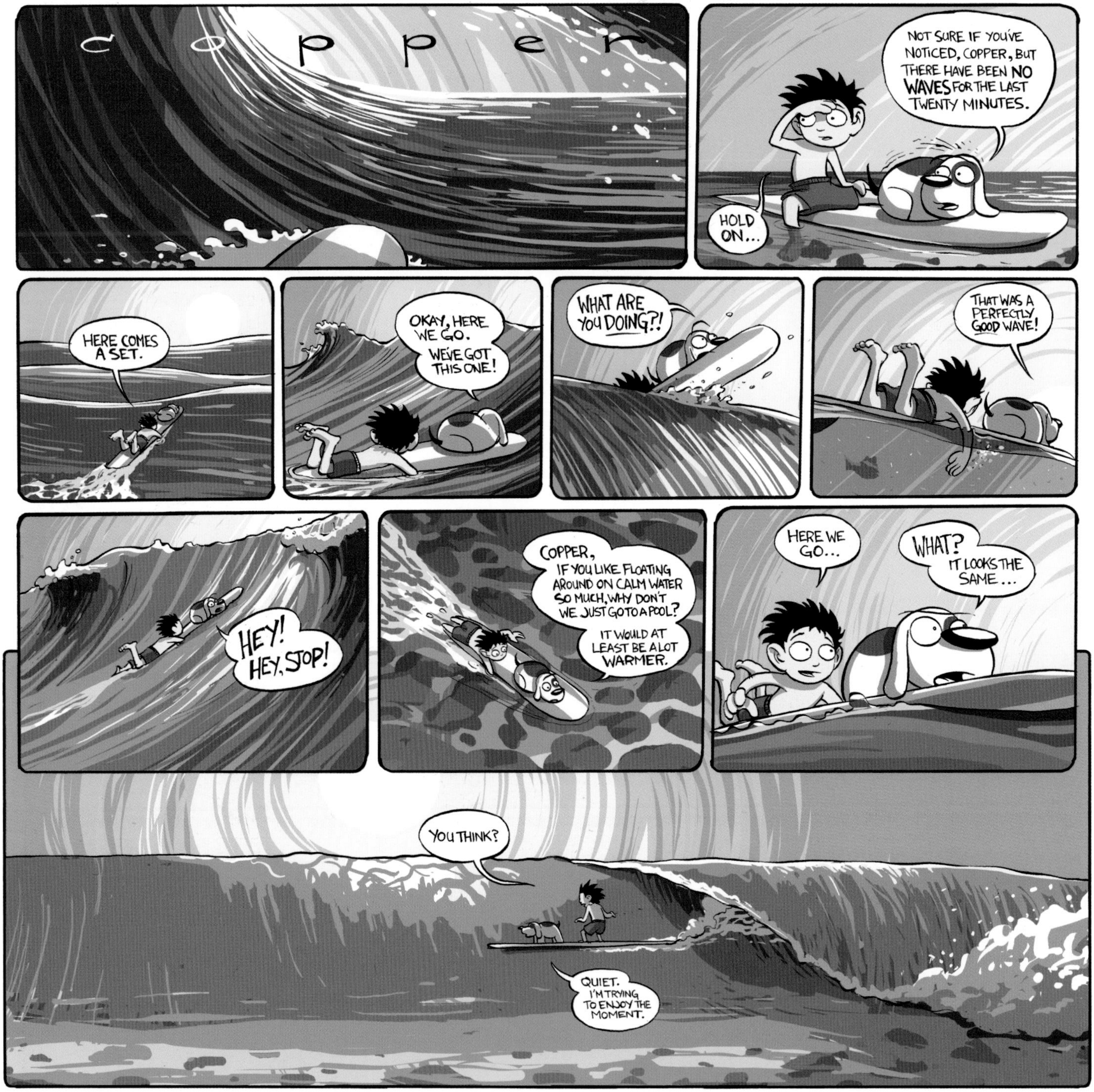
copper
NOT SURE IF YOU'VE NOTICED, COPPER, BUT THERE HAVE BEEN NO WAVES FOR THE LAST TWENTY MINUTES.
HOLD ON...
HERE COMES A SET.
OKAY, HERE WE GO.
WE'VE GOT THIS ONE!
WHAT ARE YOU DOING?!
THAT WAS A PERFECTLY GOOD WAVE!
HEY! HEY, STOP!
COPPER, IF YOU LIKE FLOATING AROUND ON CALM WATER SO MUCH, WHY DON'T WE JUST GO TO A POOL?
IT WOULD AT LEAST BE A LOT WARMER.
HERE WE GO...
WHAT? IT LOOKS THE SAME...
YOU THINK?
QUIET. I'M TRYING TO ENJOY THE MOMENT.

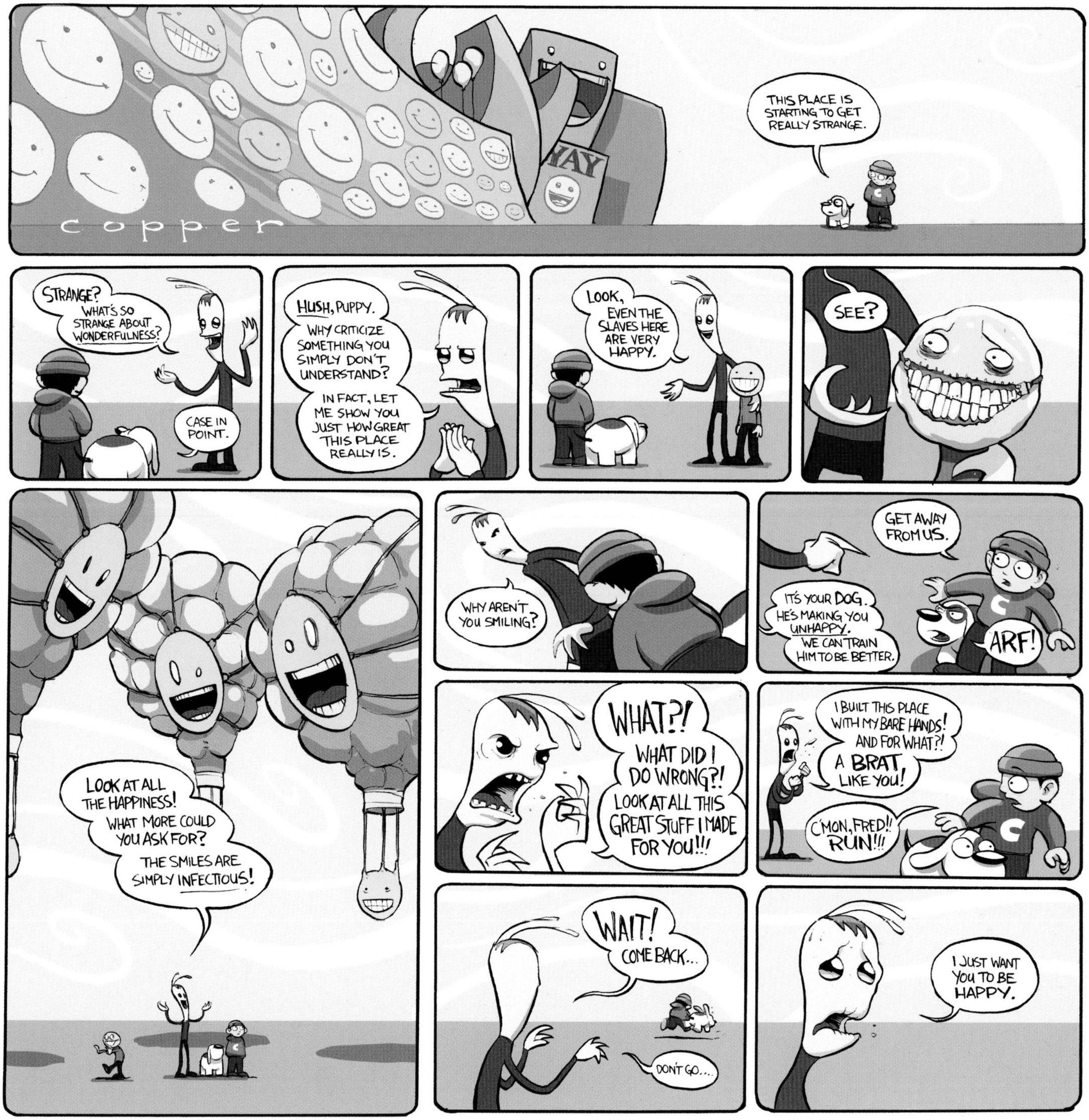
copper
THIS PLACE IS STARTING TO GET REALLY STRANGE.
YAY
STRANGE? WHAT'S SO STRANGE ABOUT WONDERFULNESS?
CASE IN POINT.
HUSH, PUPPY. WHY CRITICIZE SOMETHING YOU SIMPLY DON'T UNDERSTAND?
IN FACT, LET ME SHOW YOU JUST HOW GREAT THIS PLACE REALLY IS.
LOOK, EVEN THE SLAVES HERE ARE VERY HAPPY.
SEE?
LOOK AT ALL THE HAPPINESS!
WHAT MORE COULD YOU ASK FOR?
THE SMILES ARE SIMPLY INFECTIOUS!
WHY AREN'T YOU SMILING?
GET AWAY FROM US.
IT'S YOUR DOG. HE'S MAKING YOU UNHAPPY. WE CAN TRAIN HIM TO BE BETTER.
ARF!
WHAT?! WHAT DID I DO WRONG?! LOOK AT ALL THIS GREAT STUFF I MADE FOR YOU!!!
I BUILT THIS PLACE WITH MY BARE HANDS! AND FOR WHAT?! A BRAT LIKE YOU!
C'MON, FRED!! RUN!!!
WAIT! COME BACK...
DON'T GO...
I JUST WANT YOU TO BE HAPPY.

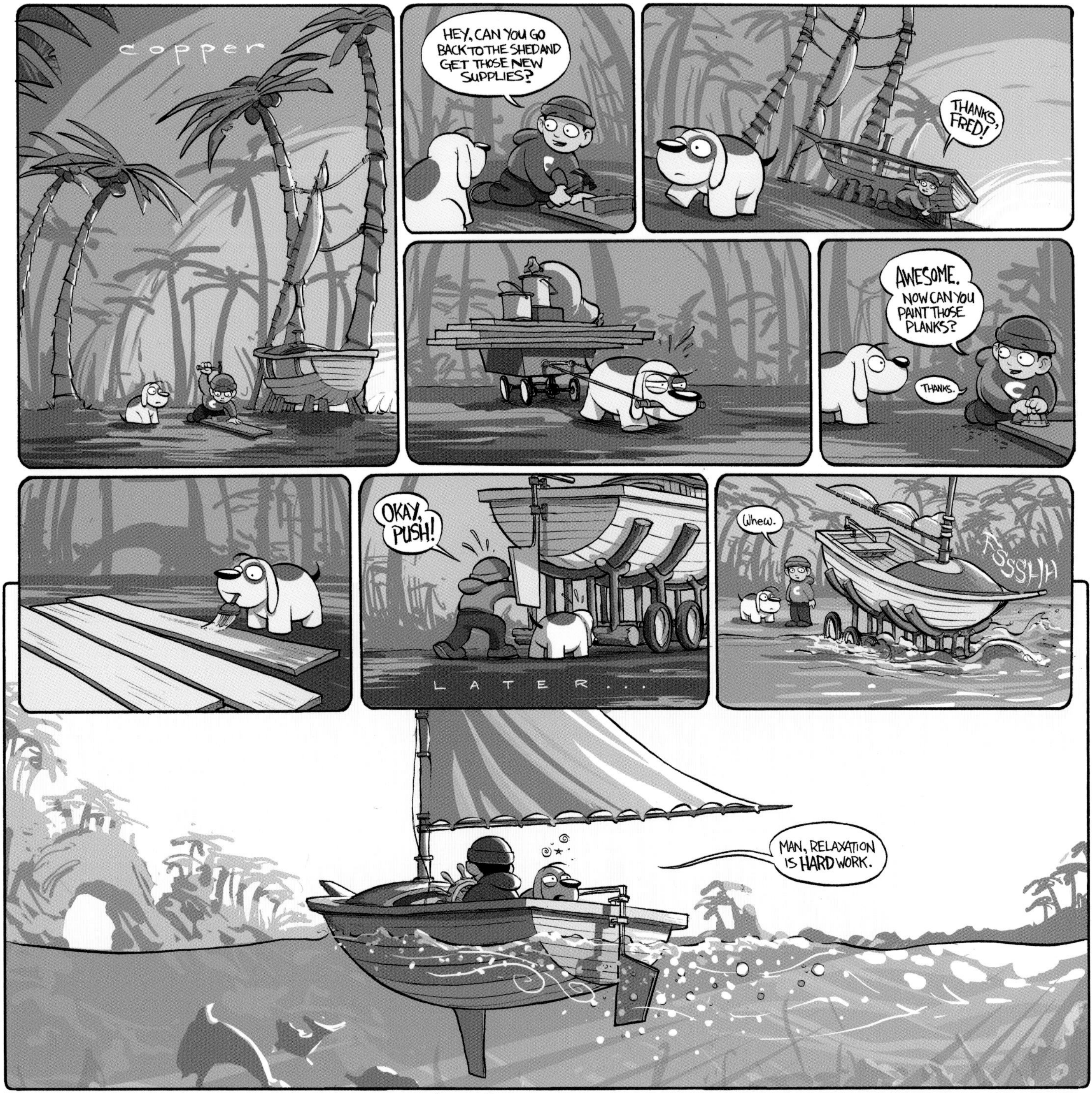
copper
HEY, CAN YOU GO BACK TO THE SHED AND GET THOSE NEW SUPPLIES?
THANKS, FRED!
AWESOME. NOW CAN YOU PAINT THOSE PLANKS?
THANKS.
OKAY, PUSH!
LATER...
Whew.
FSSSHH
MAN, RELAXATION IS HARD WORK.

WATERFALL

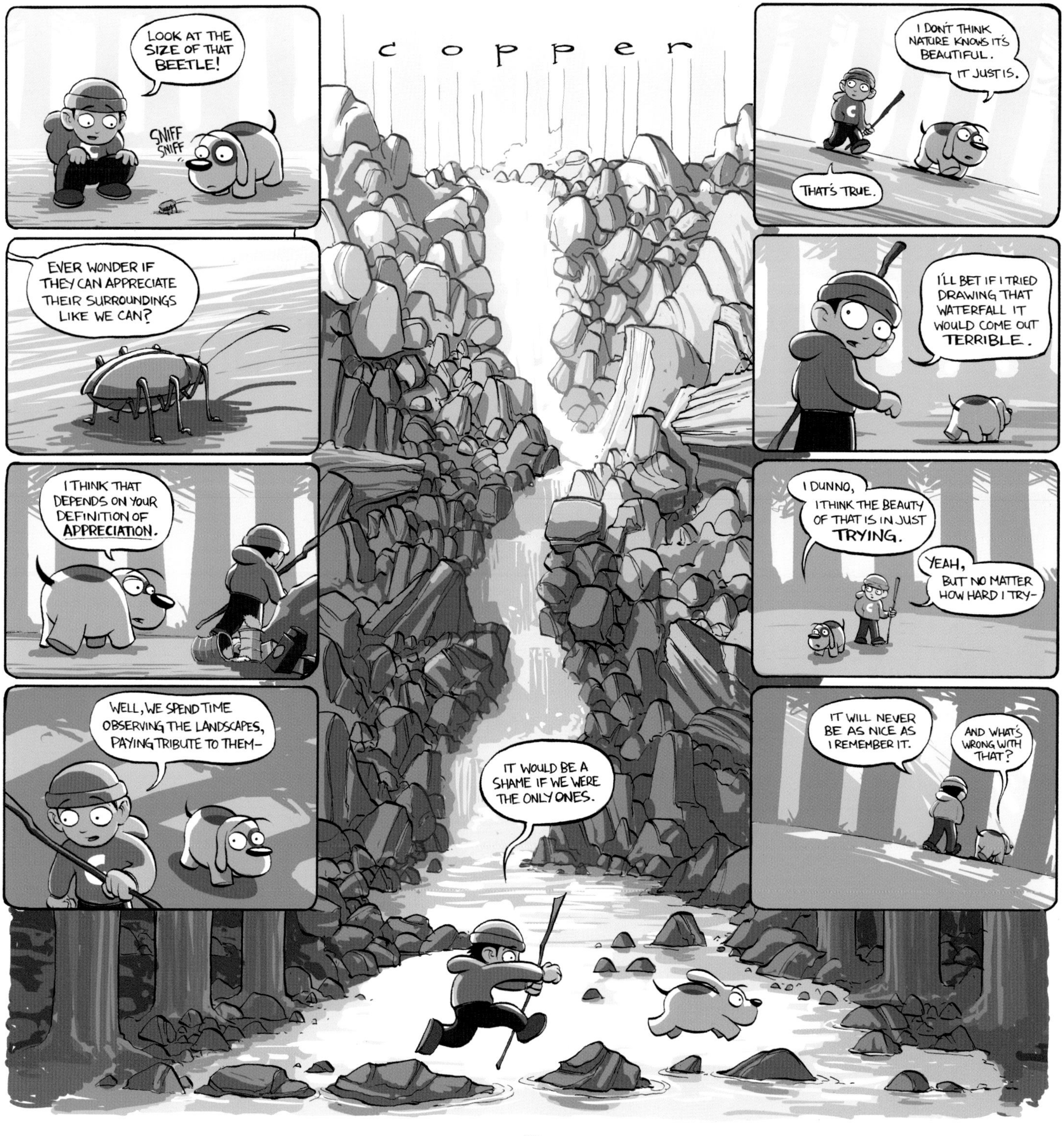
copper
LOOK AT THE SIZE OF THAT BEETLE!
SNIFF SNIFF
EVER WONDER IF THEY CAN APPRECIATE THEIR SURROUNDINGS LIKE WE CAN?
I THINK THAT DEPENDS ON YOUR DEFINITION OF APPRECIATION.
WELL, WE SPEND TIME OBSERVING THE LANDSCAPES, PAYING TRIBUTE TO THEM-
IT WOULD BE A SHAME IF WE WERE THE ONLY ONES.
I DON'T THINK NATURE KNOWS IT'S BEAUTIFUL.
IT JUST IS.
THAT'S TRUE.
I'LL BET IF I TRIED DRAWING THAT WATERFALL IT WOULD COME OUT TERRIBLE.
I DUNNO, I THINK THE BEAUTY OF THAT IS IN JUST TRYING.
YEAH, BUT NO MATTER HOW HARD I TRY-
IT WILL NEVER BE AS NICE AS I REMEMBER IT.
AND WHAT'S WRONG WITH THAT?

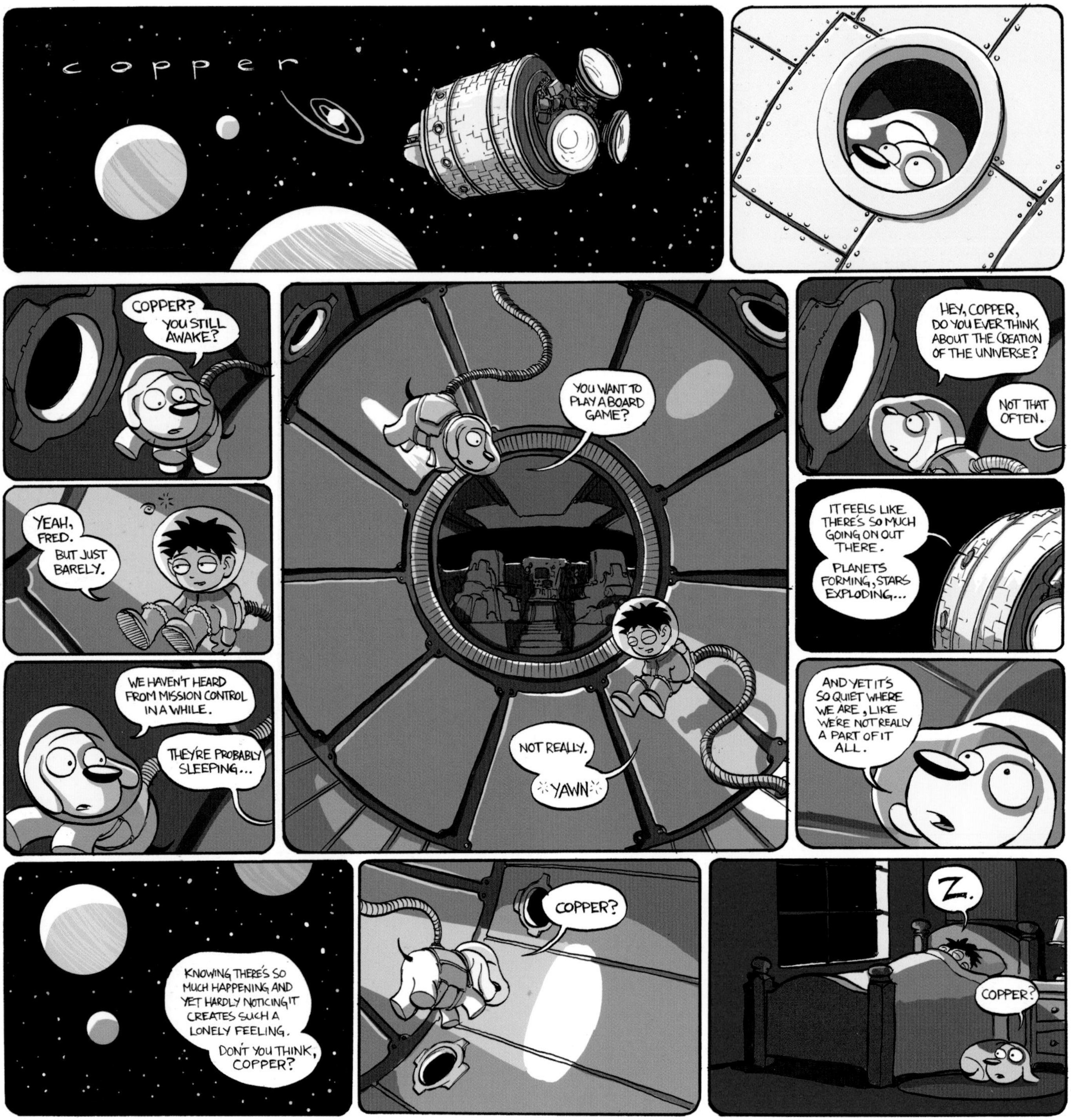
copper
COPPER? YOU STILL AWAKE?
YOU WANT TO PLAY A BOARD GAME?
HEY, COPPER, DO YOU EVER THINK ABOUT THE CREATION OF THE UNIVERSE?
NOT THAT OFTEN.
YEAH, FRED. BUT JUST BARELY.
IT FEELS LIKE THERE'S SO MUCH GOING ON OUT THERE.
PLANETS FORMING, STARS EXPLODING...
WE HAVEN'T HEARD FROM MISSION CONTROL IN A WHILE.
THEY'RE PROBABLY SLEEPING...
NOT REALLY.
YAWN
AND YET IT'S SO QUIET WHERE WE ARE, LIKE WE'RE NOT REALLY A PART OF IT ALL.
KNOWING THERE'S SO MUCH HAPPENING AND YET HARDLY NOTICING IT CREATES SUCH A LONELY FEELING.
DON'T YOU THINK, COPPER?
COPPER?
Z.
COPPER?

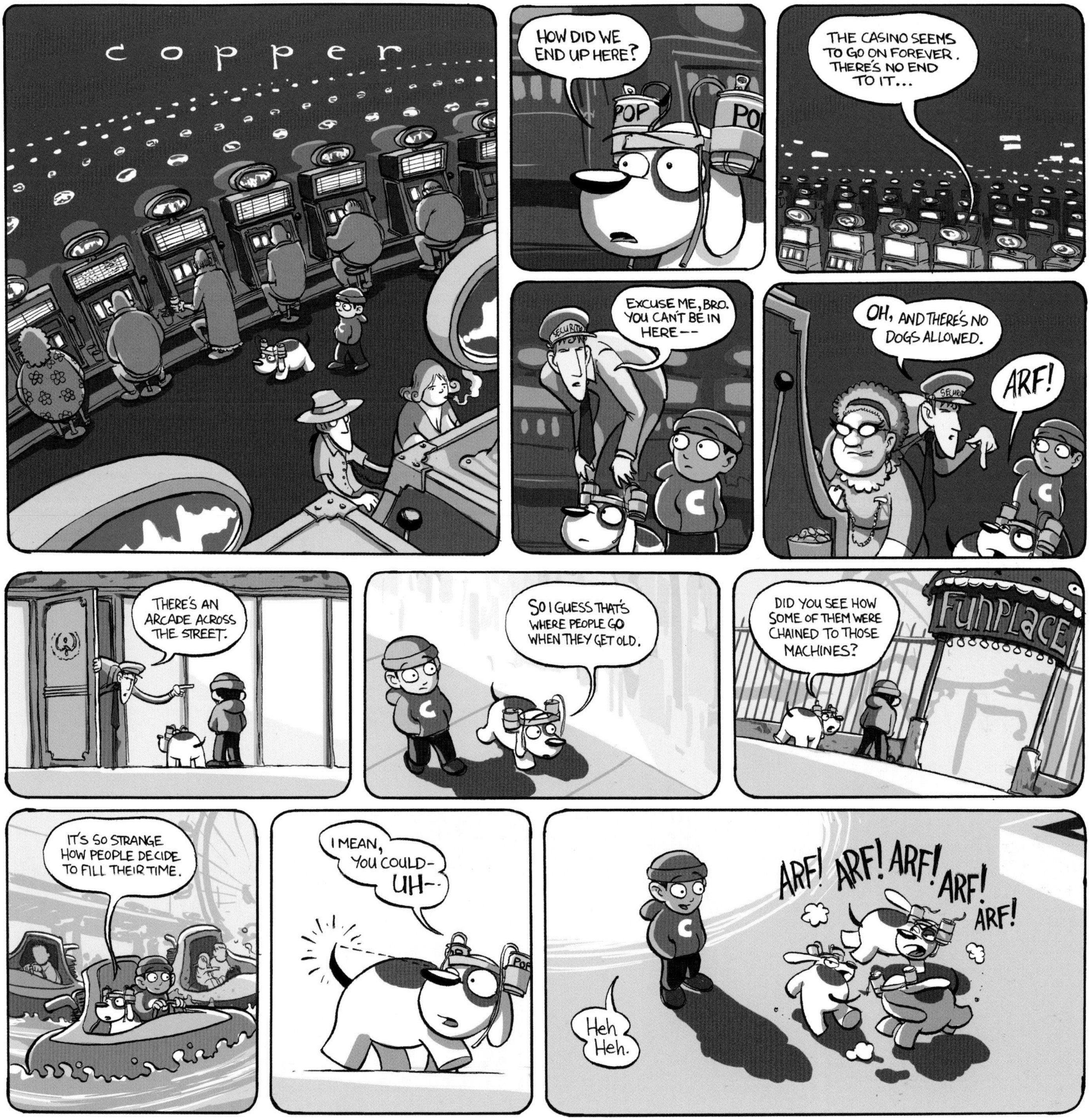
copper
HOW DID WE END UP HERE?
POP
THE CASINO SEEMS TO GO ON FOREVER. THERE'S NO END TO IT...
EXCUSE ME, BRO. YOU CAN'T BE IN HERE--
OH, AND THERE'S NO DOGS ALLOWED.
ARF!
THERE'S AN ARCADE ACROSS THE STREET.
SO I GUESS THAT'S WHERE PEOPLE GO WHEN THEY GET OLD.
DID YOU SEE HOW SOME OF THEM WERE CHAINED TO THOSE MACHINES?
FUNPLACE
IT'S SO STRANGE HOW PEOPLE DECIDE TO FILL THEIR TIME.
I MEAN, YOU COULD-
UH-
ARF! ARF! ARF! ARF! ARF!
Heh Heh.

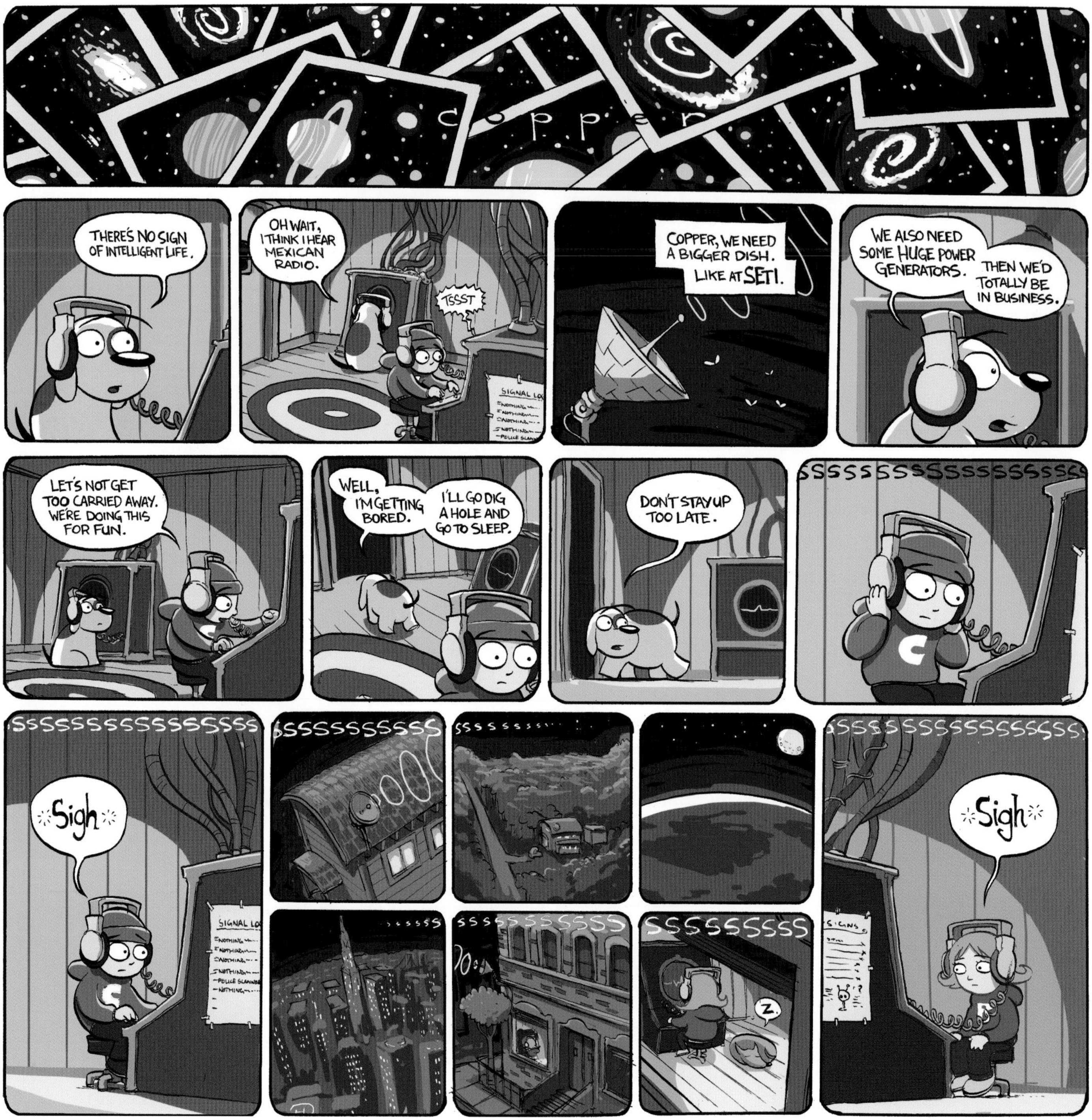
copper
THERE'S NO SIGN OF INTELLIGENT LIFE.
OH WAIT, I THINK I HEAR MEXICAN RADIO.
TSSST
COPPER, WE NEED A BIGGER DISH. LIKE AT SETI.
WE ALSO NEED SOME HUGE POWER GENERATORS.
THEN WE'D TOTALLY BE IN BUSINESS.
LET'S NOT GET TOO CARRIED AWAY. WE'RE DOING THIS FOR FUN.
WELL, I'M GETTING BORED.
I'LL GO DIG A HOLE AND GO TO SLEEP.
DON'T STAY UP TOO LATE.
SSSSSSSSSSSSSSSSSSSS
SSSSSSSSSSSSSSSS
Sigh
SSSSSSSSSS
SSSSSSSS
SSSSS
SSSSSSSSSSS
SSSSSSSSS
Z
SSSSSSSSSSSSSSSSS
Sigh

PURCHASE

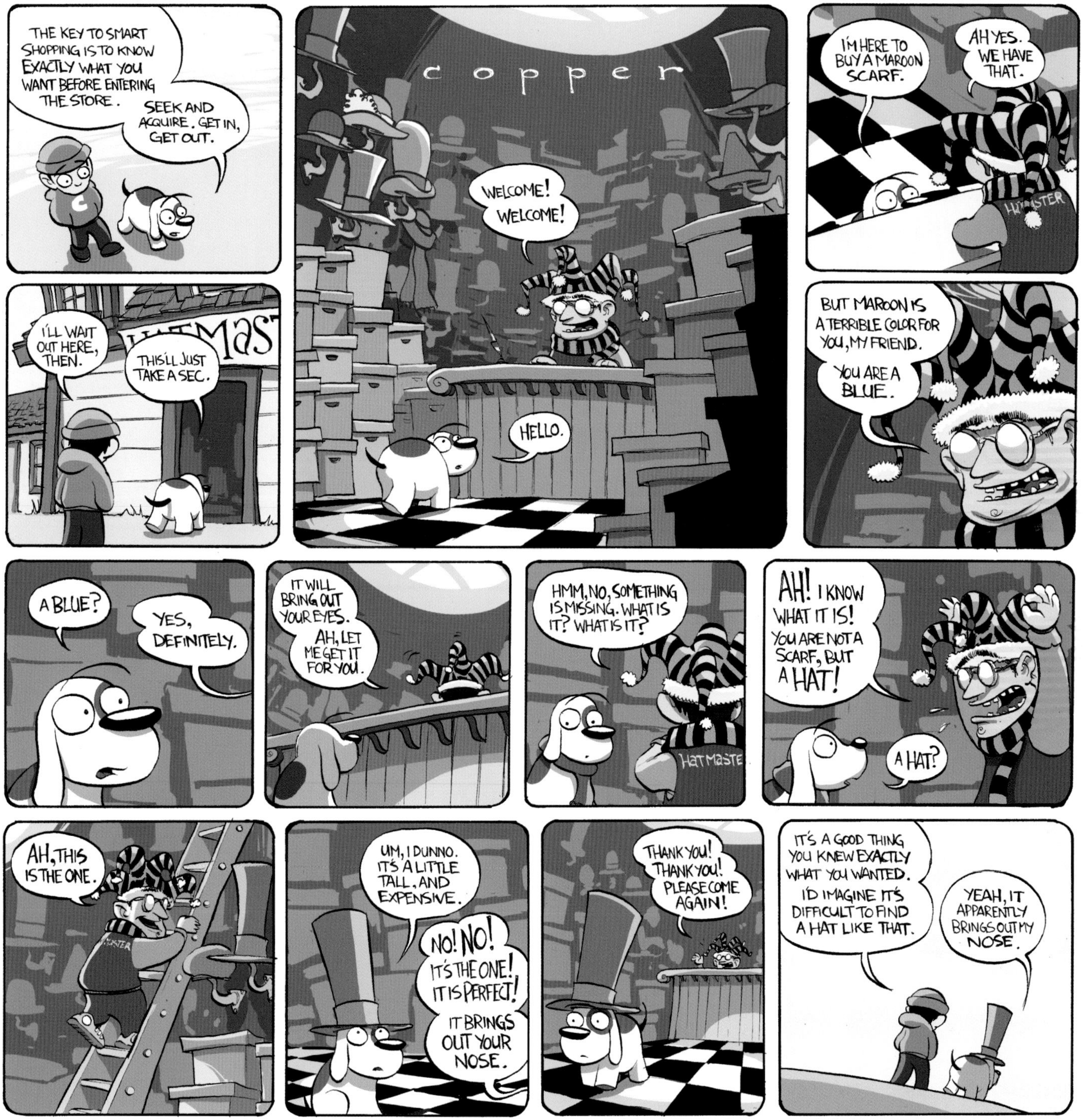

THE KEY TO SMART SHOPPING IS TO KNOW EXACTLY WHAT YOU WANT BEFORE ENTERING THE STORE.
SEEK AND ACQUIRE. GET IN, GET OUT.
I'LL WAIT OUT HERE, THEN.
THIS'LL JUST TAKE A SEC.
copper
WELCOME! WELCOME!
HELLO.
I'M HERE TO BUY A MAROON SCARF.
AH YES. WE HAVE THAT.
BUT MAROON IS A TERRIBLE COLOR FOR YOU, MY FRIEND.
YOU ARE A BLUE.
A BLUE?
YES, DEFINITELY.
IT WILL BRING OUT YOUR EYES.
AH, LET ME GET IT FOR YOU.
HMM, NO, SOMETHING IS MISSING. WHAT IS IT? WHAT IS IT?
AH! I KNOW WHAT IT IS! YOU ARE NOT A SCARF, BUT A HAT!
A HAT?
AH, THIS IS THE ONE.
UM, I DUNNO. IT'S A LITTLE TALL, AND EXPENSIVE.
NO! NO! IT'S THE ONE! IT IS PERFECT!
IT BRINGS OUT YOUR NOSE.
THANK YOU! THANK YOU! PLEASE COME AGAIN!
IT'S A GOOD THING YOU KNEW EXACTLY WHAT YOU WANTED.
I'D IMAGINE IT'S DIFFICULT TO FIND A HAT LIKE THAT.
YEAH, IT APPARENTLY BRINGS OUT MY NOSE.

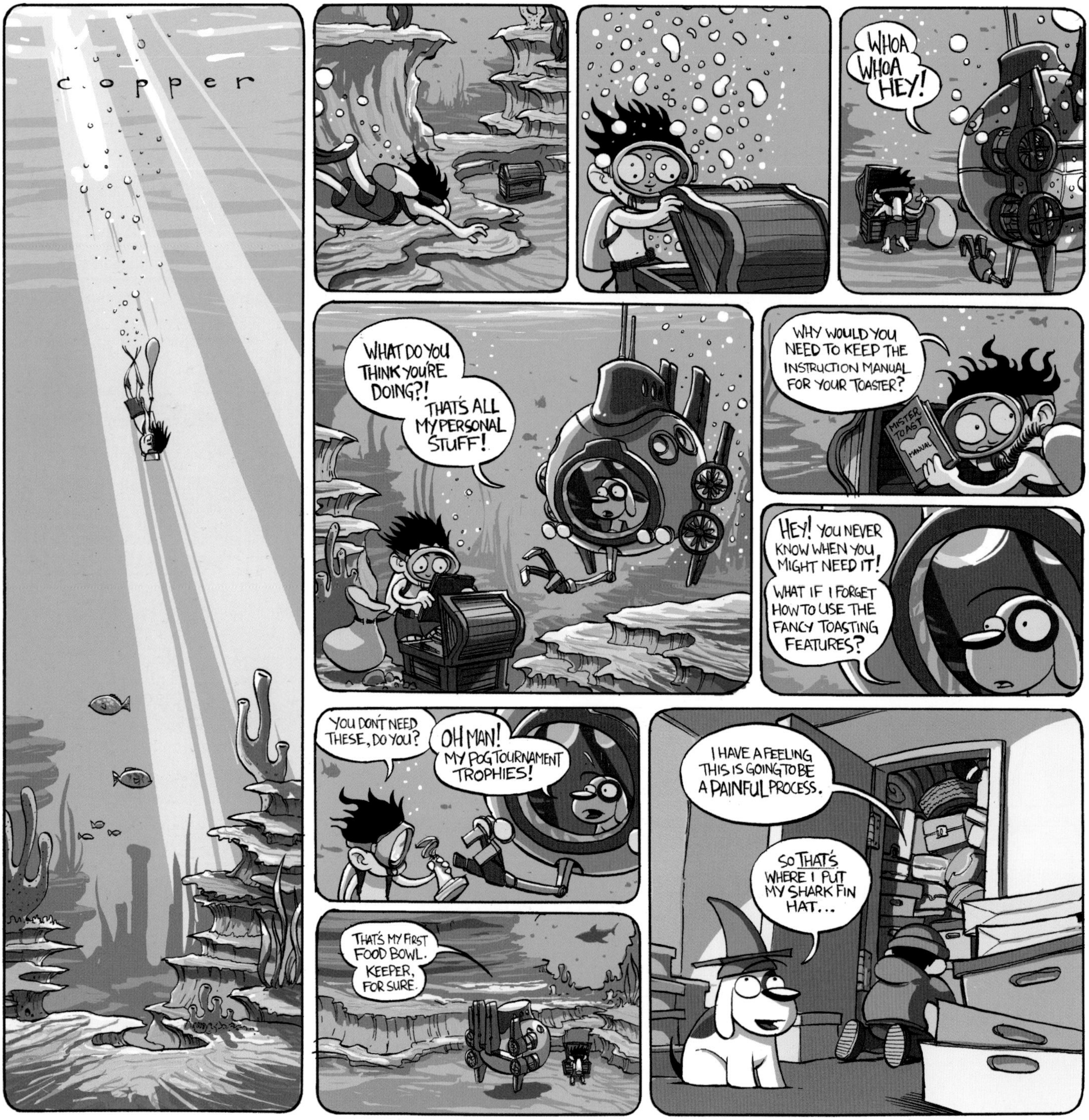
copper
WHOA WHOA HEY!
WHAT DO YOU THINK YOU'RE DOING?!
THAT'S ALL MY PERSONAL STUFF!
WHY WOULD YOU NEED TO KEEP THE INSTRUCTION MANUAL FOR YOUR TOASTER?
MISTER TOAST MANUAL
HEY! YOU NEVER KNOW WHEN YOU MIGHT NEED IT!
WHAT IF I FORGET HOW TO USE THE FANCY TOASTING FEATURES?
YOU DON'T NEED THESE, DO YOU?
OH MAN! MY POG TOURNAMENT TROPHIES!
THAT'S MY FIRST FOOD BOWL. KEEPER, FOR SURE.
I HAVE A FEELING THIS IS GOING TO BE A PAINFUL PROCESS.
SO THAT'S WHERE I PUT MY SHARK FIN HAT...

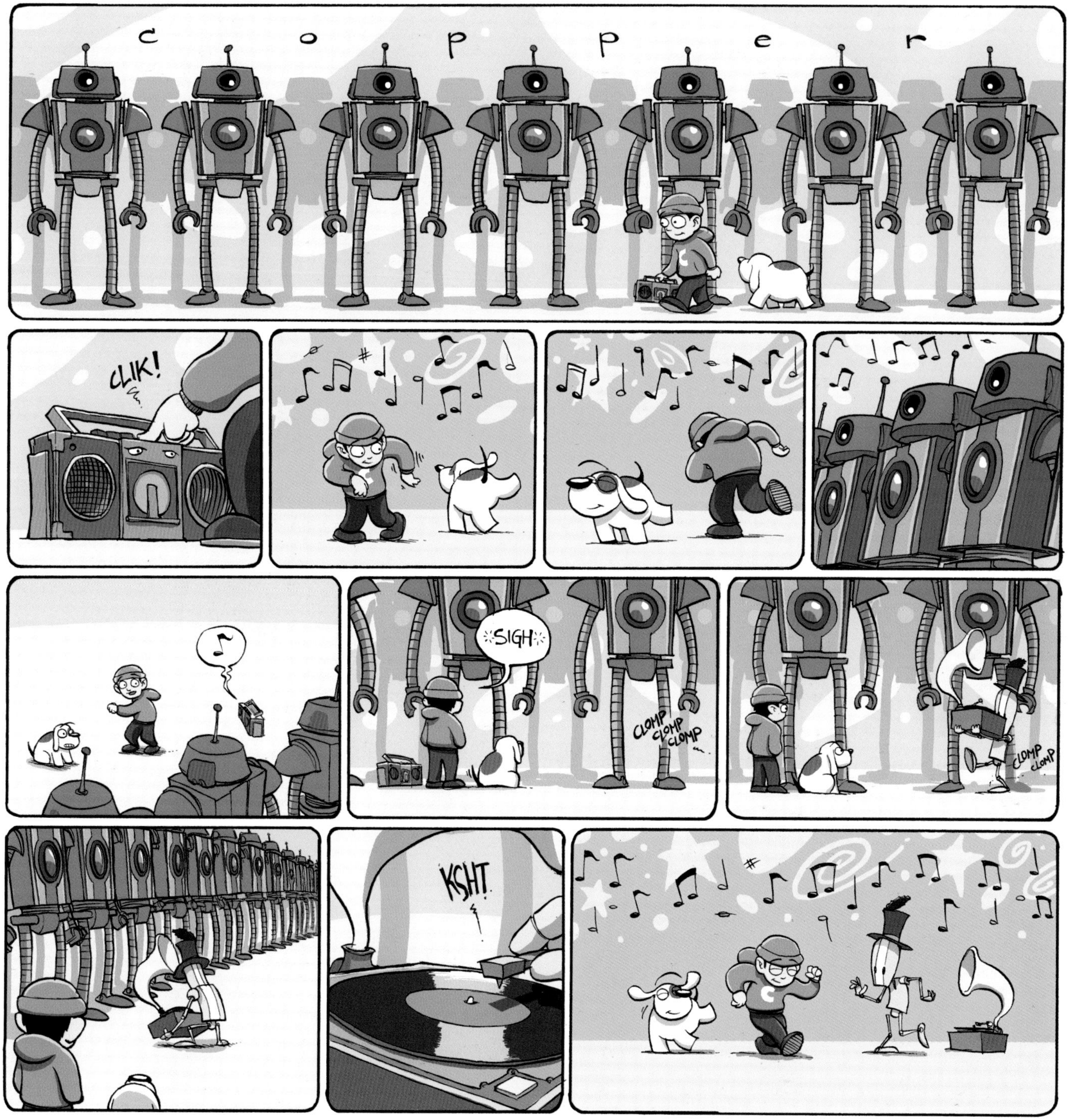
c o p p e r
CLIK!
SIGH
CLOMP CLOMP CLOMP
CLOMP CLOMP
KSHT.

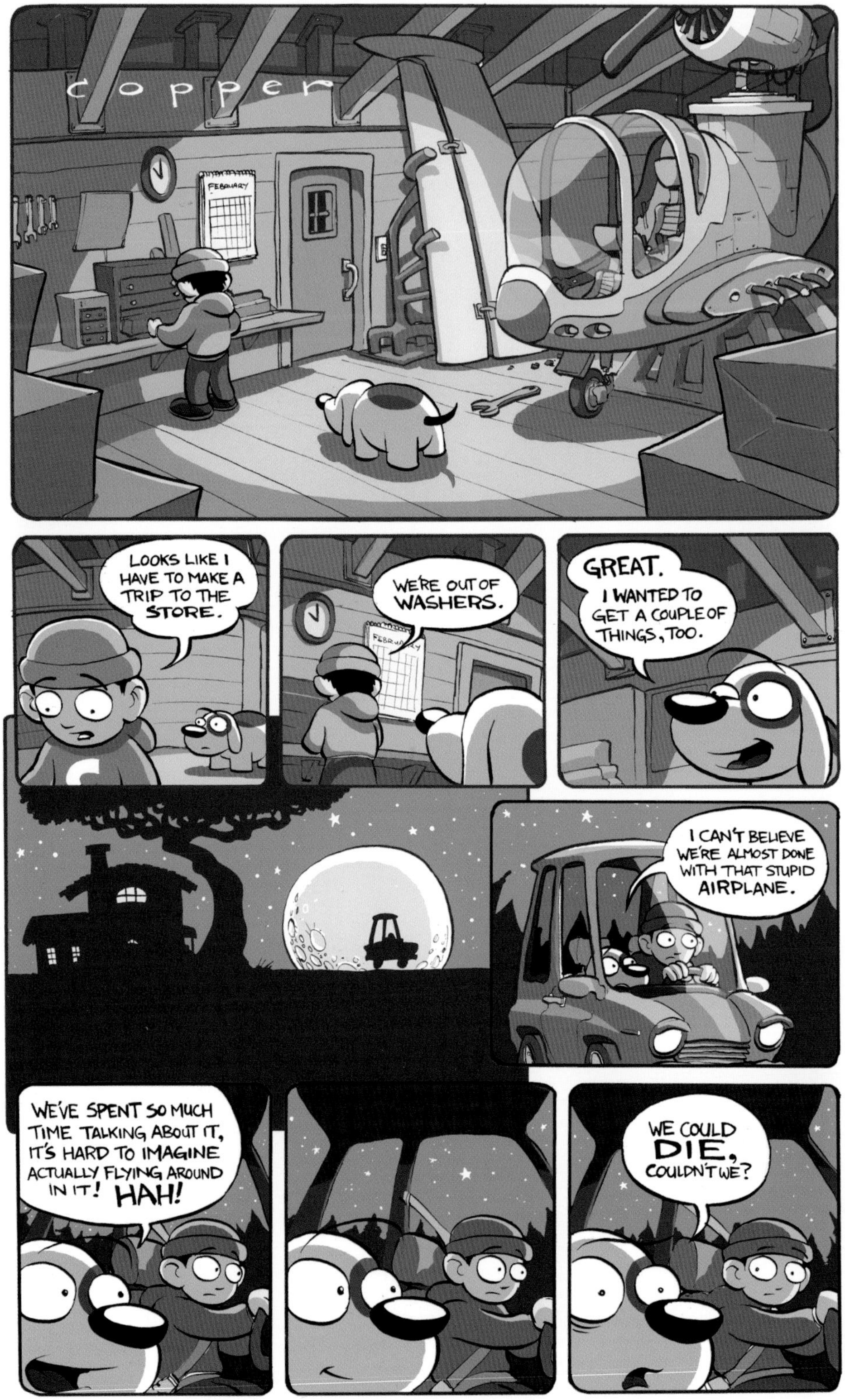
copper
FEBRUARY
LOOKS LIKE I HAVE TO MAKE A TRIP TO THE STORE.
WE'RE OUT OF WASHERS.
GREAT. I WANTED TO GET A COUPLE OF THINGS, TOO.
I CAN'T BELIEVE WE'RE ALMOST DONE WITH THAT STUPID AIRPLANE.
WE'VE SPENT SO MUCH TIME TALKING ABOUT IT, IT'S HARD TO IMAGINE ACTUALLY FLYING AROUND IN IT! HAH!
WE COULD DIE, COULDN'T WE?

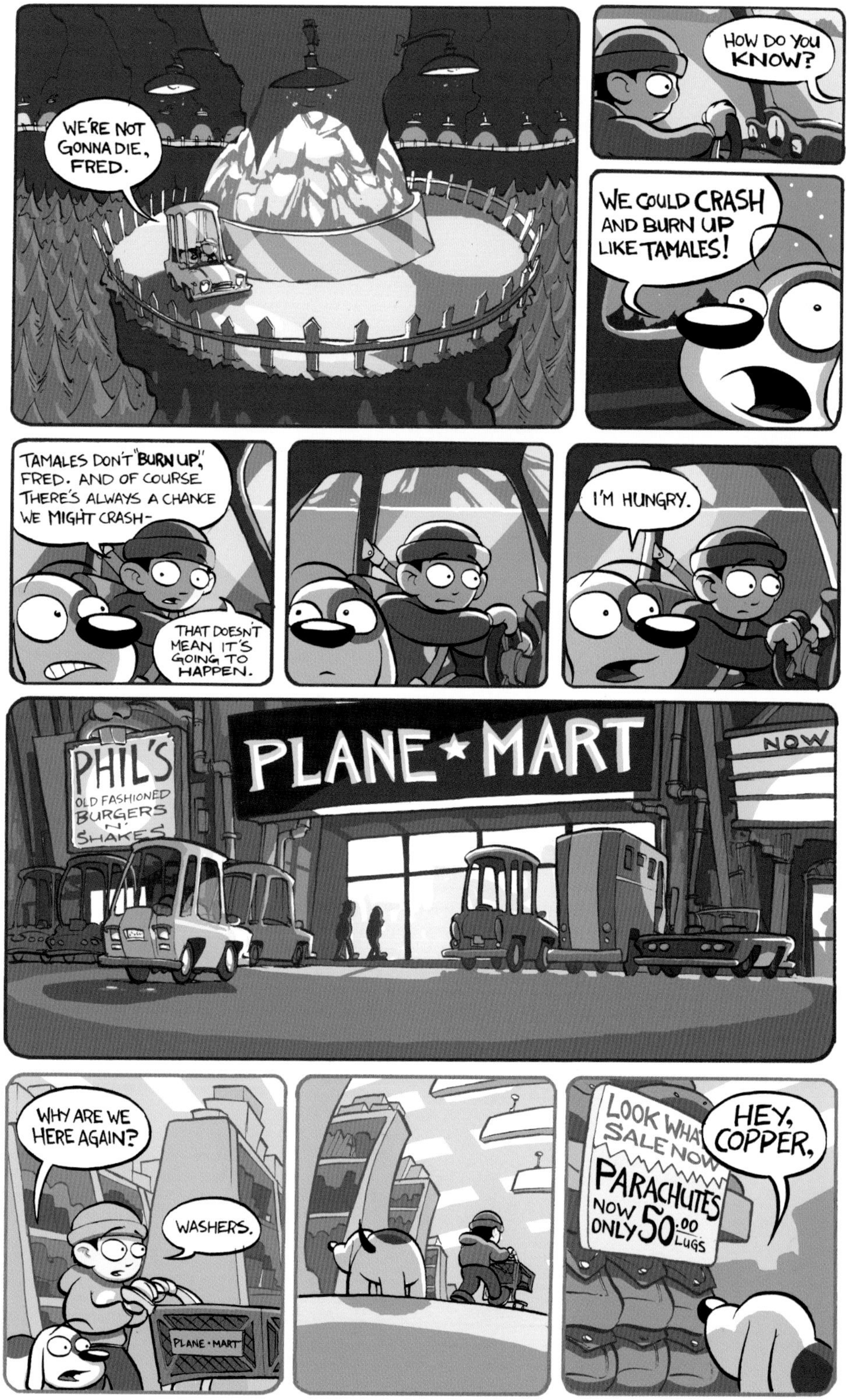
WE'RE NOT GONNA DIE, FRED.
HOW DO YOU KNOW?
WE COULD CRASH AND BURN UP LIKE TAMALES!
TAMALES DON'T "BURN UP," FRED. AND OF COURSE THERE'S ALWAYS A CHANCE WE MIGHT CRASH-
THAT DOESN'T MEAN IT'S GOING TO HAPPEN.
I'M HUNGRY.
PHIL'S OLD FASHIONED BURGERS N' SHAKES
PLANE ★ MART
NOW
WHY ARE WE HERE AGAIN?
WASHERS.
PLANE • MART
LOOK WHAT'S ON SALE NOW
PARACHUTES NOW ONLY 50.00 LUGS
HEY, COPPER,

MAIDEN VOYAGE

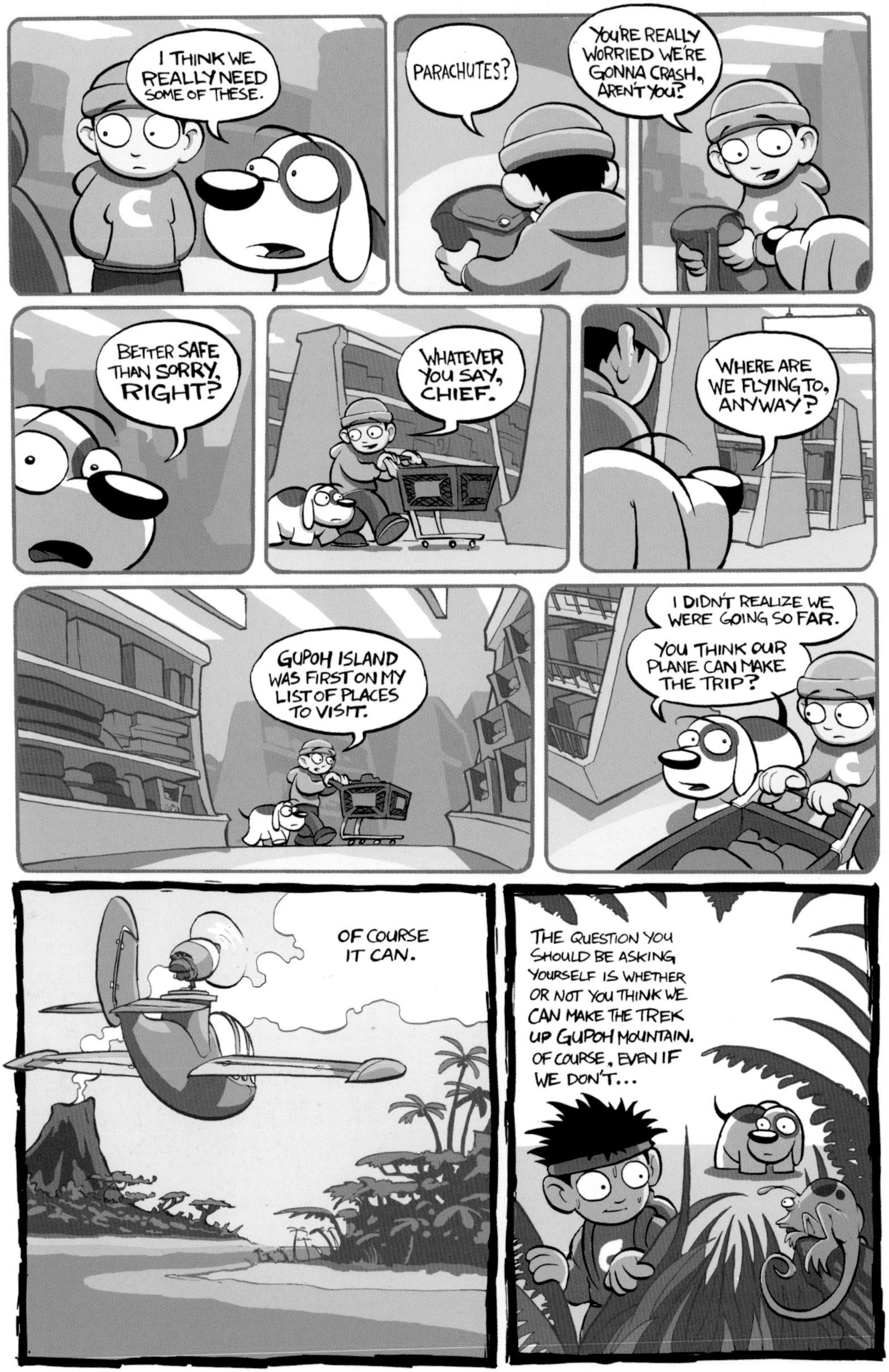
I THINK WE REALLY NEED SOME OF THESE.
PARACHUTES?
YOU'RE REALLY WORRIED WE'RE GONNA CRASH, AREN'T YOU?
BETTER SAFE THAN SORRY, RIGHT?
WHATEVER YOU SAY, CHIEF.
WHERE ARE WE FLYING TO, ANYWAY?
GUPOH ISLAND WAS FIRST ON MY LIST OF PLACES TO VISIT.
I DIDN'T REALIZE WE WERE GOING SO FAR.
YOU THINK OUR PLANE CAN MAKE THE TRIP?
OF COURSE IT CAN.
THE QUESTION YOU SHOULD BE ASKING YOURSELF IS WHETHER OR NOT YOU THINK WE CAN MAKE THE TREK UP GUPOH MOUNTAIN. OF COURSE, EVEN IF WE DON'T...

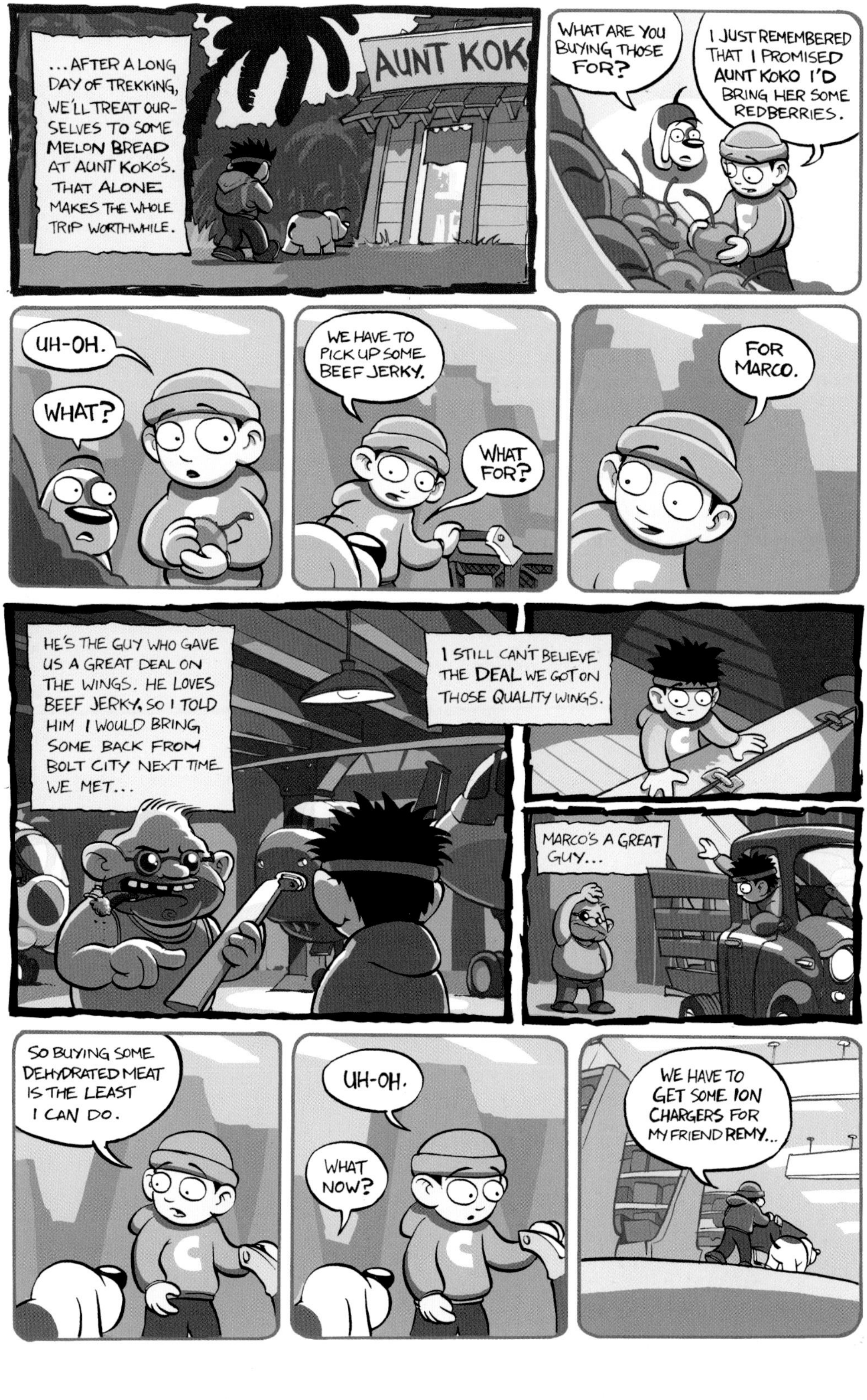

AUNT KOK
...AFTER A LONG DAY OF TREKKING, WE'LL TREAT OURSELVES TO SOME MELON BREAD AT AUNT KOKO'S. THAT ALONE MAKES THE WHOLE TRIP WORTHWHILE.
WHAT ARE YOU BUYING THOSE FOR?
I JUST REMEMBERED THAT I PROMISED AUNT KOKO I'D BRING HER SOME REDBERRIES.
UH-OH.
WHAT?
WE HAVE TO PICK UP SOME BEEF JERKY.
WHAT FOR?
FOR MARCO.
HE'S THE GUY WHO GAVE US A GREAT DEAL ON THE WINGS. HE LOVES BEEF JERKY, SO I TOLD HIM I WOULD BRING SOME BACK FROM BOLT CITY NEXT TIME WE MET...
I STILL CAN'T BELIEVE THE DEAL WE GOT ON THOSE QUALITY WINGS.
MARCO'S A GREAT GUY...
SO BUYING SOME DEHYDRATED MEAT IS THE LEAST I CAN DO.
UH-OH.
WHAT NOW?
WE HAVE TO GET SOME ION CHARGERS FOR MY FRIEND REMY...

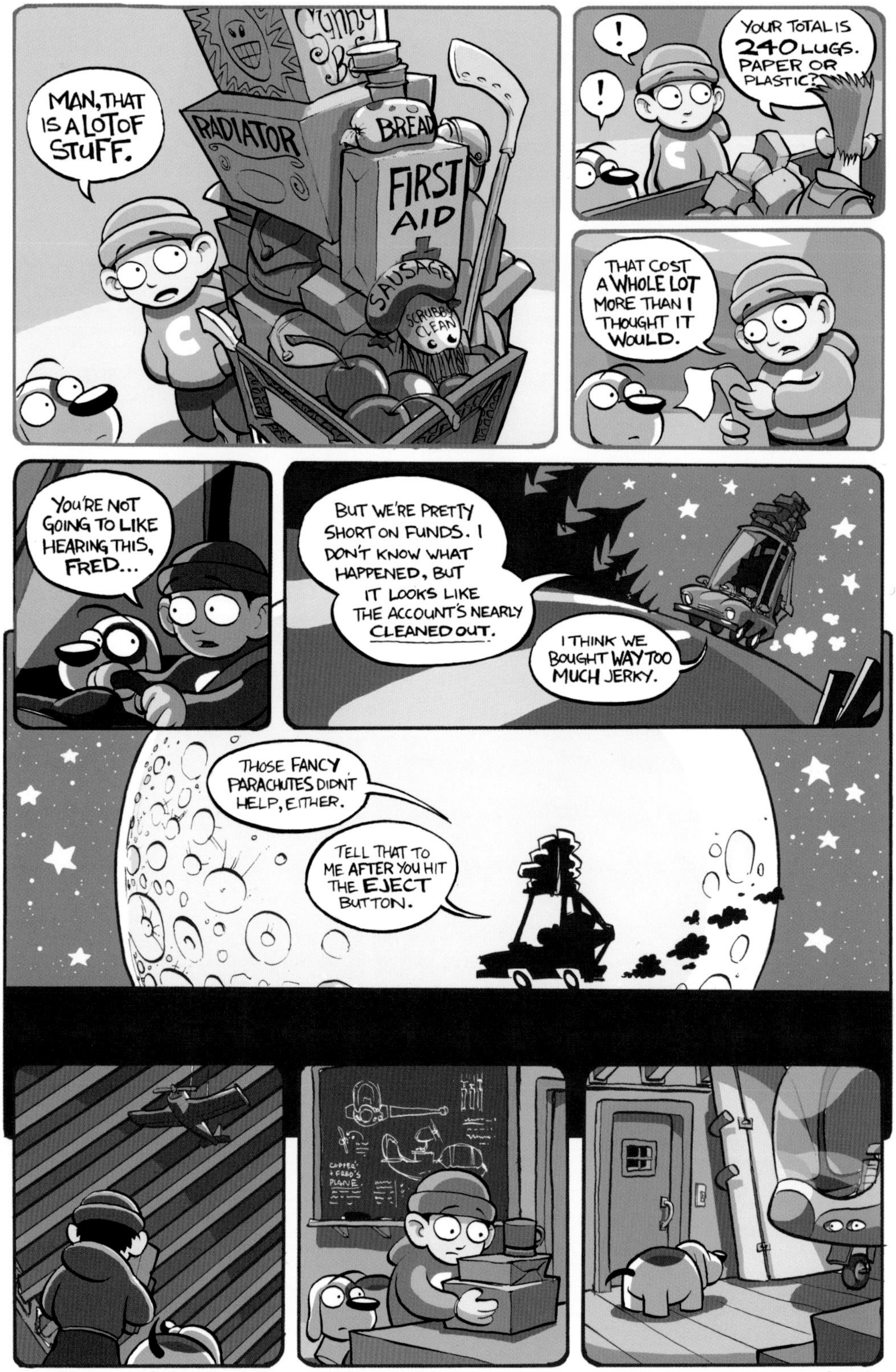
MAN, THAT IS A LOT OF STUFF.
RADIATOR
BREAD
FIRST AID
SAUSAGE
SCRUBBY CLEAN
!
!
YOUR TOTAL IS 240 LUGS. PAPER OR PLASTIC?
THAT COST A WHOLE LOT MORE THAN I THOUGHT IT WOULD.
YOU'RE NOT GOING TO LIKE HEARING THIS, FRED...
BUT WE'RE PRETTY SHORT ON FUNDS. I DON'T KNOW WHAT HAPPENED, BUT IT LOOKS LIKE THE ACCOUNT'S NEARLY CLEANED OUT.
I THINK WE BOUGHT WAY TOO MUCH JERKY.
THOSE FANCY PARACHUTES DIDN'T HELP, EITHER.
TELL THAT TO ME AFTER YOU HIT THE EJECT BUTTON.
COPPER'S + FRED'S PLANE

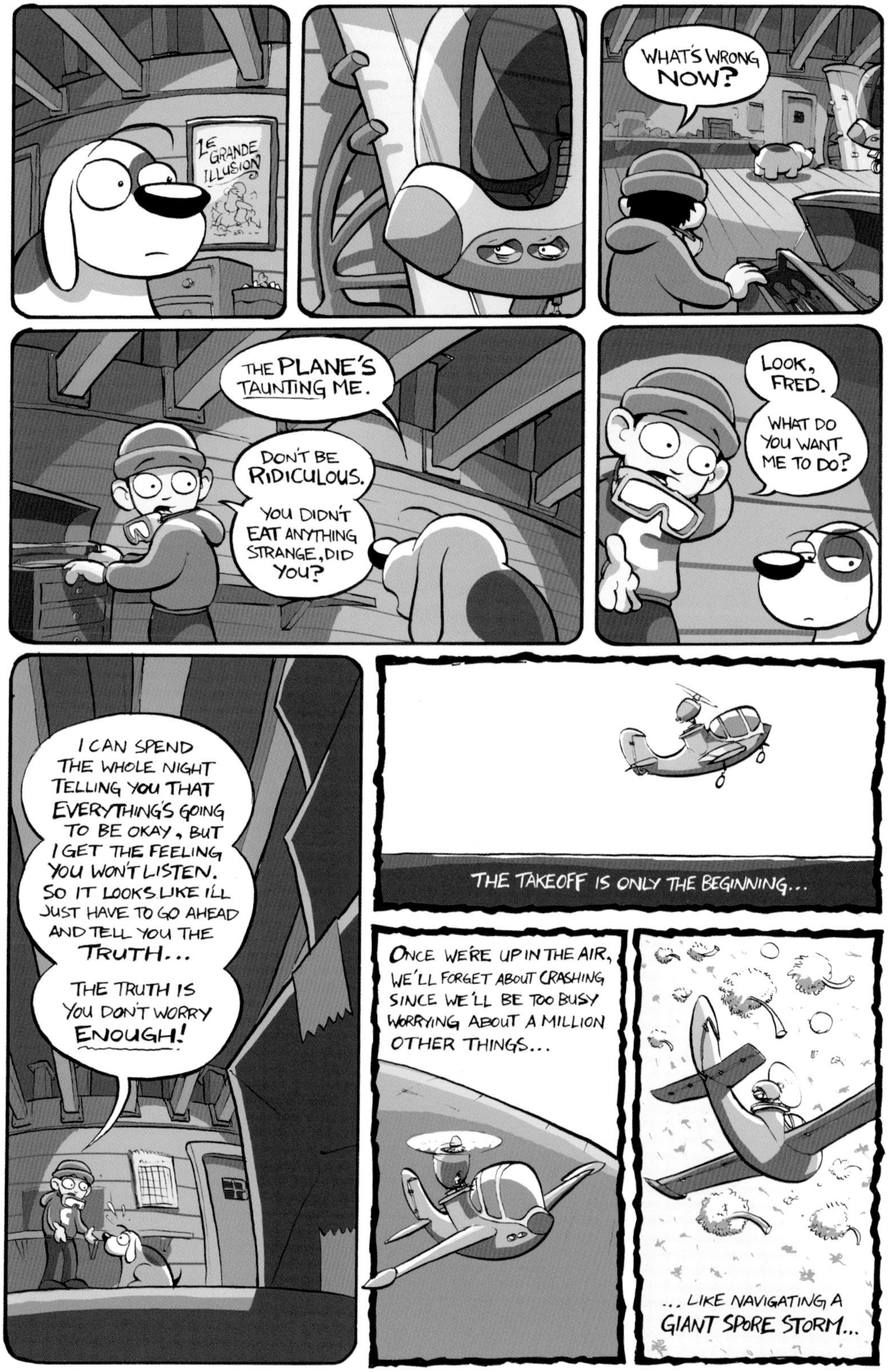
LE GRANDE ILLUSION
WHAT'S WRONG NOW?
THE PLANE'S TAUNTING ME.
DON'T BE RIDICULOUS.
YOU DIDN'T EAT ANYTHING STRANGE, DID YOU?
LOOK, FRED.
WHAT DO YOU WANT ME TO DO?
I CAN SPEND THE WHOLE NIGHT TELLING YOU THAT EVERYTHING'S GOING TO BE OKAY, BUT I GET THE FEELING YOU WON'T LISTEN. SO IT LOOKS LIKE I'LL JUST HAVE TO GO AHEAD AND TELL YOU THE TRUTH...
THE TRUTH IS YOU DON'T WORRY ENOUGH!
THE TAKEOFF IS ONLY THE BEGINNING...
ONCE WE'RE UP IN THE AIR, WE'LL FORGET ABOUT CRASHING SINCE WE'LL BE TOO BUSY WORRYING ABOUT A MILLION OTHER THINGS...
...LIKE NAVIGATING A GIANT SPORE STORM...

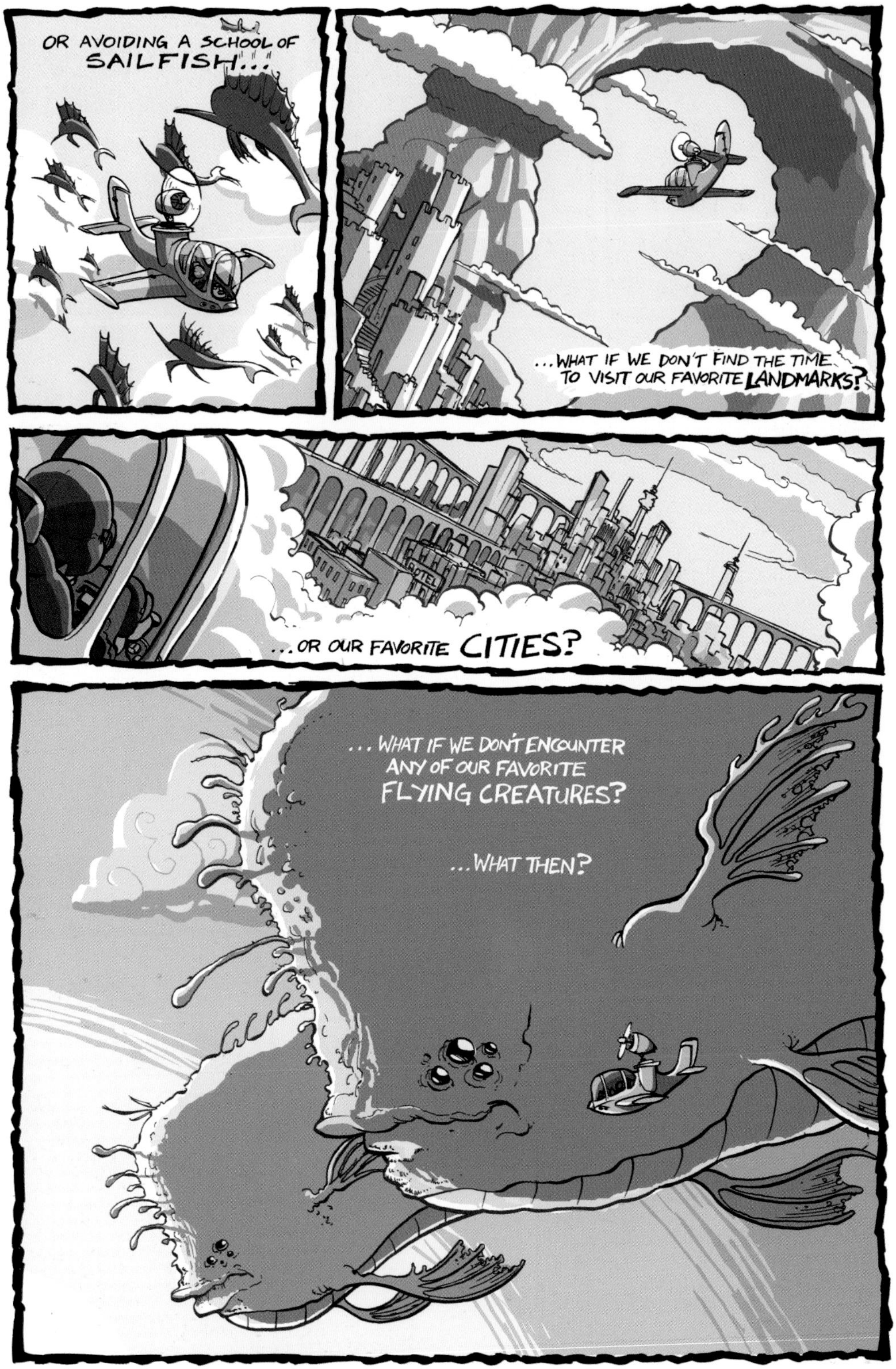
OR AVOIDING A SCHOOL OF SAILFISH...
...WHAT IF WE DON'T FIND THE TIME TO VISIT OUR FAVORITE LANDMARKS?
...OR OUR FAVORITE CITIES?
...WHAT IF WE DON'T ENCOUNTER ANY OF OUR FAVORITE FLYING CREATURES?
...WHAT THEN?

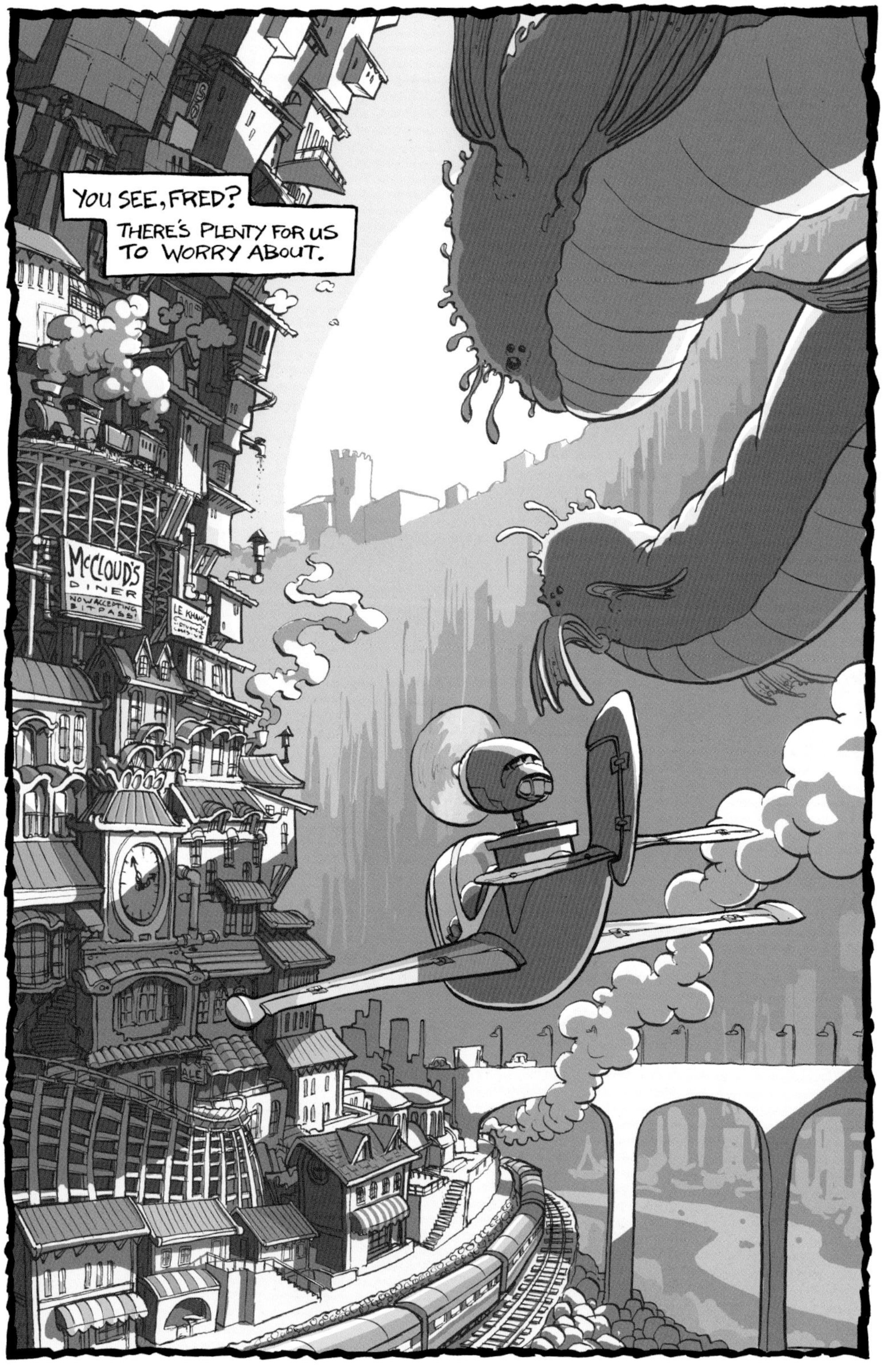
YOU SEE, FRED?
THERE'S PLENTY FOR US TO WORRY ABOUT.
McCLOUD'S DINER
NOW ACCEPTING BITPASS!

MAIDEN VOYAGE

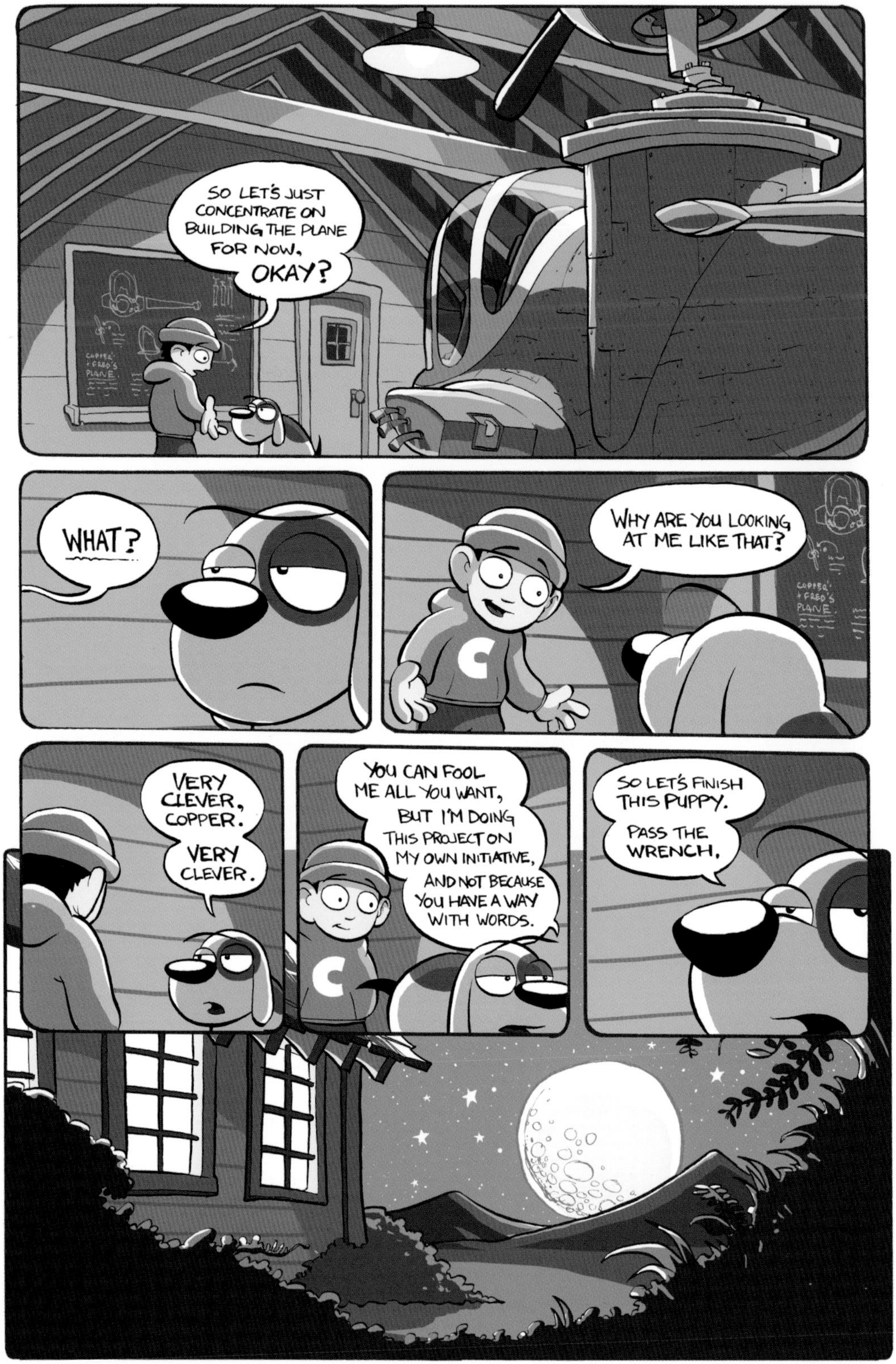
SO LET'S JUST CONCENTRATE ON BUILDING THE PLANE FOR NOW, OKAY?
COPPER + FRED'S PLANE
WHAT?
WHY ARE YOU LOOKING AT ME LIKE THAT?
VERY CLEVER, COPPER.
VERY CLEVER.
YOU CAN FOOL ME ALL YOU WANT,
BUT I'M DOING THIS PROJECT ON MY OWN INITIATIVE,
AND NOT BECAUSE YOU HAVE A WAY WITH WORDS.
SO LET'S FINISH THIS PUPPY.
PASS THE WRENCH.

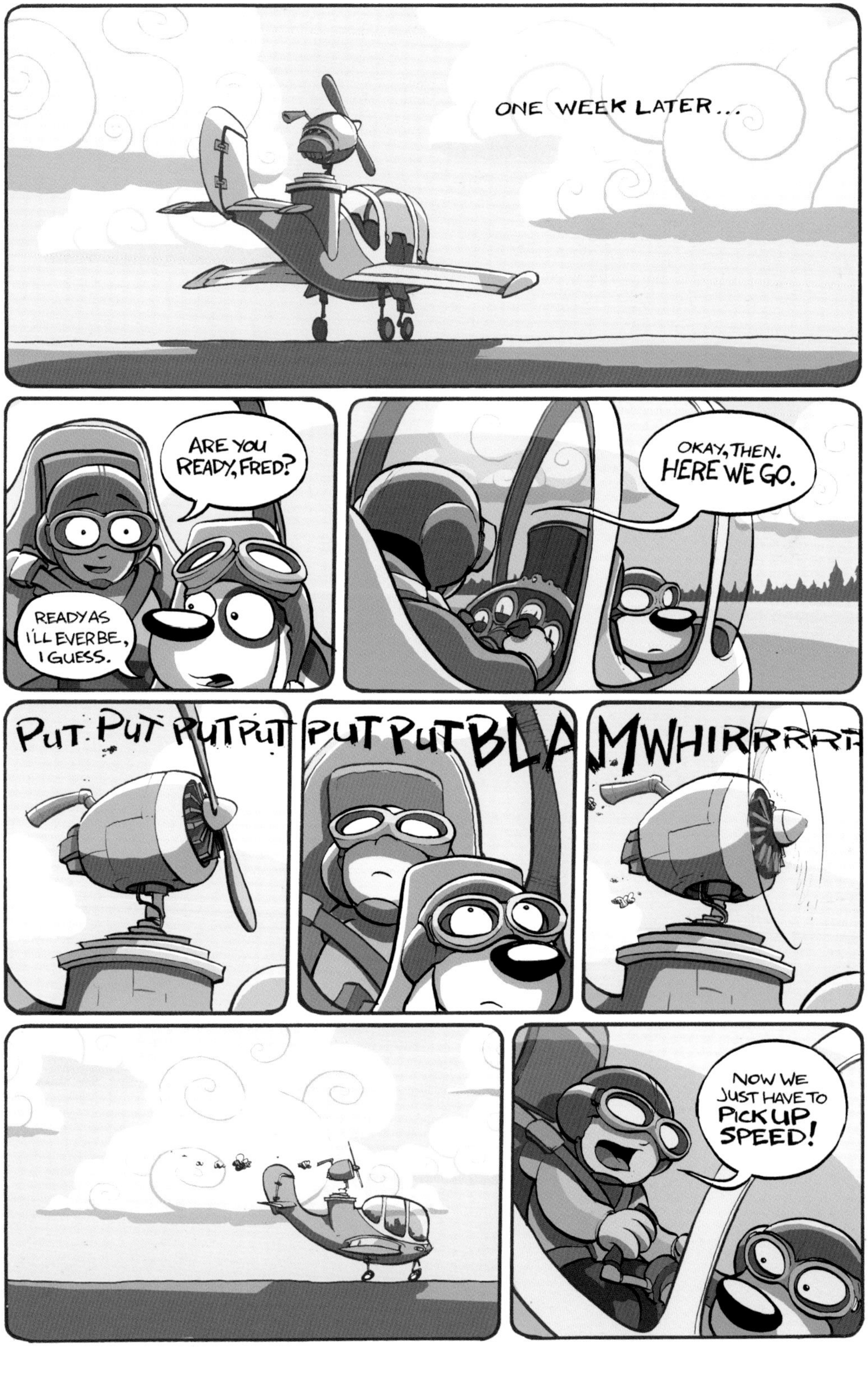
ONE WEEK LATER...
ARE YOU READY, FRED?
READY AS I'LL EVER BE, I GUESS.
OKAY, THEN. HERE WE GO.
PUT. PUT PUTPUT
PUT PUT BLAM
WHIRRRRR
NOW WE JUST HAVE TO PICK UP SPEED!

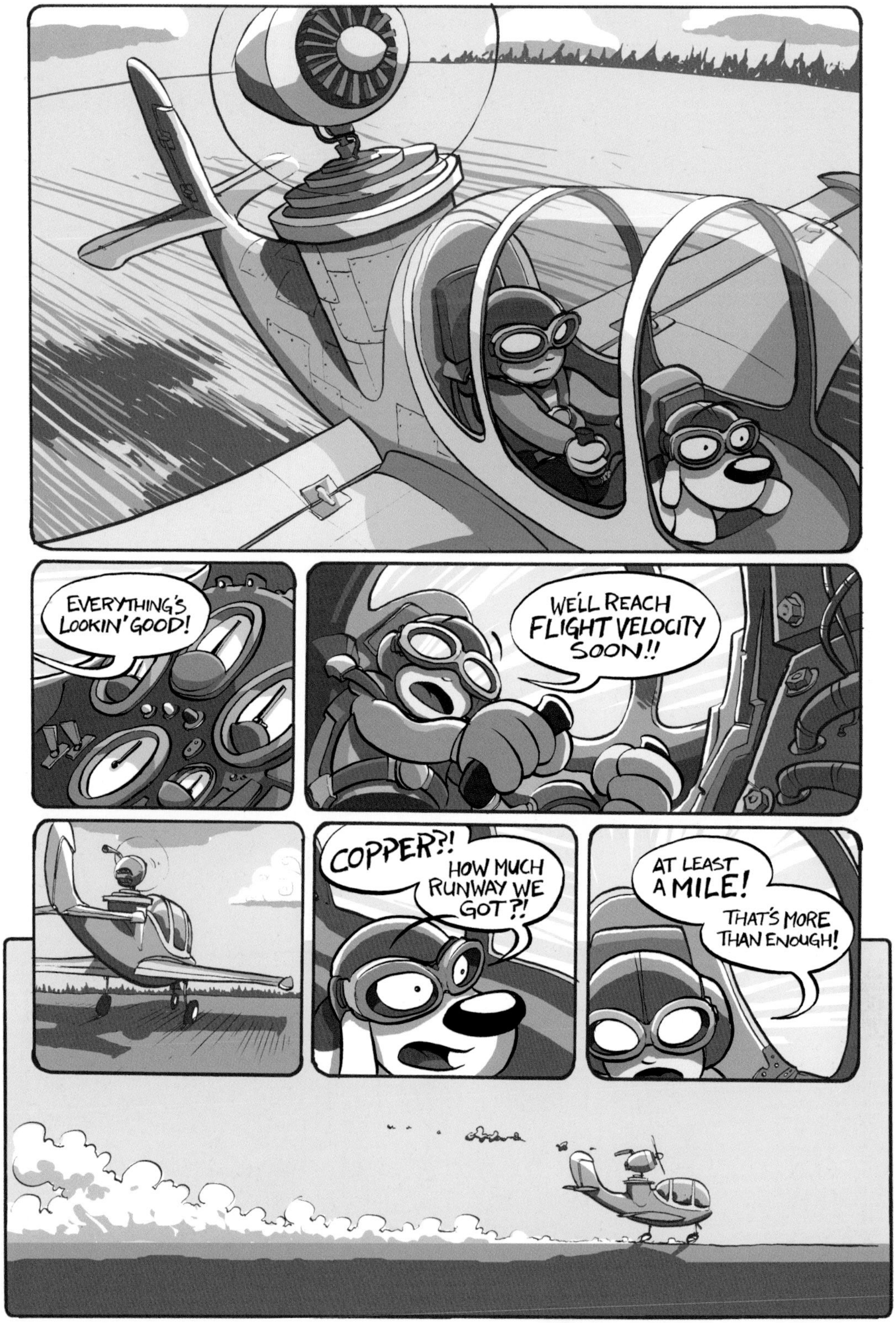
EVERYTHING'S LOOKIN' GOOD!
WE'LL REACH FLIGHT VELOCITY SOON!!
COPPER?!
HOW MUCH RUNWAY WE GOT?!
AT LEAST A MILE!
THAT'S MORE THAN ENOUGH!

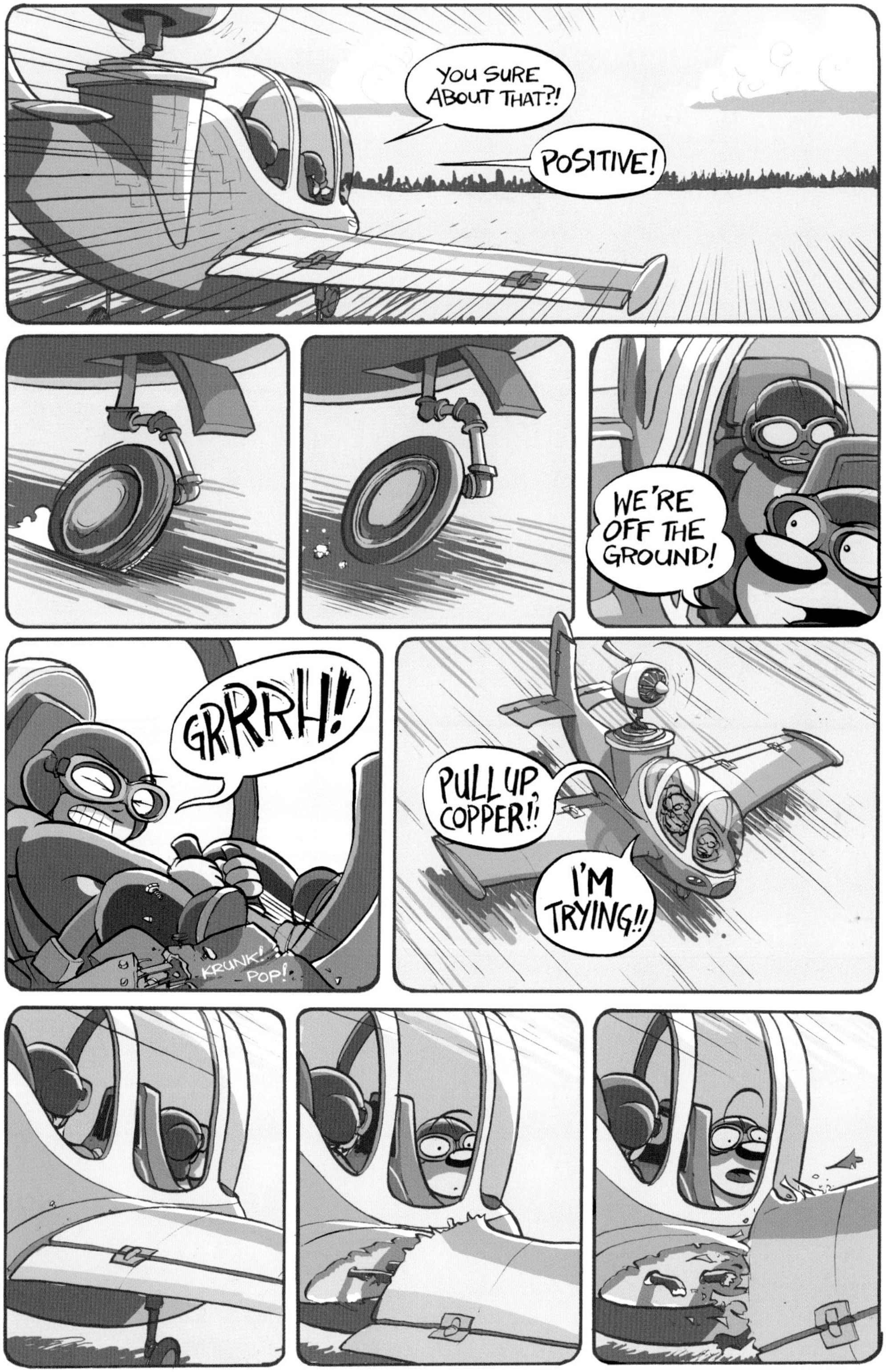
YOU SURE ABOUT THAT?!
POSITIVE!
WE'RE OFF THE GROUND!
GRRRH!
KRUNK!
POP!
PULL UP, COPPER!!
I'M TRYING!!

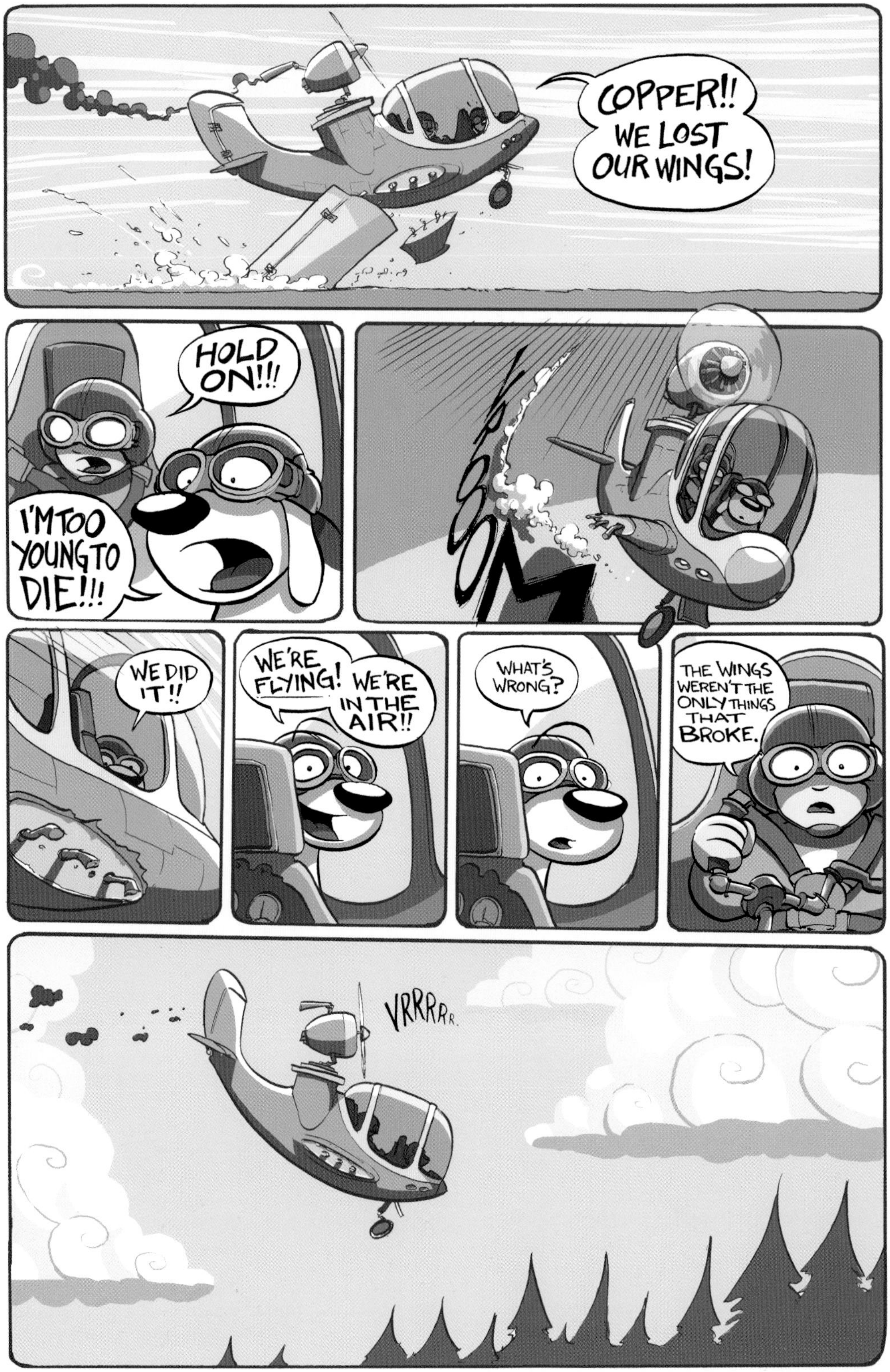
COPPER!! WE LOST OUR WINGS!
HOLD ON!!!
I'M TOO YOUNG TO DIE!!!
VROOOM
WE DID IT!!
WE'RE FLYING!
WE'RE IN THE AIR!!
WHAT'S WRONG?
THE WINGS WEREN'T THE ONLY THINGS THAT BROKE.
VRRRRR.

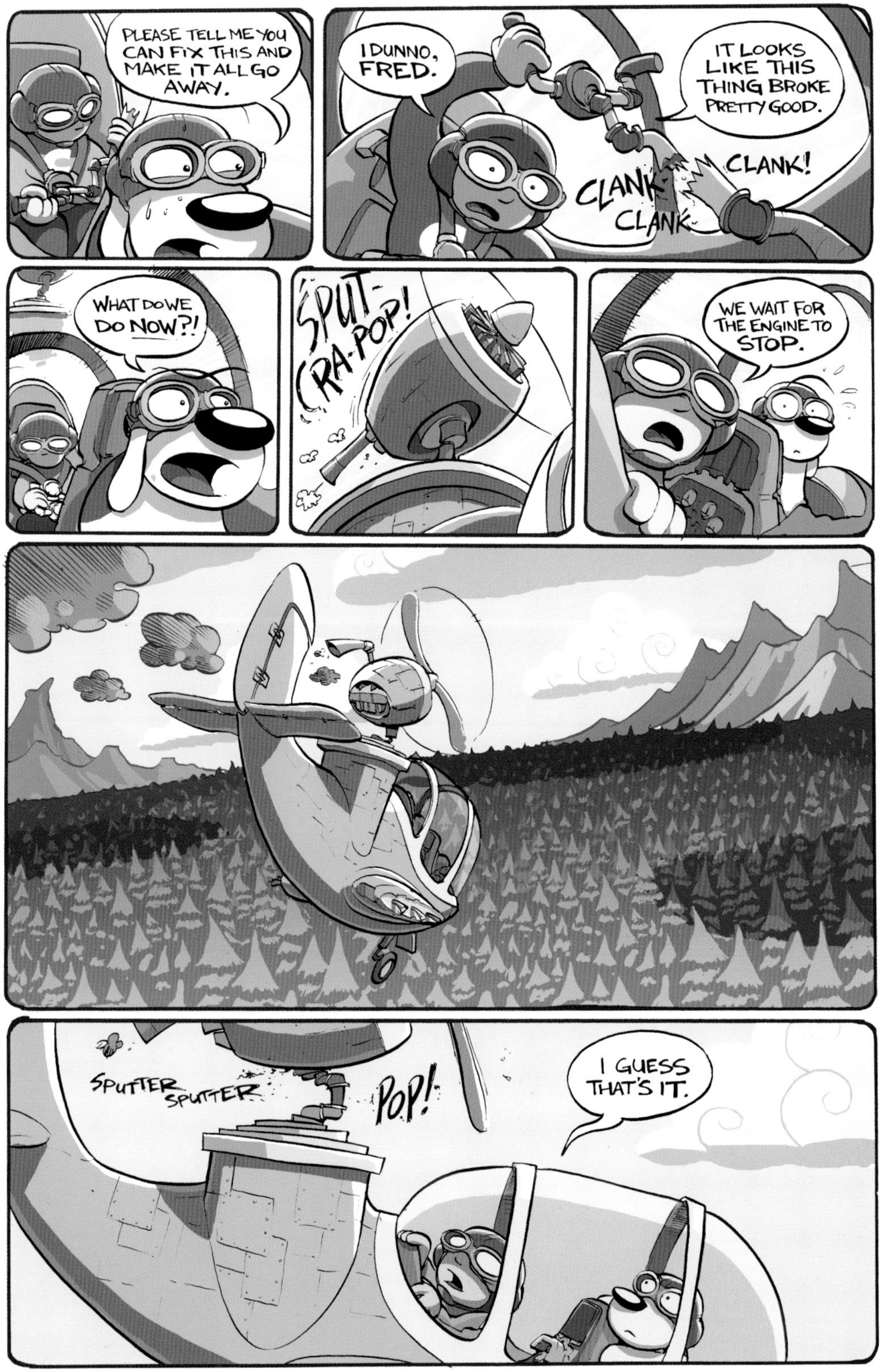
PLEASE TELL ME YOU CAN FIX THIS AND MAKE IT ALL GO AWAY.
I DUNNO, FRED.
IT LOOKS LIKE THIS THING BROKE PRETTY GOOD.
CLANK CLANK
CLANK!
WHAT DO WE DO NOW?!
SPUT-CRA-POP!
WE WAIT FOR THE ENGINE TO STOP.
SPUTTER SPUTTER
POP!
I GUESS THAT'S IT.

MAIDEN VOYAGE

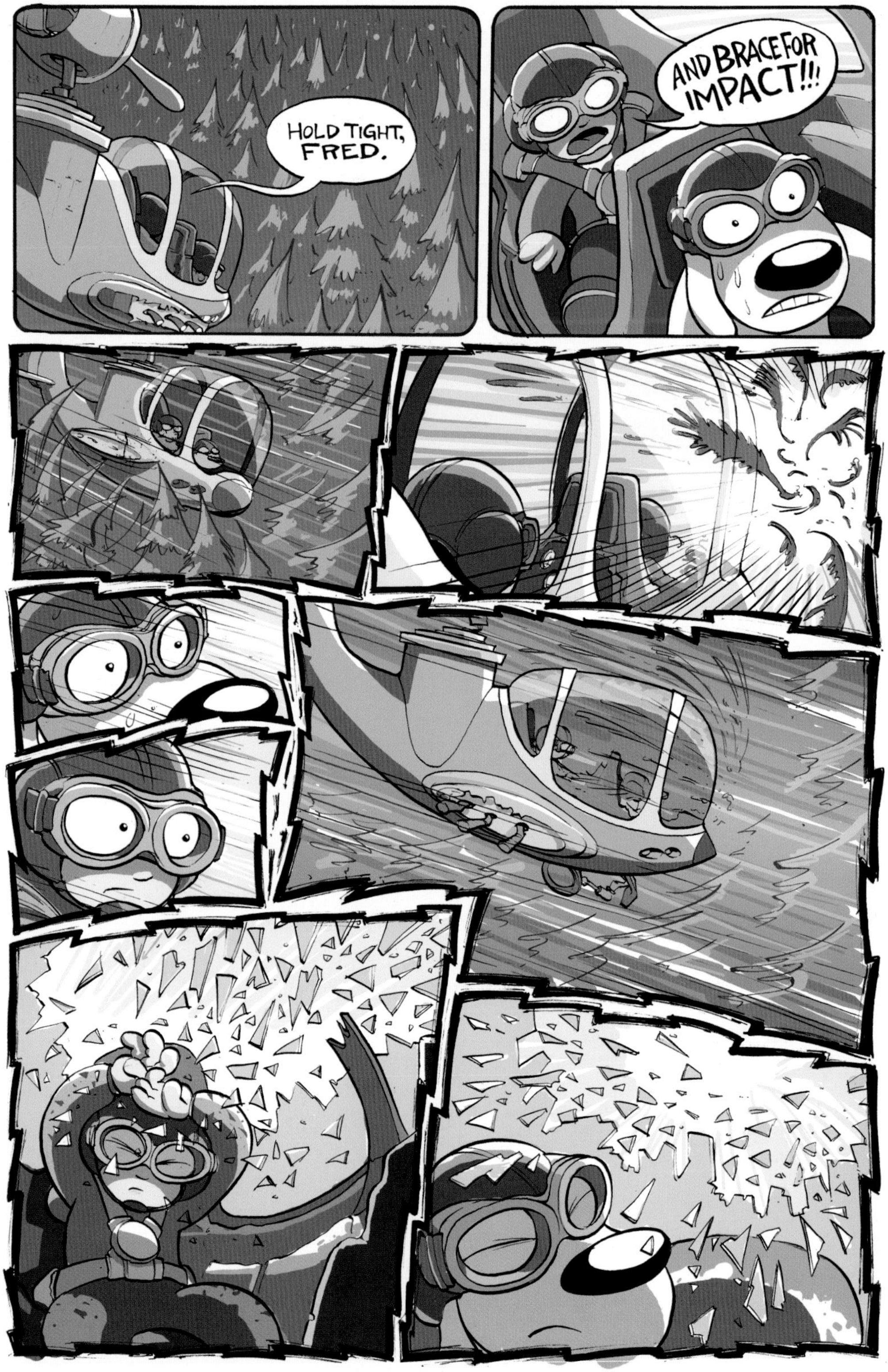
HOLD TIGHT, FRED.
AND BRACE FOR IMPACT!!!

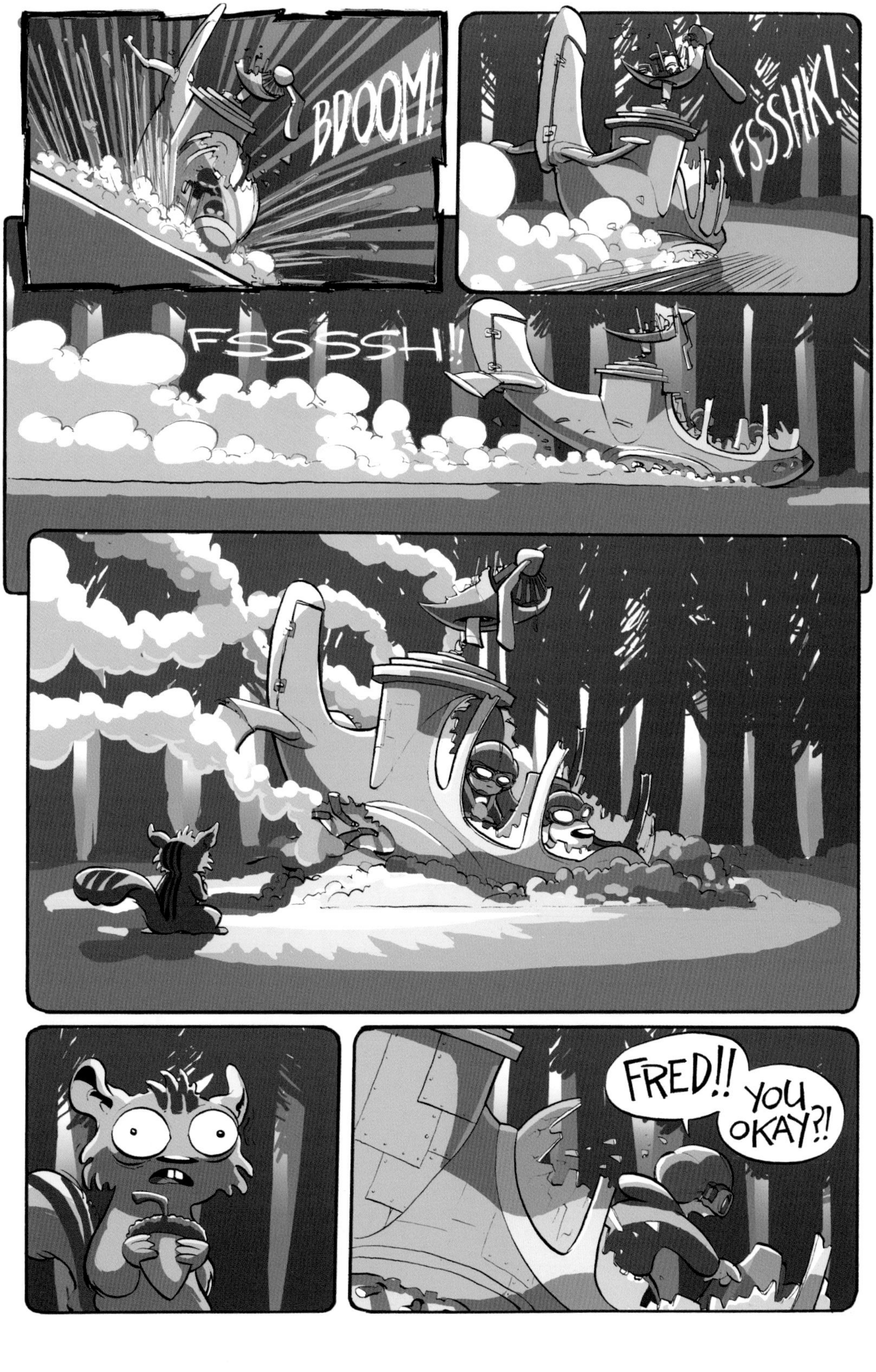
BDOOM!
FSSSHK!
FSSSSH!!
FRED!!
YOU OKAY?!

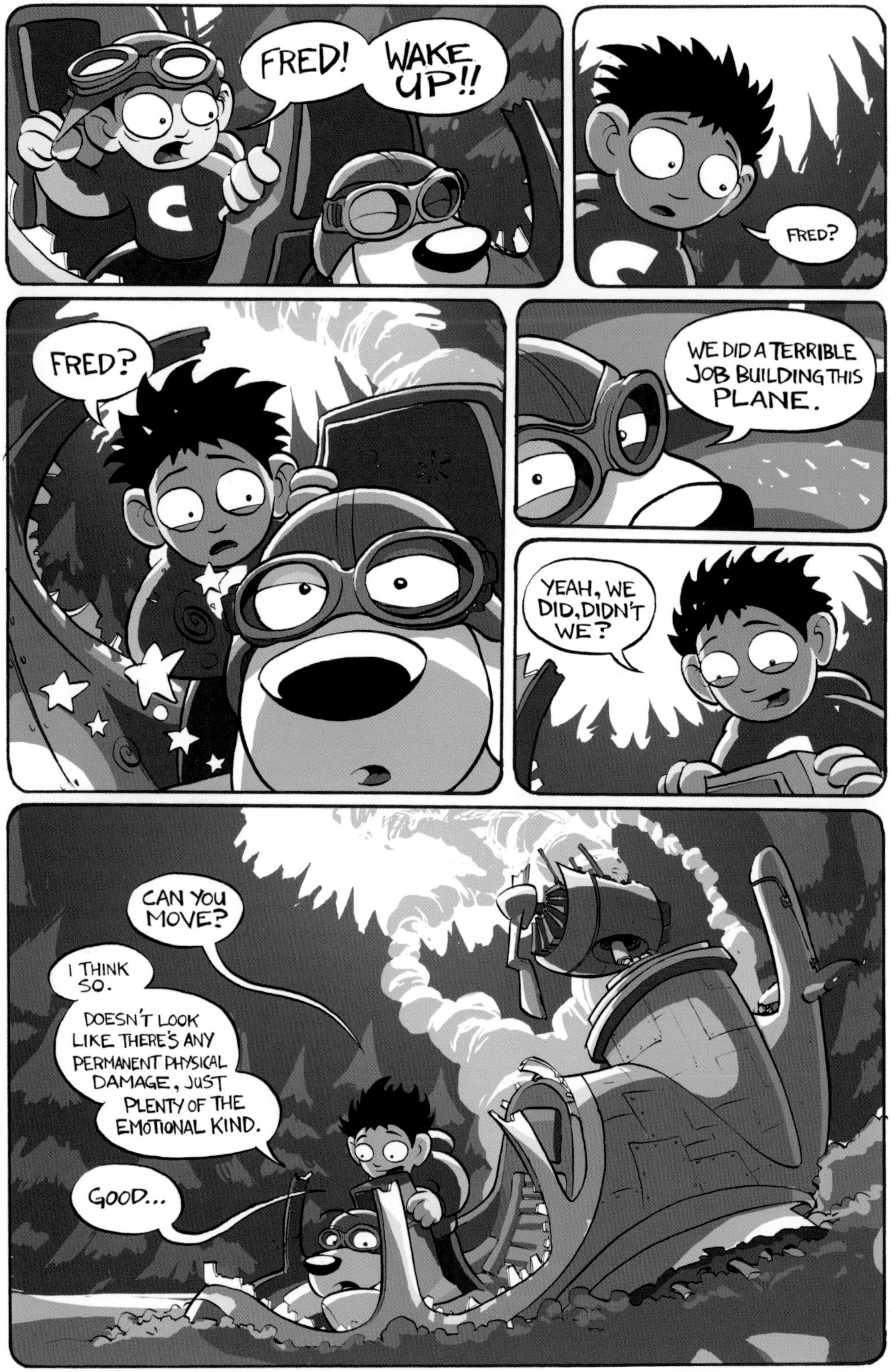
FRED!
WAKE UP!!
FRED?
FRED?
WE DID A TERRIBLE JOB BUILDING THIS PLANE.
YEAH, WE DID, DIDN'T WE?
CAN YOU MOVE?
I THINK SO.
DOESN'T LOOK LIKE THERE'S ANY PERMANENT PHYSICAL DAMAGE, JUST PLENTY OF THE EMOTIONAL KIND.
GOOD...

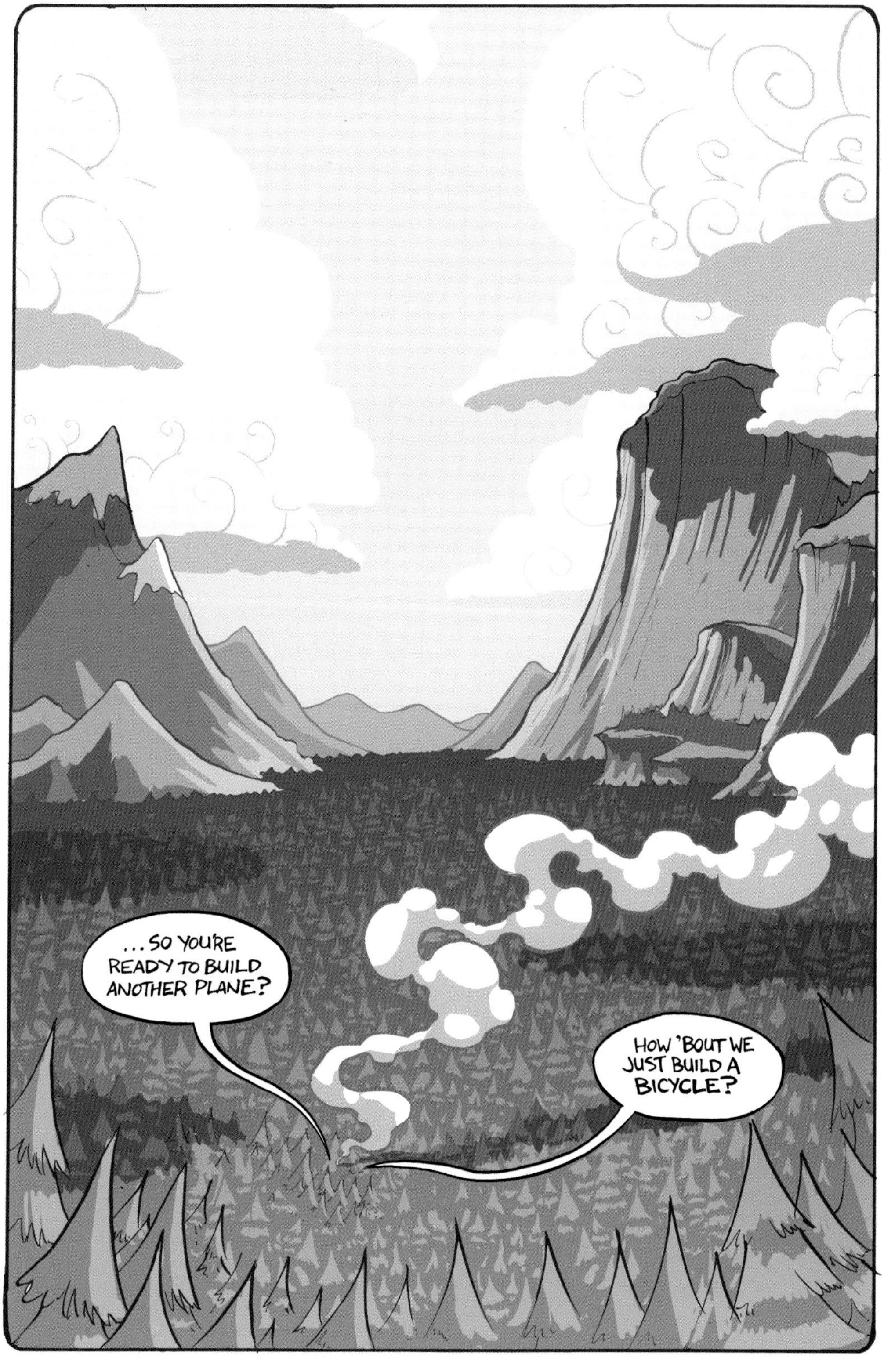
...SO YOU'RE READY TO BUILD ANOTHER PLANE?
HOW 'BOUT WE JUST BUILD A BICYCLE?

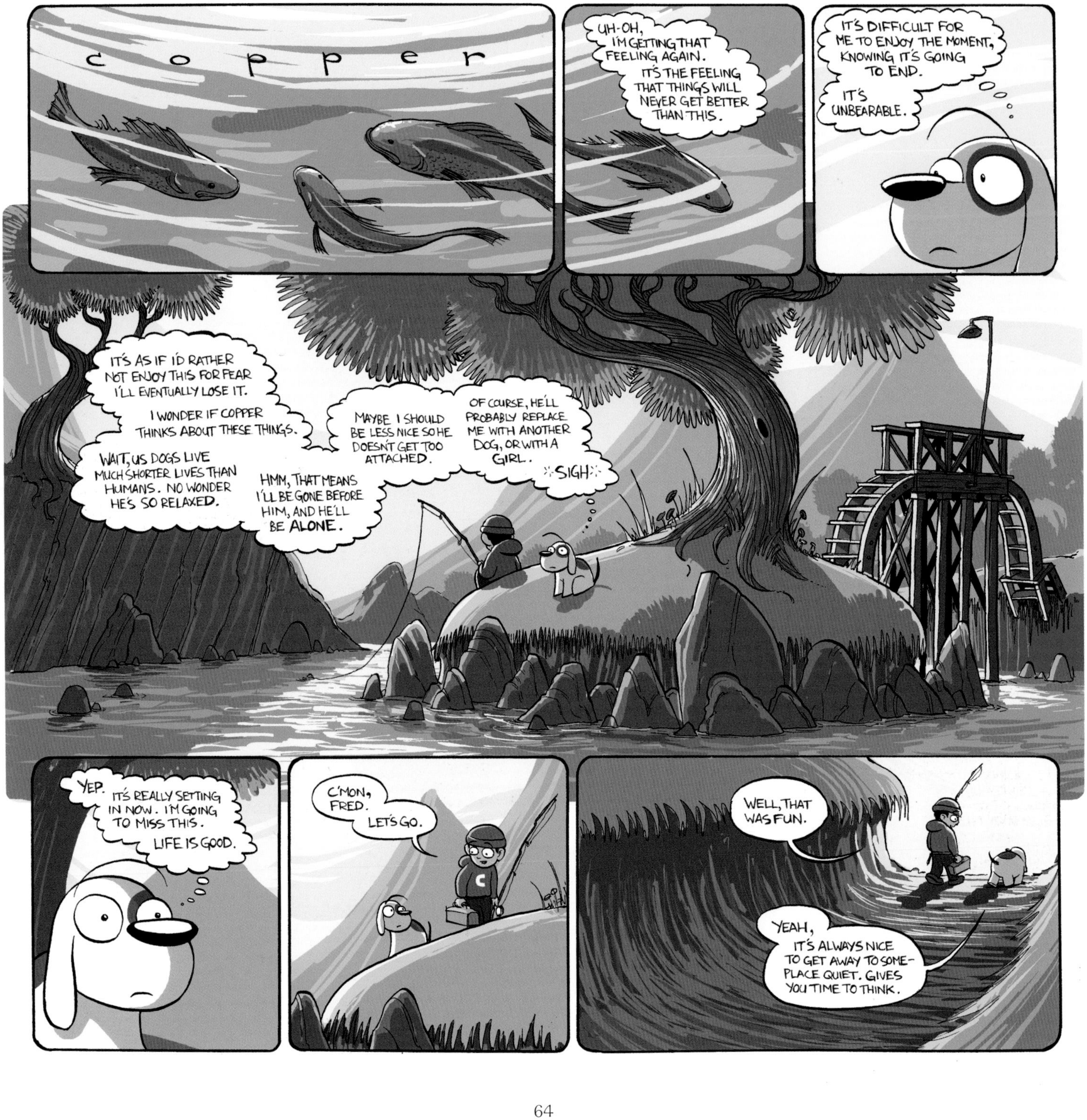
copper
UH-OH, I'M GETTING THAT FEELING AGAIN.
IT'S THE FEELING THAT THINGS WILL NEVER GET BETTER THAN THIS.
IT'S DIFFICULT FOR ME TO ENJOY THE MOMENT, KNOWING IT'S GOING TO END.
IT'S UNBEARABLE.
IT'S AS IF I'D RATHER NOT ENJOY THIS FOR FEAR I'LL EVENTUALLY LOSE IT.
I WONDER IF COPPER THINKS ABOUT THESE THINGS.
WAIT, US DOGS LIVE MUCH SHORTER LIVES THAN HUMANS. NO WONDER HE'S SO RELAXED.
HMM, THAT MEANS I'LL BE GONE BEFORE HIM, AND HE'LL BE ALONE.
MAYBE I SHOULD BE LESS NICE SO HE DOESN'T GET TOO ATTACHED.
OF COURSE, HE'LL PROBABLY REPLACE ME WITH ANOTHER DOG, OR WITH A GIRL.
SIGH
YEP. IT'S REALLY SETTING IN NOW. I'M GOING TO MISS THIS.
LIFE IS GOOD.
C'MON, FRED.
LET'S GO.
WELL, THAT WAS FUN.
YEAH, IT'S ALWAYS NICE TO GET AWAY TO SOME-PLACE QUIET. GIVES YOU TIME TO THINK.

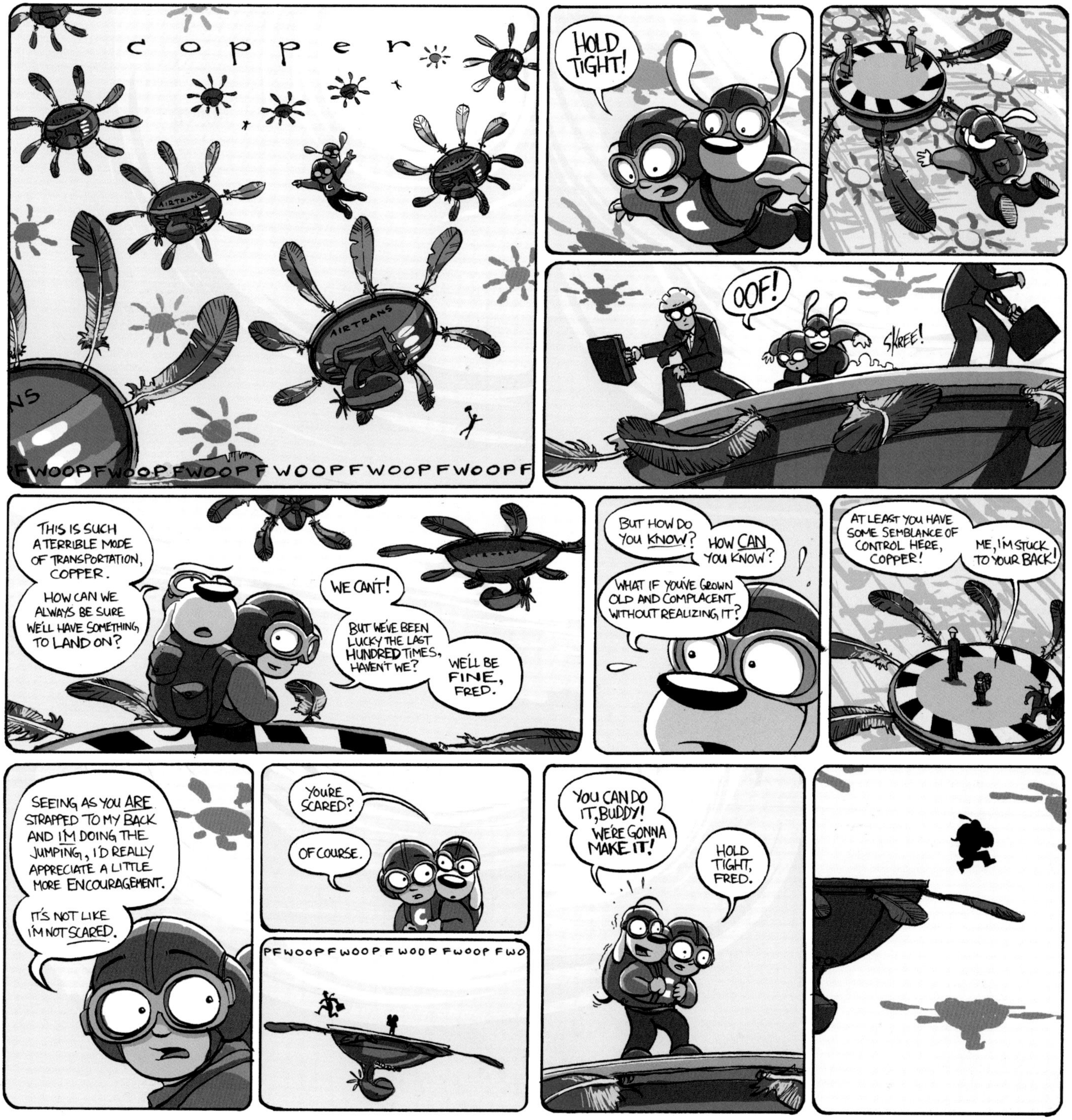
copper
AIRTRANS
FWOOPFWOOPFWOOPFWOOPFWOOPFWOOPF
HOLD TIGHT!
OOF!
SKREE!
THIS IS SUCH A TERRIBLE MODE OF TRANSPORTATION, COPPER.
HOW CAN WE ALWAYS BE SURE WE'LL HAVE SOMETHING TO LAND ON?
WE CAN'T!
BUT WE'VE BEEN LUCKY THE LAST HUNDRED TIMES, HAVEN'T WE?
WE'LL BE FINE, FRED.
BUT HOW DO YOU KNOW?
HOW CAN YOU KNOW?
WHAT IF YOU'VE GROWN OLD AND COMPLACENT WITHOUT REALIZING IT?
AT LEAST YOU HAVE SOME SEMBLANCE OF CONTROL HERE, COPPER!
ME, I'M STUCK TO YOUR BACK!
SEEING AS YOU ARE STRAPPED TO MY BACK AND I'M DOING THE JUMPING, I'D REALLY APPRECIATE A LITTLE MORE ENCOURAGEMENT.
IT'S NOT LIKE I'M NOT SCARED.
YOU'RE SCARED?
OF COURSE.
PFWOOPFWOOPFWOOPFWOOPFWO
YOU CAN DO IT, BUDDY! WE'RE GONNA MAKE IT!
HOLD TIGHT, FRED.

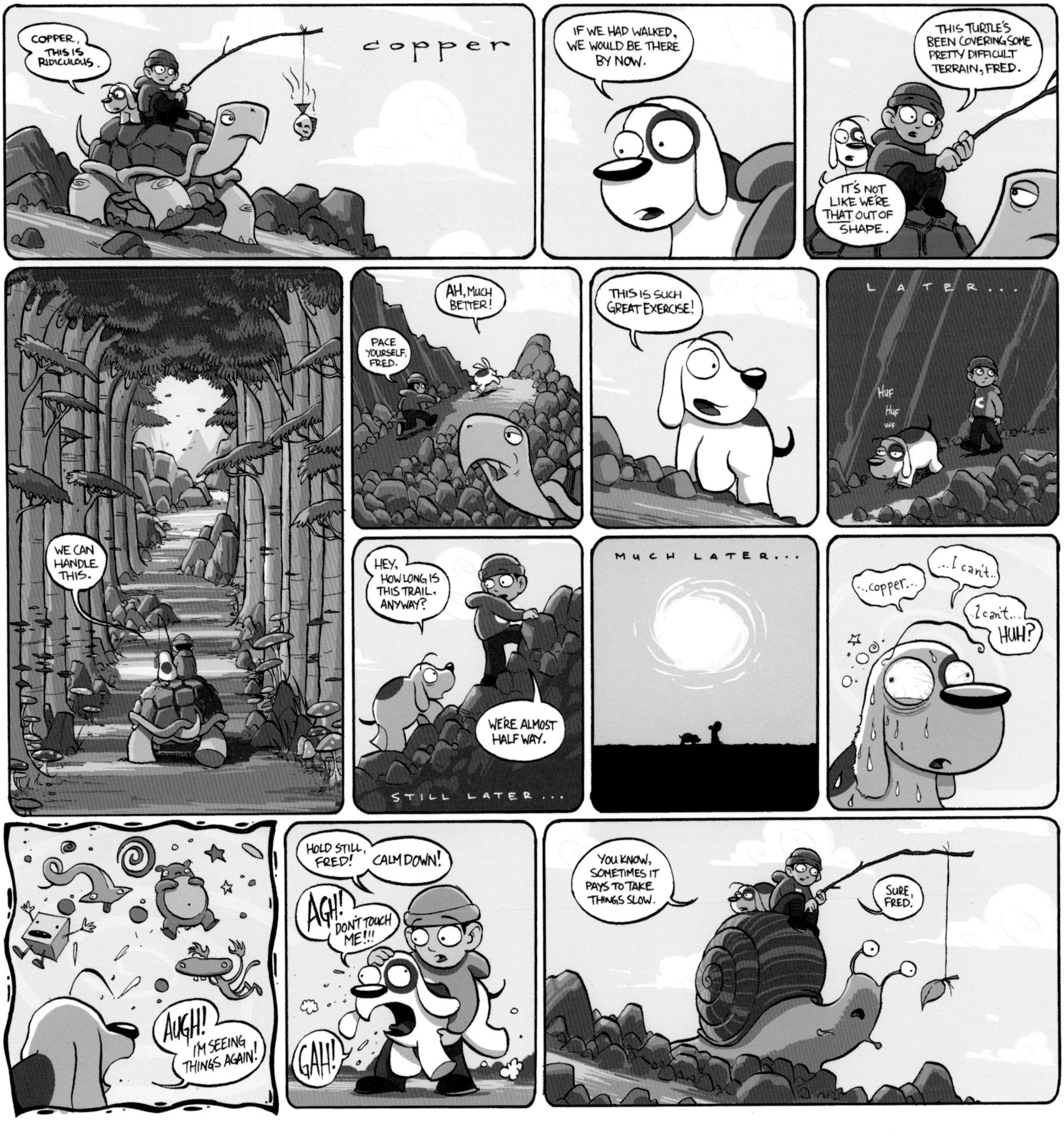
copper
COPPER, THIS IS RIDICULOUS.
IF WE HAD WALKED, WE WOULD BE THERE BY NOW.
THIS TURTLE'S BEEN COVERING SOME PRETTY DIFFICULT TERRAIN, FRED.
IT'S NOT LIKE WE'RE THAT OUT OF SHAPE.
WE CAN HANDLE THIS.
AH, MUCH BETTER!
PACE YOURSELF, FRED.
THIS IS SUCH GREAT EXERCISE!
LATER...
HUF
HUF
HUF
HEY, HOW LONG IS THIS TRAIL, ANYWAY?
WE'RE ALMOST HALF WAY.
STILL LATER...
MUCH LATER...
...copper...
...I can't...
...I can't... HUH?
AUGH! I'M SEEING THINGS AGAIN!
HOLD STILL, FRED!
CALM DOWN!
AGH! DON'T TOUCH ME!!!
GAH!
YOU KNOW, SOMETIMES IT PAYS TO TAKE THINGS SLOW.
SURE, FRED.

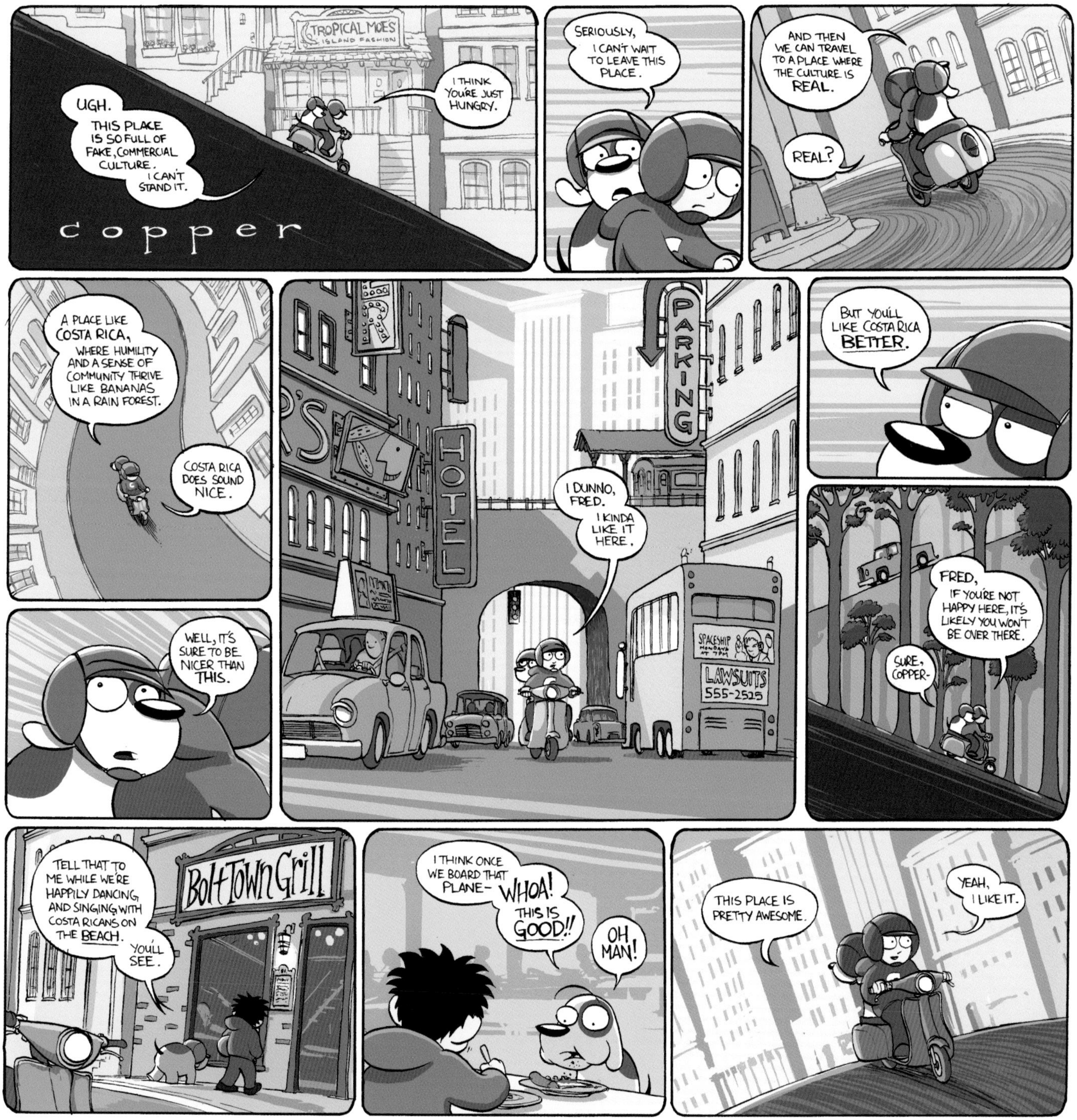
TROPICAL MOES
ISLAND FASHION
UGH.
THIS PLACE IS SO FULL OF FAKE, COMMERCIAL CULTURE. I CAN'T STAND IT.
I THINK YOU'RE JUST HUNGRY.
copper
SERIOUSLY, I CAN'T WAIT TO LEAVE THIS PLACE.
AND THEN WE CAN TRAVEL TO A PLACE WHERE THE CULTURE IS REAL.
REAL?
A PLACE LIKE COSTA RICA, WHERE HUMILITY AND A SENSE OF COMMUNITY THRIVE LIKE BANANAS IN A RAIN FOREST.
COSTA RICA DOES SOUND NICE.
PARKING
HOTEL
I DUNNO, FRED. I KINDA LIKE IT HERE.
SPACESHIP
LAWSUITS 555-2515
BUT YOU'LL LIKE COSTA RICA BETTER.
WELL, IT'S SURE TO BE NICER THAN THIS.
FRED, IF YOU'RE NOT HAPPY HERE, IT'S LIKELY YOU WON'T BE OVER THERE.
SURE, COPPER-
TELL THAT TO ME WHILE WE'RE HAPPILY DANCING, AND SINGING WITH COSTA RICANS ON THE BEACH.
YOU'LL SEE.
BoltTown Grill
I THINK ONCE WE BOARD THAT PLANE-
WHOA! THIS IS GOOD!!
OH MAN!
THIS PLACE IS PRETTY AWESOME.
YEAH, I LIKE IT.

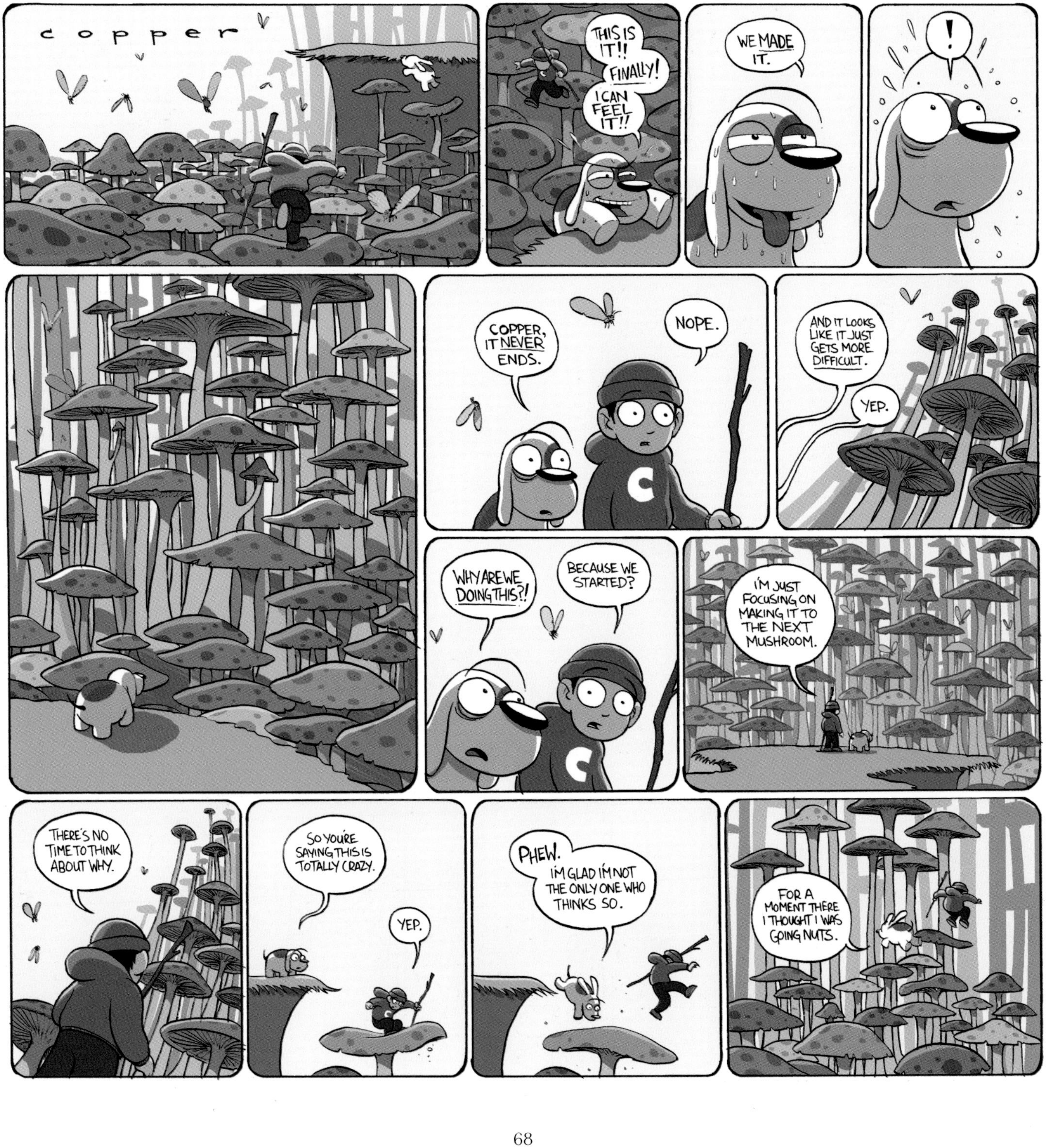
copper
THIS IS IT!!
FINALLY!
I CAN FEEL IT!!
WE MADE IT.
!
COPPER, IT NEVER ENDS.
NOPE.
AND IT LOOKS LIKE IT JUST GETS MORE DIFFICULT.
YEP.
WHY ARE WE DOING THIS?!
BECAUSE WE STARTED?
I'M JUST FOCUSING ON MAKING IT TO THE NEXT MUSHROOM.
THERE'S NO TIME TO THINK ABOUT WHY.
SO YOU'RE SAYING THIS IS TOTALLY CRAZY.
YEP.
PHEW.
I'M GLAD I'M NOT THE ONLY ONE WHO THINKS SO.
FOR A MOMENT THERE I THOUGHT I WAS GOING NUTS.

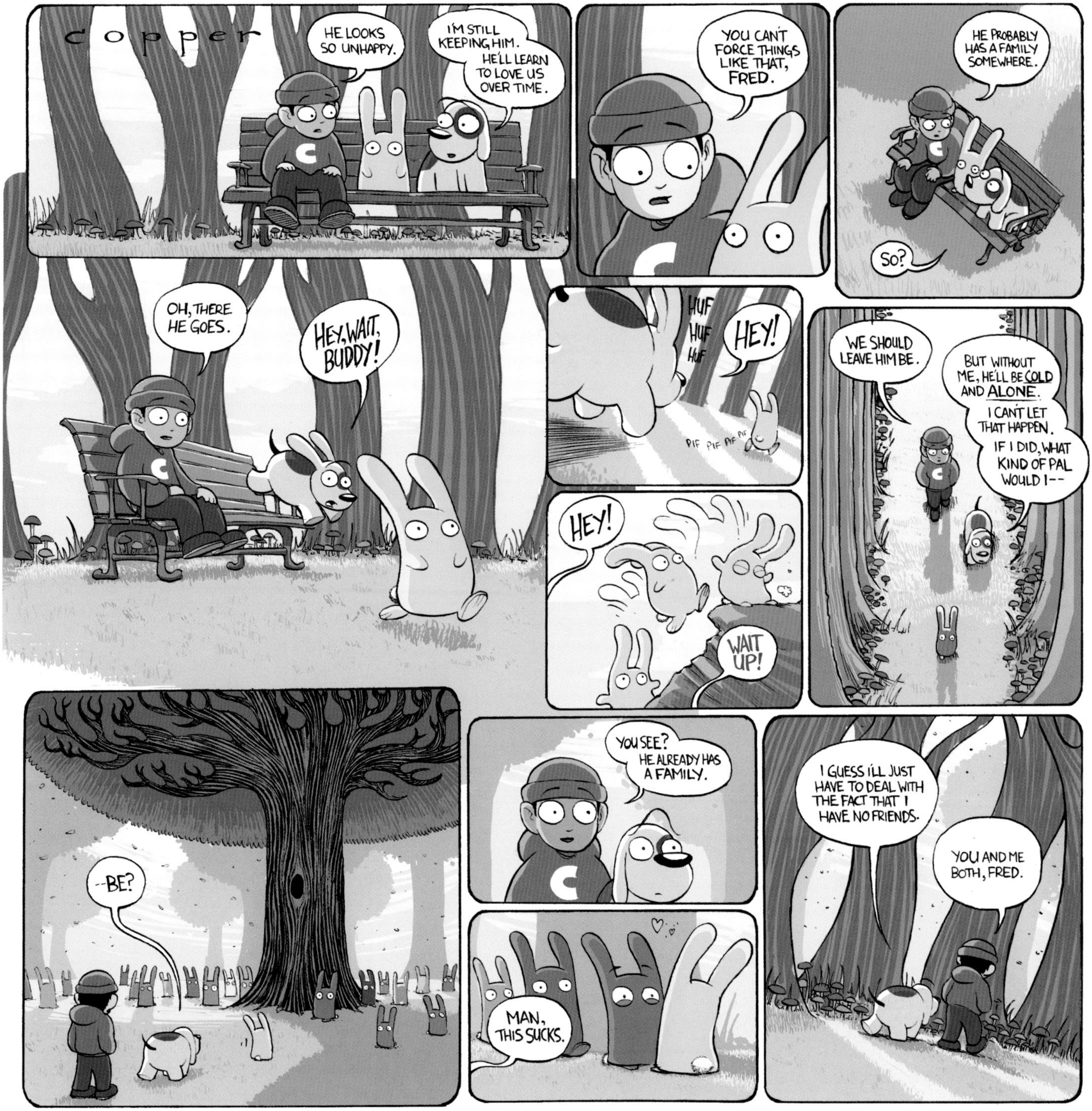
copper
HE LOOKS SO UNHAPPY.
I'M STILL KEEPING HIM. HE'LL LEARN TO LOVE US OVER TIME.
YOU CAN'T FORCE THINGS LIKE THAT, FRED.
HE PROBABLY HAS A FAMILY SOMEWHERE.
SO?
OH, THERE HE GOES.
HEY, WAIT, BUDDY!
HUF HUF HUF
HEY!
PIF PIF PIF PIF
HEY!
WAIT UP!
WE SHOULD LEAVE HIM BE.
BUT WITHOUT ME, HE'LL BE COLD AND ALONE.
I CAN'T LET THAT HAPPEN.
IF I DID, WHAT KIND OF PAL WOULD I--
--BE?
YOU SEE? HE ALREADY HAS A FAMILY.
MAN, THIS SUCKS.
I GUESS I'LL JUST HAVE TO DEAL WITH THE FACT THAT I HAVE NO FRIENDS.
YOU AND ME BOTH, FRED.

SIGNPOST

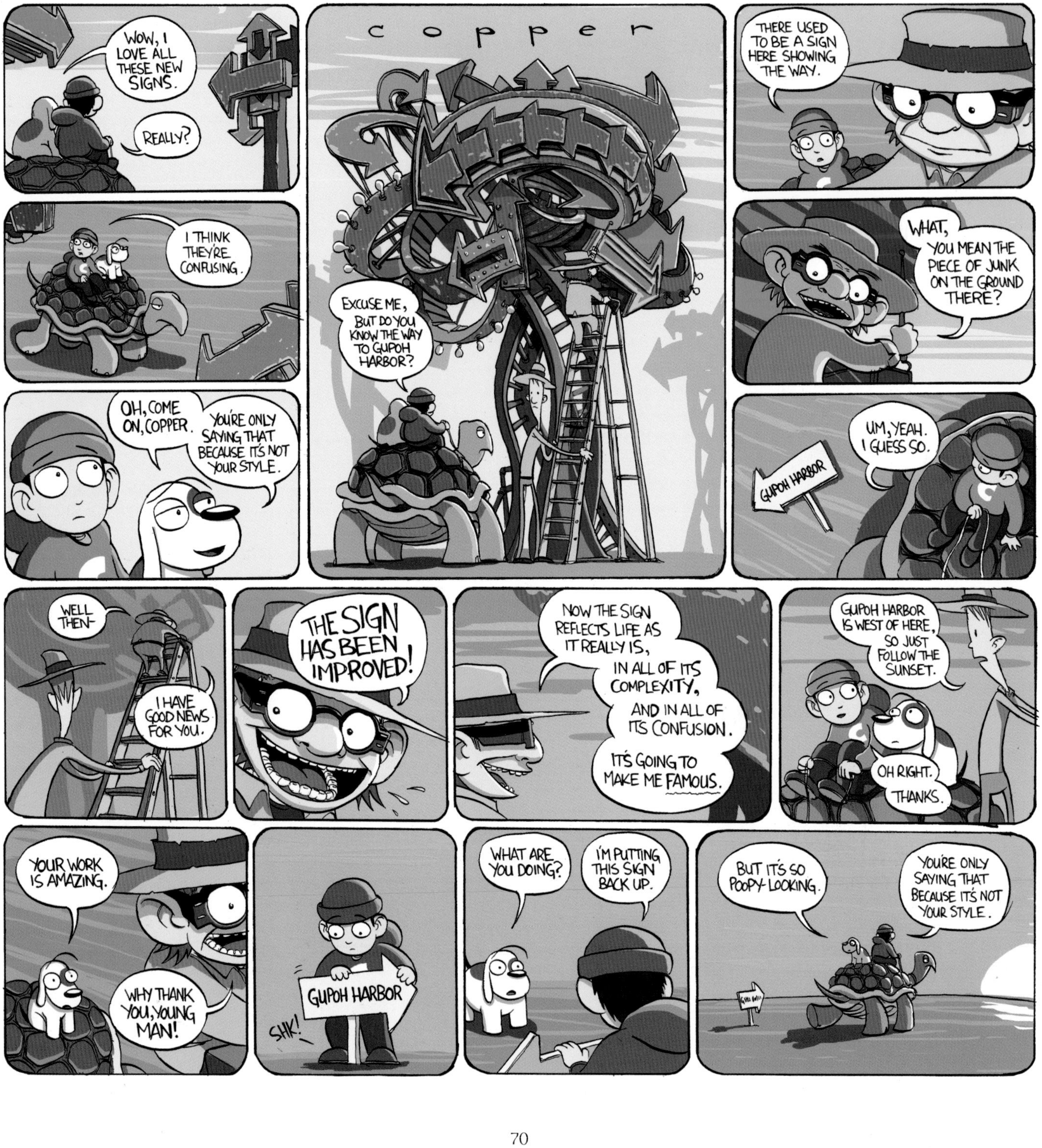
WOW, I LOVE ALL THESE NEW SIGNS.
REALLY?
I THINK THEY'RE CONFUSING.
OH, COME ON, COPPER.
YOU'RE ONLY SAYING THAT BECAUSE IT'S NOT YOUR STYLE.
copper
EXCUSE ME, BUT DO YOU KNOW THE WAY TO GUPOH HARBOR?
THERE USED TO BE A SIGN HERE SHOWING THE WAY.
WHAT, YOU MEAN THE PIECE OF JUNK ON THE GROUND THERE?
GUPOH HARBOR
UM, YEAH. I GUESS SO.
WELL THEN-
I HAVE GOOD NEWS FOR YOU.
THE SIGN HAS BEEN IMPROVED!
NOW THE SIGN REFLECTS LIFE AS IT REALLY IS,
IN ALL OF ITS COMPLEXITY,
AND IN ALL OF ITS CONFUSION.
IT'S GOING TO MAKE ME FAMOUS.
GUPOH HARBOR IS WEST OF HERE, SO JUST FOLLOW THE SUNSET.
OH RIGHT.
THANKS.
YOUR WORK IS AMAZING.
WHY THANK YOU, YOUNG MAN!
GUPOH HARBOR
SHK!
WHAT ARE YOU DOING?
I'M PUTTING THIS SIGN BACK UP.
BUT IT'S SO POOPY-LOOKING.
YOU'RE ONLY SAYING THAT BECAUSE IT'S NOT YOUR STYLE.

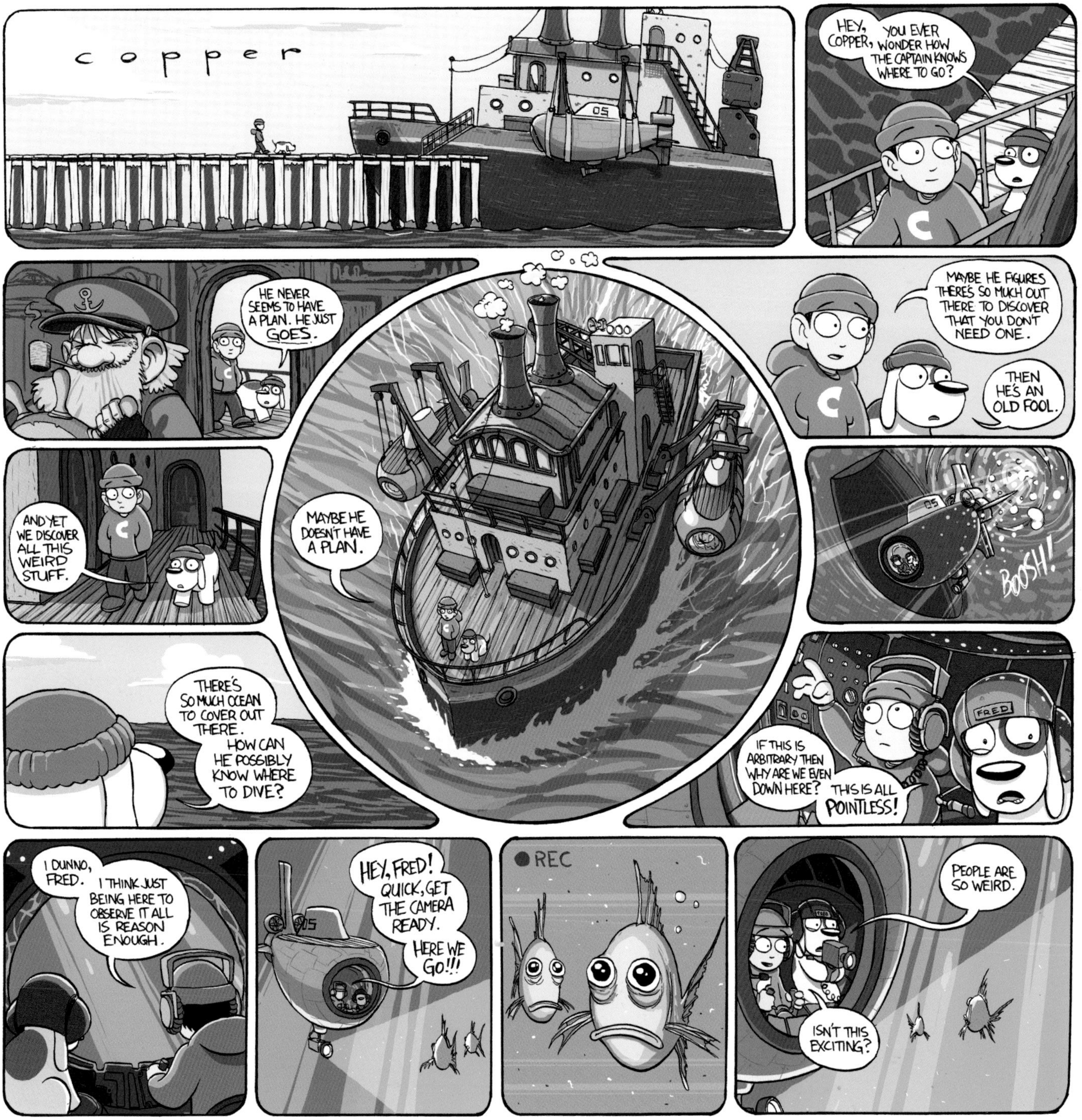
copper
HEY, COPPER, YOU EVER WONDER HOW THE CAPTAIN KNOWS WHERE TO GO?
HE NEVER SEEMS TO HAVE A PLAN. HE JUST GOES.
MAYBE HE DOESN'T HAVE A PLAN.
MAYBE HE FIGURES THERE'S SO MUCH OUT THERE TO DISCOVER THAT YOU DON'T NEED ONE.
THEN HE'S AN OLD FOOL.
AND YET WE DISCOVER ALL THIS WEIRD STUFF.
BOOSH!
THERE'S SO MUCH OCEAN TO COVER OUT THERE.
HOW CAN HE POSSIBLY KNOW WHERE TO DIVE?
IF THIS IS ARBITRARY THEN WHY ARE WE EVEN DOWN HERE?
THIS IS ALL POINTLESS!
I DUNNO, FRED.
I THINK JUST BEING HERE TO OBSERVE IT ALL IS REASON ENOUGH.
HEY, FRED! QUICK, GET THE CAMERA READY.
HERE WE GO!!!
REC
PEOPLE ARE SO WEIRD.
ISN'T THIS EXCITING?

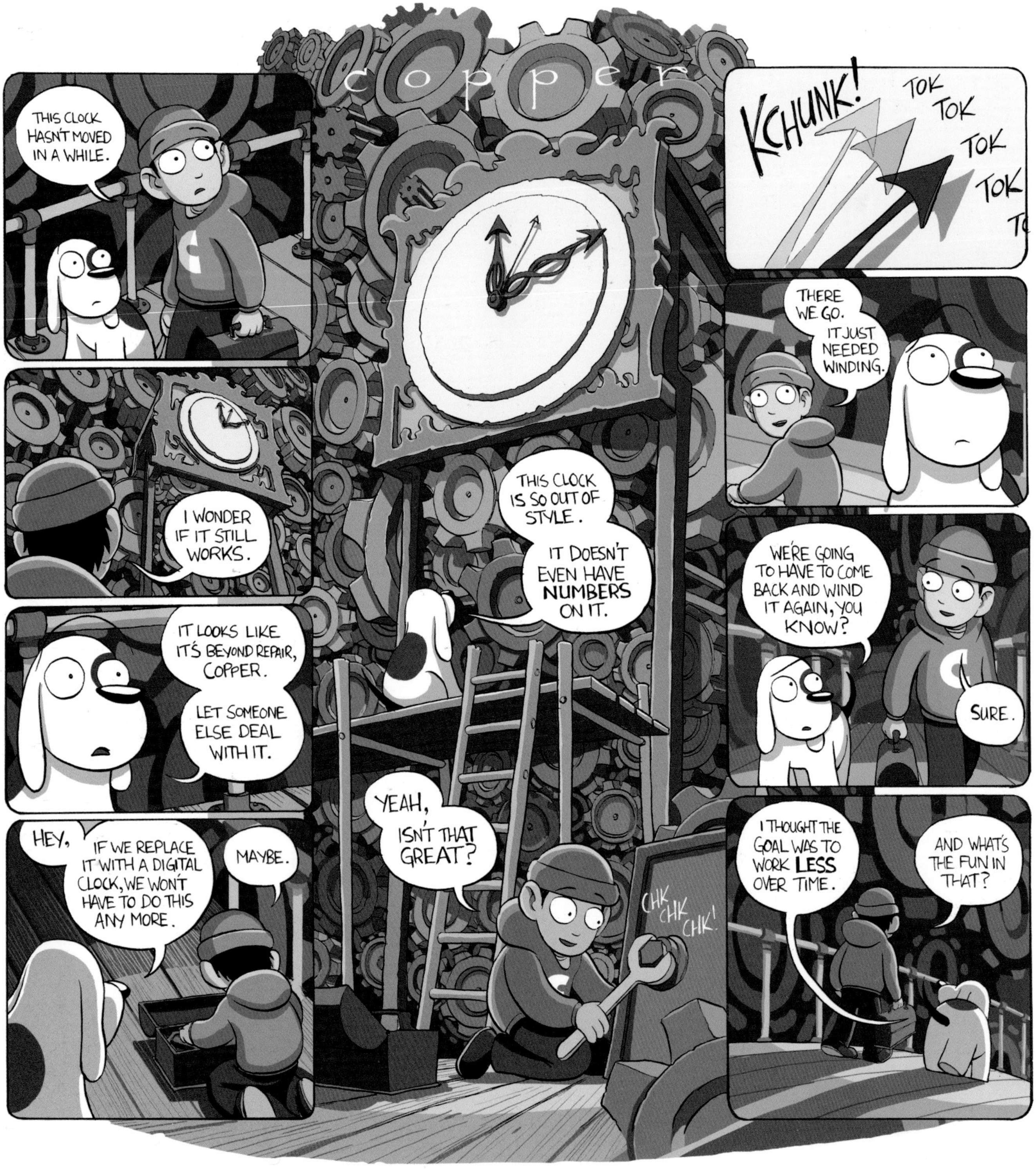
copper
THIS CLOCK HASN'T MOVED IN A WHILE.
I WONDER IF IT STILL WORKS.
IT LOOKS LIKE IT'S BEYOND REPAIR, COPPER.
LET SOMEONE ELSE DEAL WITH IT.
HEY,
IF WE REPLACE IT WITH A DIGITAL CLOCK, WE WON'T HAVE TO DO THIS ANY MORE.
MAYBE.
THIS CLOCK IS SO OUT OF STYLE.
IT DOESN'T EVEN HAVE NUMBERS ON IT.
YEAH, ISN'T THAT GREAT?
CHK CHK CHK!
KCHUNK!
TOK TOK TOK TOK
THERE WE GO.
IT JUST NEEDED WINDING.
WE'RE GOING TO HAVE TO COME BACK AND WIND IT AGAIN, YOU KNOW?
SURE.
I THOUGHT THE GOAL WAS TO WORK LESS OVER TIME.
AND WHAT'S THE FUN IN THAT?

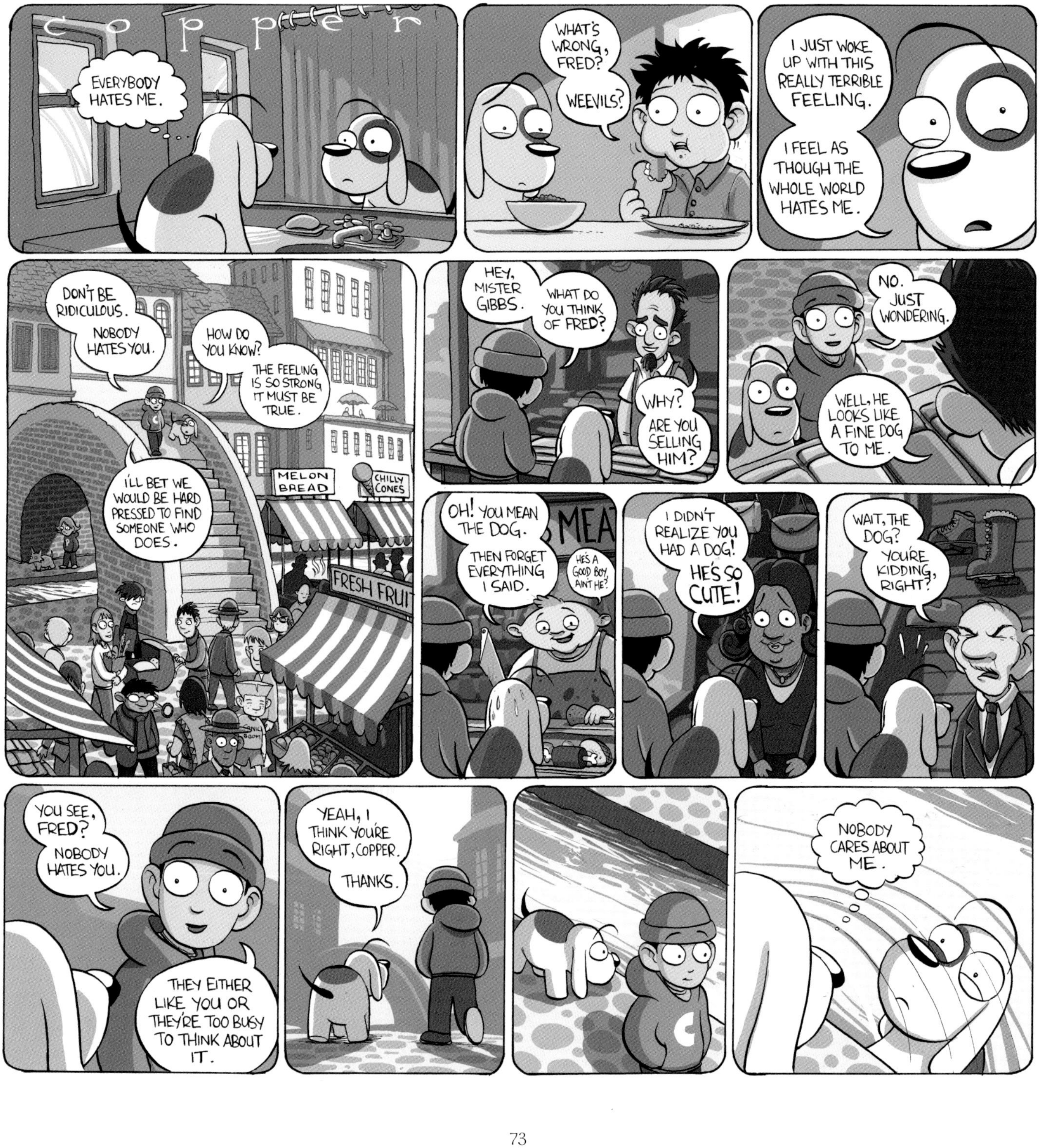
copper
EVERYBODY HATES ME.
WHAT'S WRONG, FRED?
WEEVILS?
I JUST WOKE UP WITH THIS REALLY TERRIBLE FEELING.
I FEEL AS THOUGH THE WHOLE WORLD HATES ME.
DON'T BE RIDICULOUS.
NOBODY HATES YOU.
HOW DO YOU KNOW?
THE FEELING IS SO STRONG IT MUST BE TRUE.
I'LL BET WE WOULD BE HARD PRESSED TO FIND SOMEONE WHO DOES.
MELON BREAD
CHILLY CONES
FRESH FRUIT
HEY, MISTER GIBBS.
WHAT DO YOU THINK OF FRED?
WHY?
ARE YOU SELLING HIM?
NO. JUST WONDERING.
WELL, HE LOOKS LIKE A FINE DOG TO ME.
OH! YOU MEAN THE DOG.
THEN FORGET EVERYTHING I SAID.
HE'S A GOOD BOY, AIN'T HE?
MEAT
I DIDN'T REALIZE YOU HAD A DOG!
HE'S SO CUTE!
WAIT, THE DOG?
YOU'RE KIDDING, RIGHT?
YOU SEE, FRED?
NOBODY HATES YOU.
THEY EITHER LIKE YOU OR THEY'RE TOO BUSY TO THINK ABOUT IT.
YEAH, I THINK YOU'RE RIGHT, COPPER.
THANKS.
NOBODY CARES ABOUT ME.

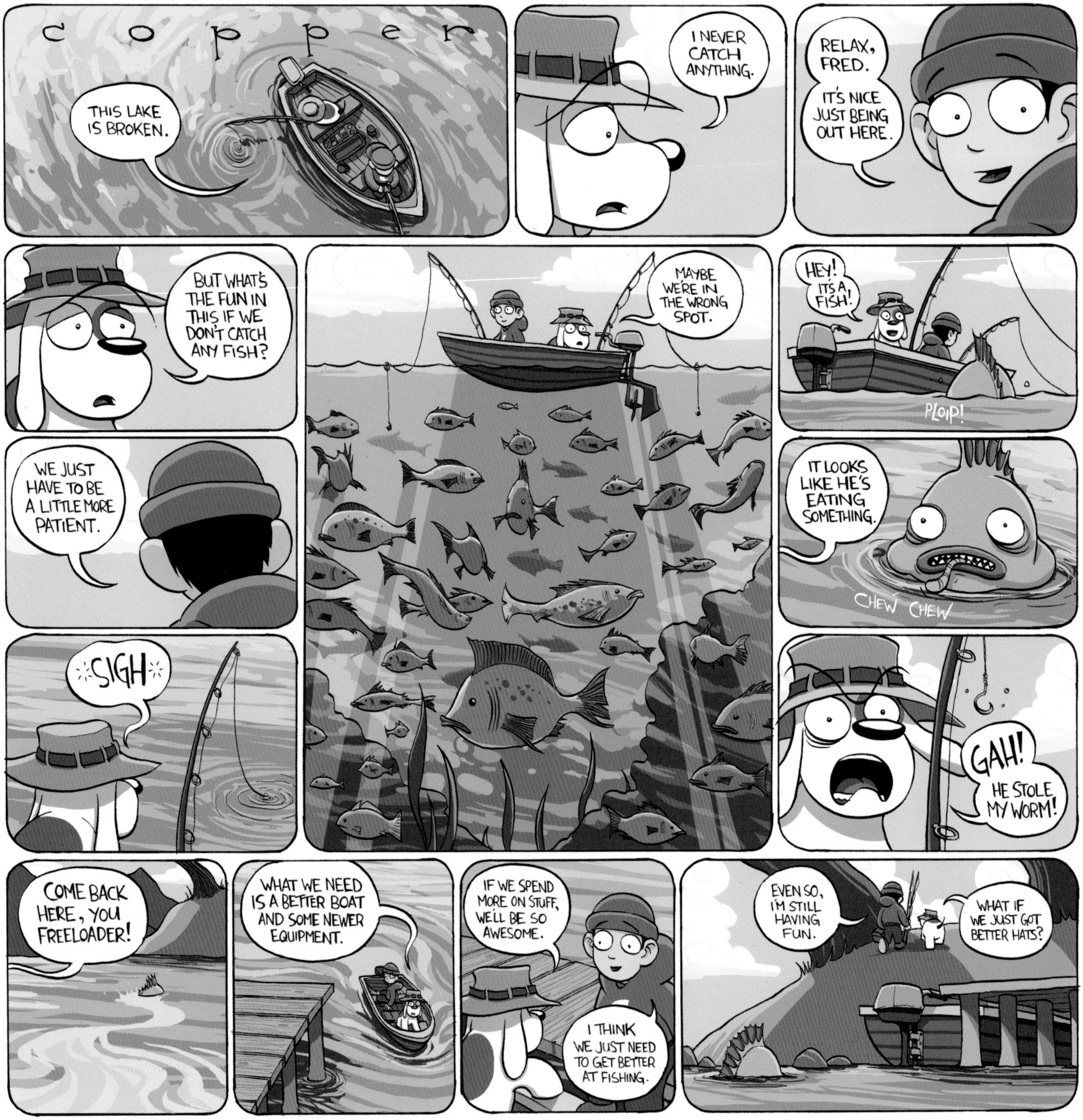
copper
THIS LAKE IS BROKEN.
I NEVER CATCH ANYTHING.
RELAX, FRED.
IT'S NICE JUST BEING OUT HERE.
BUT WHAT'S THE FUN IN THIS IF WE DON'T CATCH ANY FISH?
WE JUST HAVE TO BE A LITTLE MORE PATIENT.
SIGH
MAYBE WE'RE IN THE WRONG SPOT.
HEY! IT'S A FISH!
PLOIP!
IT LOOKS LIKE HE'S EATING SOMETHING.
CHEW CHEW
GAH!
HE STOLE MY WORM!
COME BACK HERE, YOU FREELOADER!
WHAT WE NEED IS A BETTER BOAT AND SOME NEWER EQUIPMENT.
IF WE SPEND MORE ON STUFF, WE'LL BE SO AWESOME.
I THINK WE JUST NEED TO GET BETTER AT FISHING.
EVEN SO, I'M STILL HAVING FUN.
WHAT IF WE JUST GOT BETTER HATS?

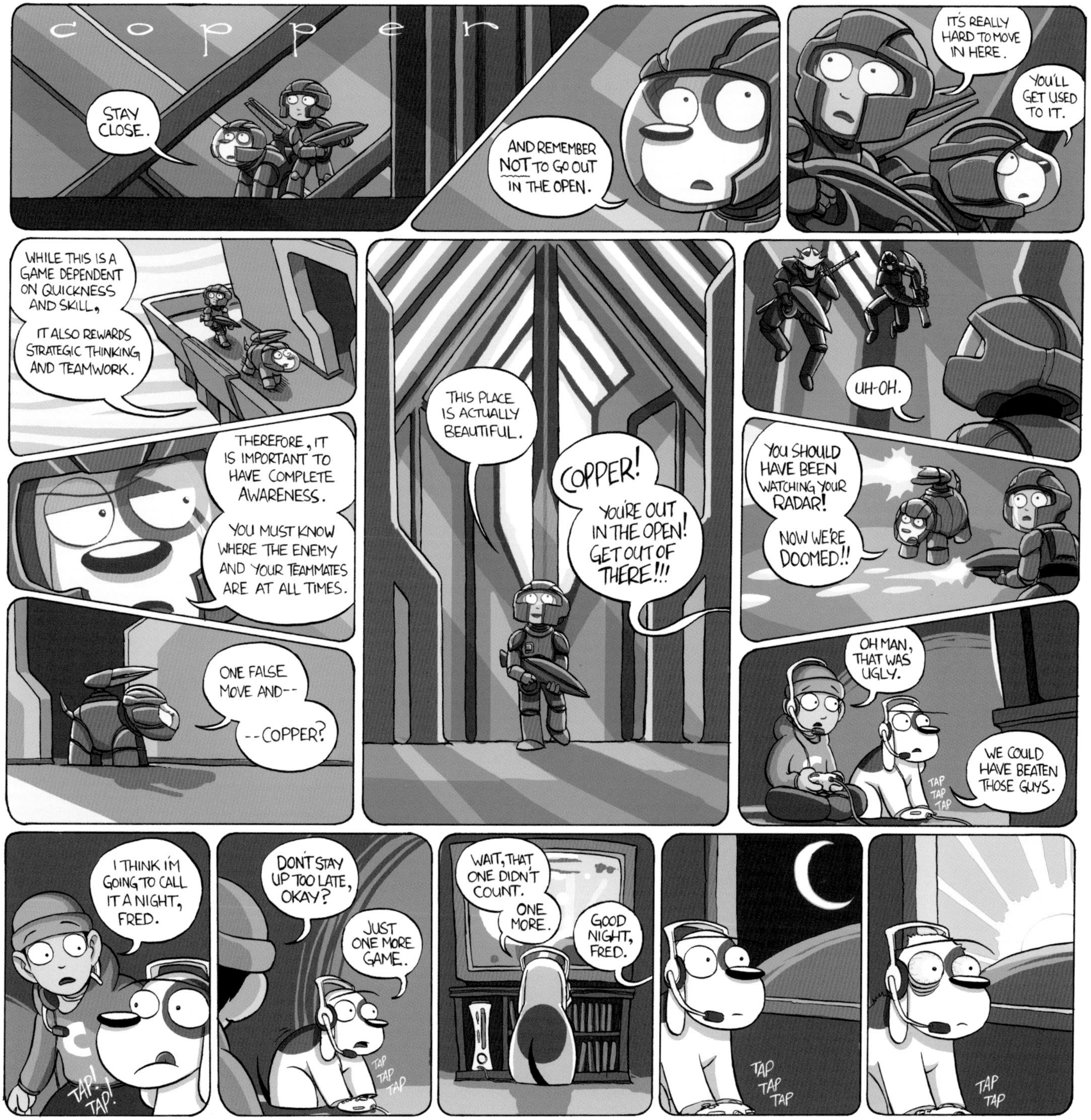
copper
STAY CLOSE.
AND REMEMBER NOT TO GO OUT IN THE OPEN.
IT'S REALLY HARD TO MOVE IN HERE.
YOU'LL GET USED TO IT.
WHILE THIS IS A GAME DEPENDENT ON QUICKNESS AND SKILL,
IT ALSO REWARDS STRATEGIC THINKING AND TEAMWORK.
THEREFORE, IT IS IMPORTANT TO HAVE COMPLETE AWARENESS.
YOU MUST KNOW WHERE THE ENEMY AND YOUR TEAMMATES ARE AT ALL TIMES.
ONE FALSE MOVE AND--
--COPPER?
THIS PLACE IS ACTUALLY BEAUTIFUL.
COPPER!
YOU'RE OUT IN THE OPEN! GET OUT OF THERE!!!
UH-OH.
YOU SHOULD HAVE BEEN WATCHING YOUR RADAR!
NOW WE'RE DOOMED!!
OH MAN, THAT WAS UGLY.
WE COULD HAVE BEATEN THOSE GUYS.
TAP TAP TAP
I THINK I'M GOING TO CALL IT A NIGHT, FRED.
TAP! TAP!
DON'T STAY UP TOO LATE, OKAY?
JUST ONE MORE GAME.
TAP TAP TAP
WAIT, THAT ONE DIDN'T COUNT.
ONE MORE.
GOOD NIGHT, FRED.
TAP TAP TAP
TAP TAP

LUNCH PACK

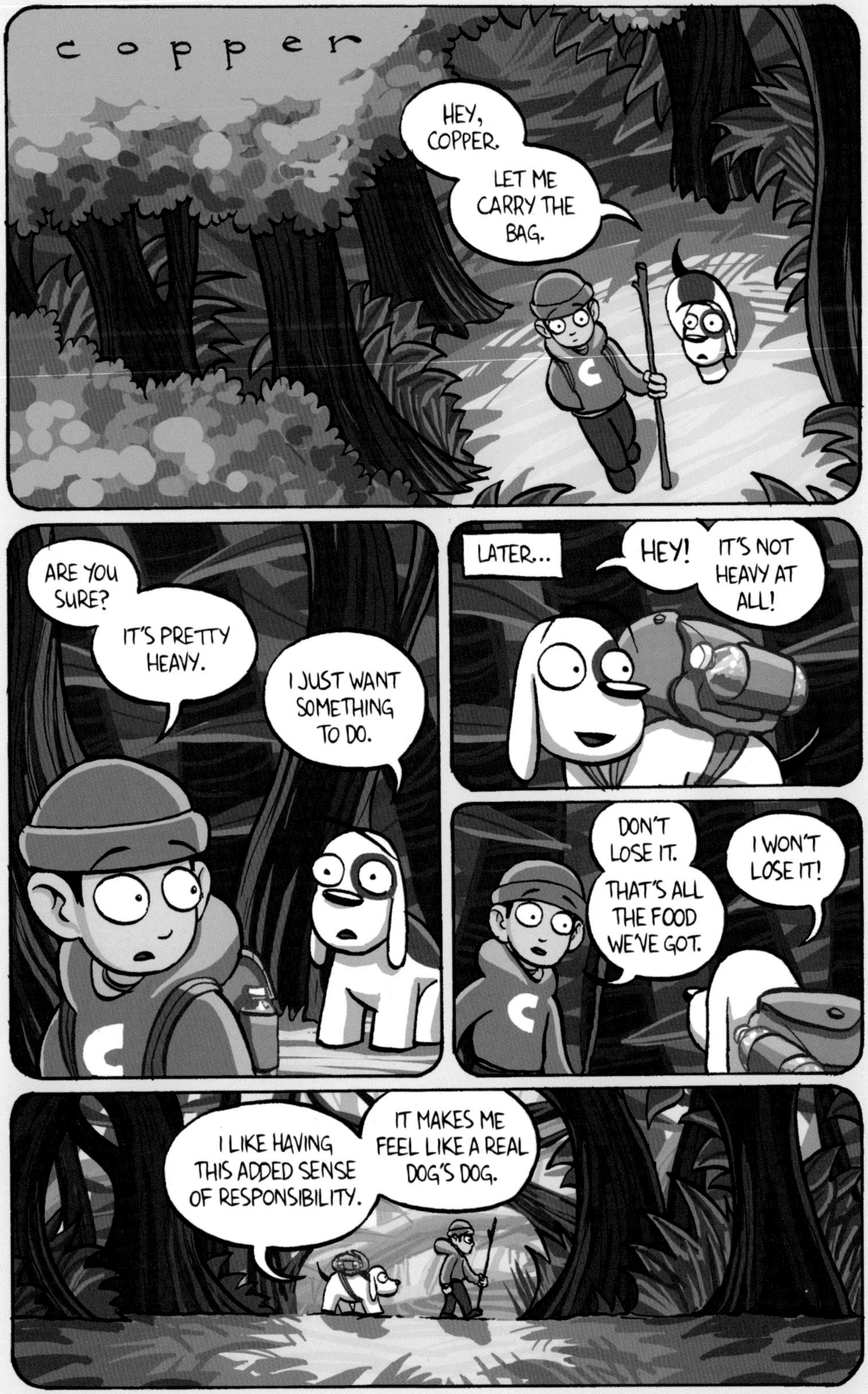
copper
HEY, COPPER.
LET ME CARRY THE BAG.
ARE YOU SURE?
IT'S PRETTY HEAVY.
I JUST WANT SOMETHING TO DO.
LATER...
HEY!
IT'S NOT HEAVY AT ALL!
DON'T LOSE IT.
THAT'S ALL THE FOOD WE'VE GOT.
I WON'T LOSE IT!
I LIKE HAVING THIS ADDED SENSE OF RESPONSIBILITY.
IT MAKES ME FEEL LIKE A REAL DOG'S DOG.

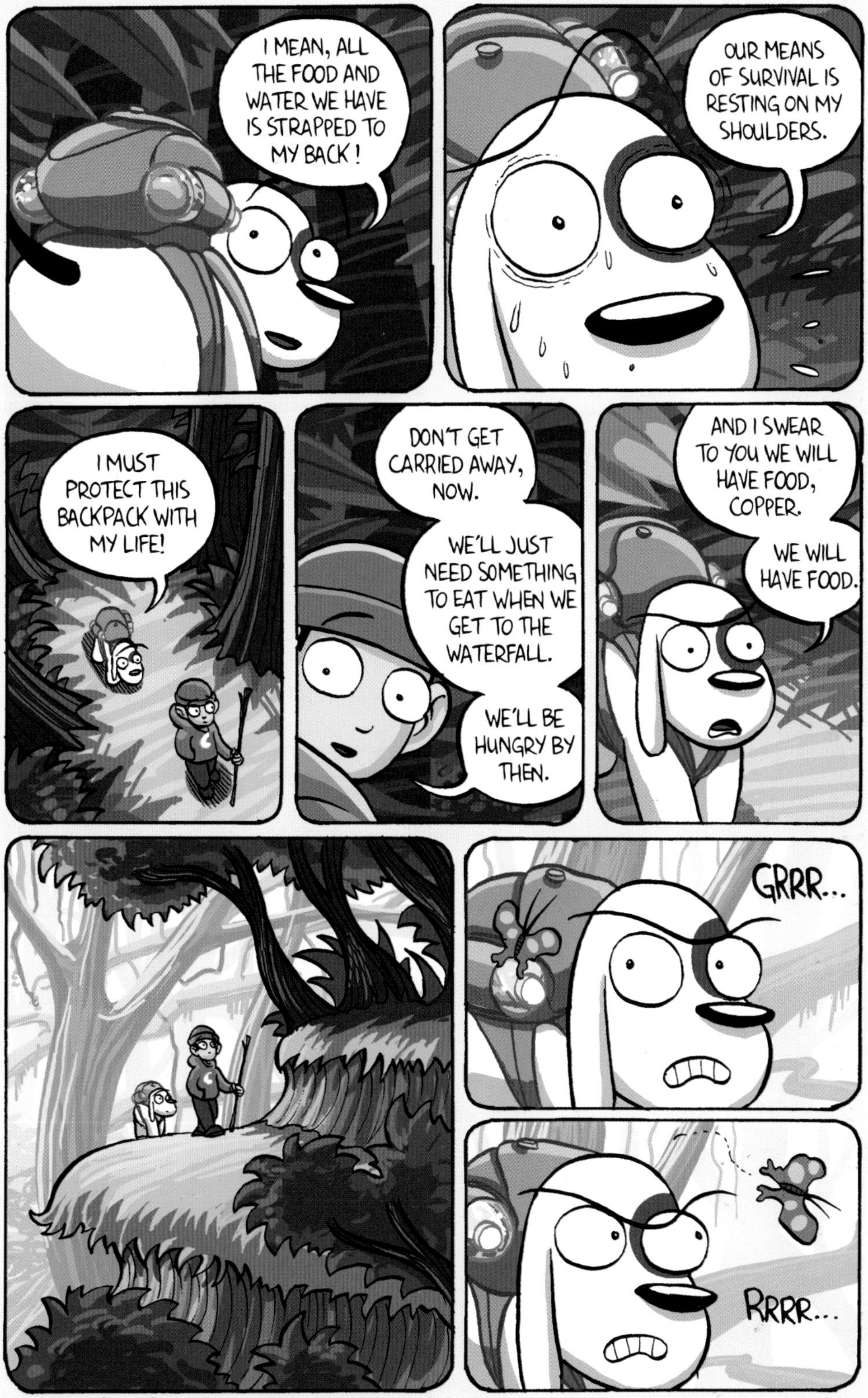
I MEAN, ALL THE FOOD AND WATER WE HAVE IS STRAPPED TO MY BACK!
OUR MEANS OF SURVIVAL IS RESTING ON MY SHOULDERS.
I MUST PROTECT THIS BACKPACK WITH MY LIFE!
DON'T GET CARRIED AWAY, NOW.
WE'LL JUST NEED SOMETHING TO EAT WHEN WE GET TO THE WATERFALL.
WE'LL BE HUNGRY BY THEN.
AND I SWEAR TO YOU WE WILL HAVE FOOD, COPPER.
WE WILL HAVE FOOD.
GRRR...
RRRR...

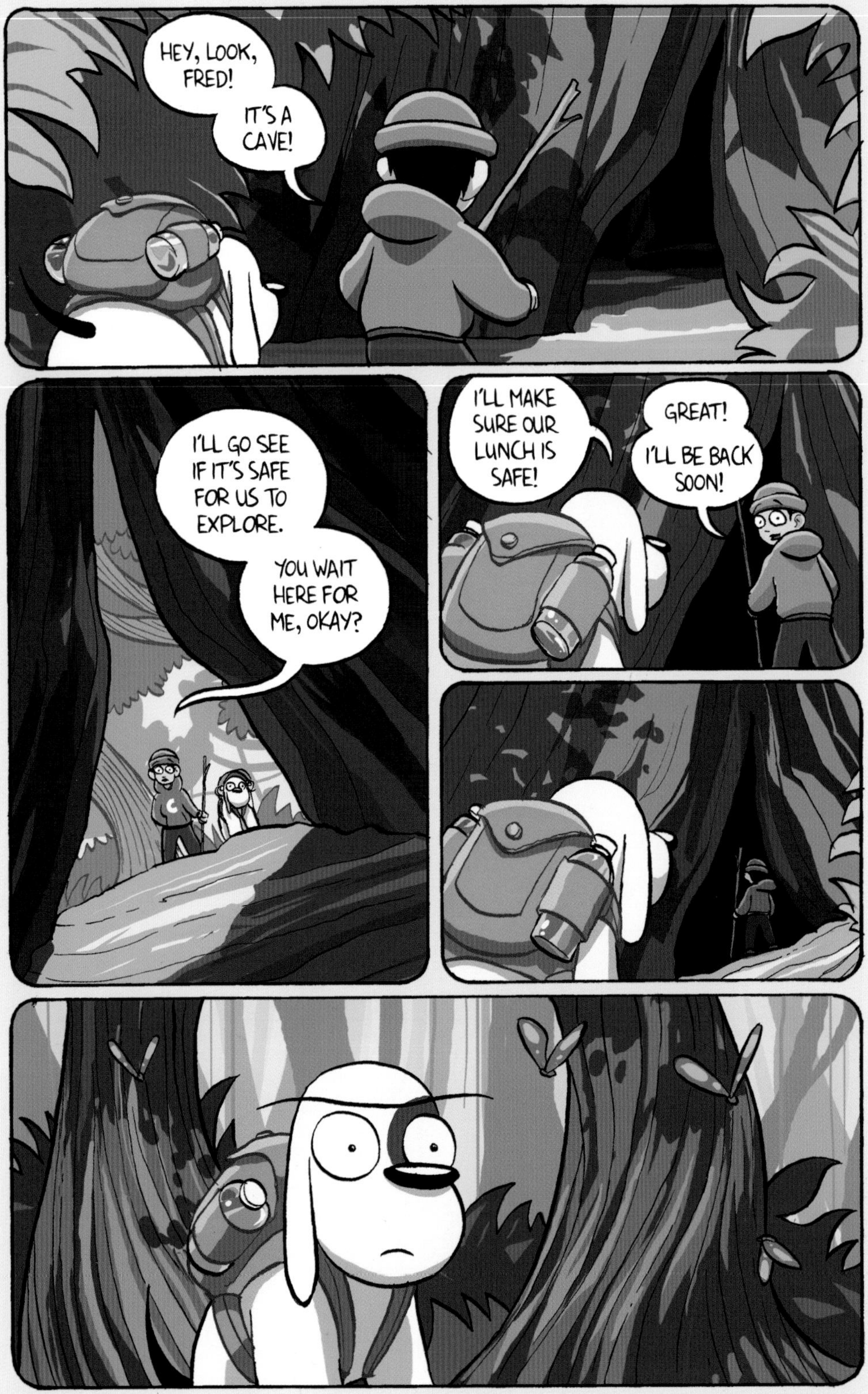
HEY, LOOK, FRED!
IT'S A CAVE!
I'LL GO SEE IF IT'S SAFE FOR US TO EXPLORE.
YOU WAIT HERE FOR ME, OKAY?
I'LL MAKE SURE OUR LUNCH IS SAFE!
GREAT!
I'LL BE BACK SOON!

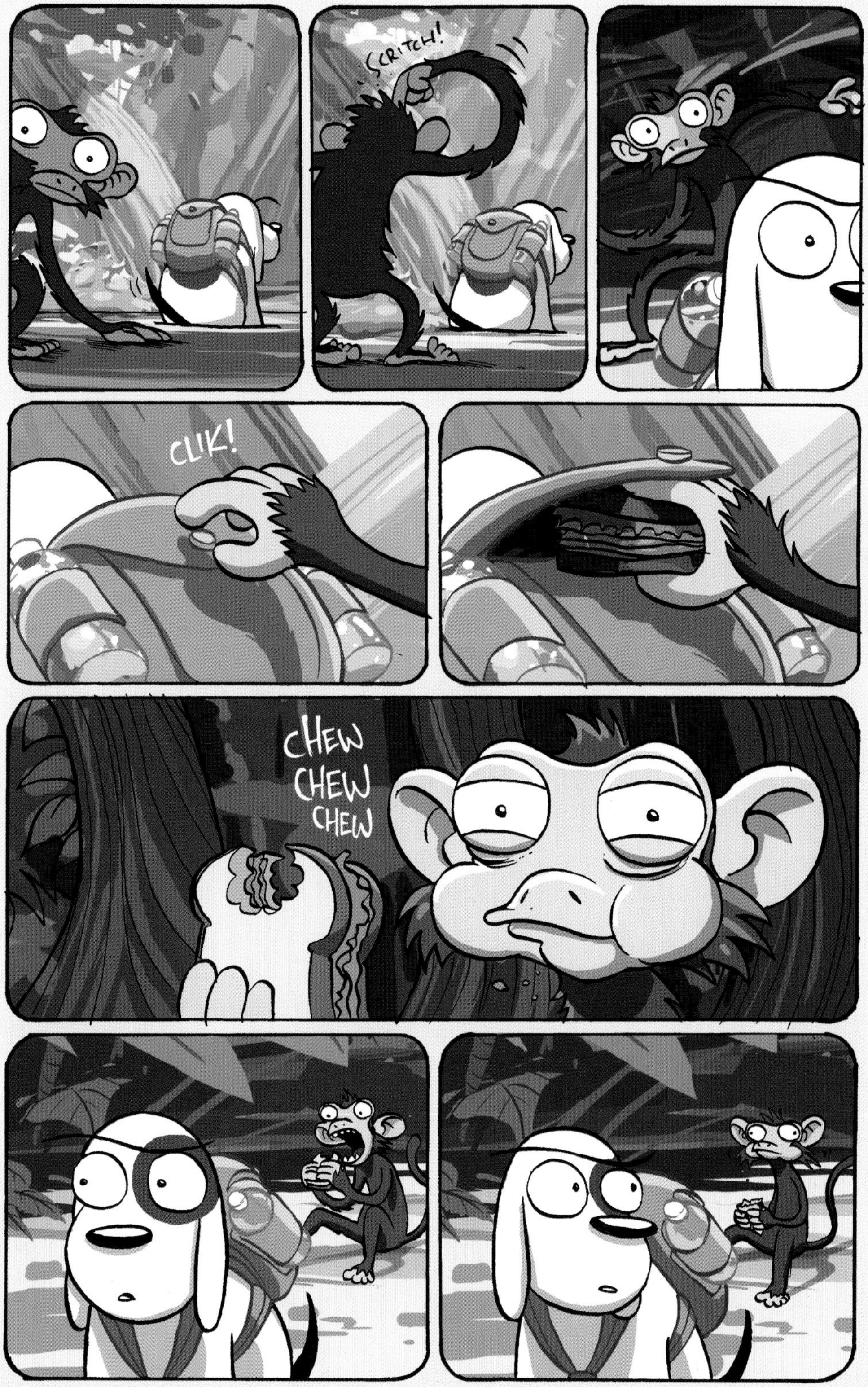
SCRITCH!
CLIK!
CHEW
CHEW
CHEW

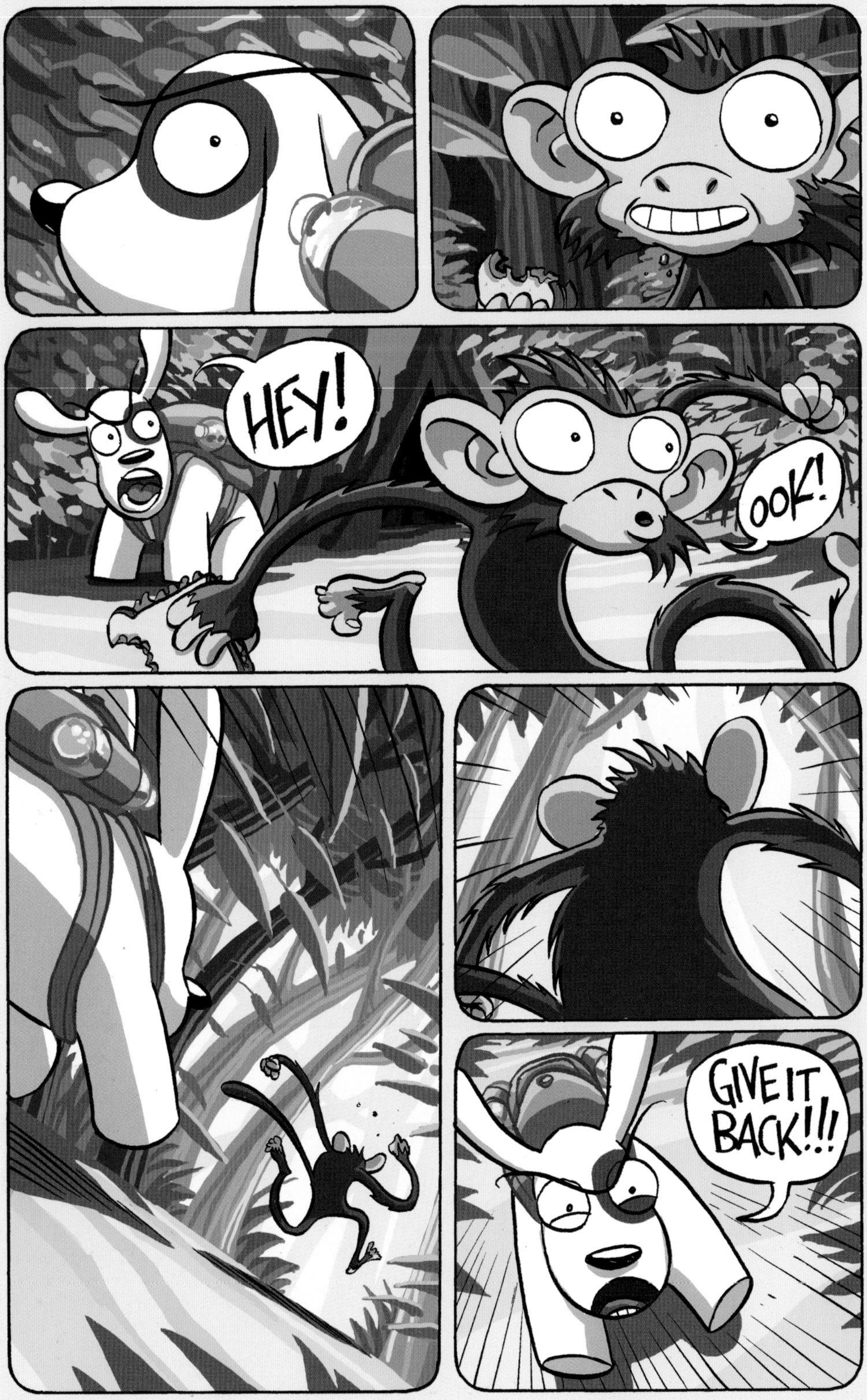
HEY!
OOK!
GIVE IT BACK!!!

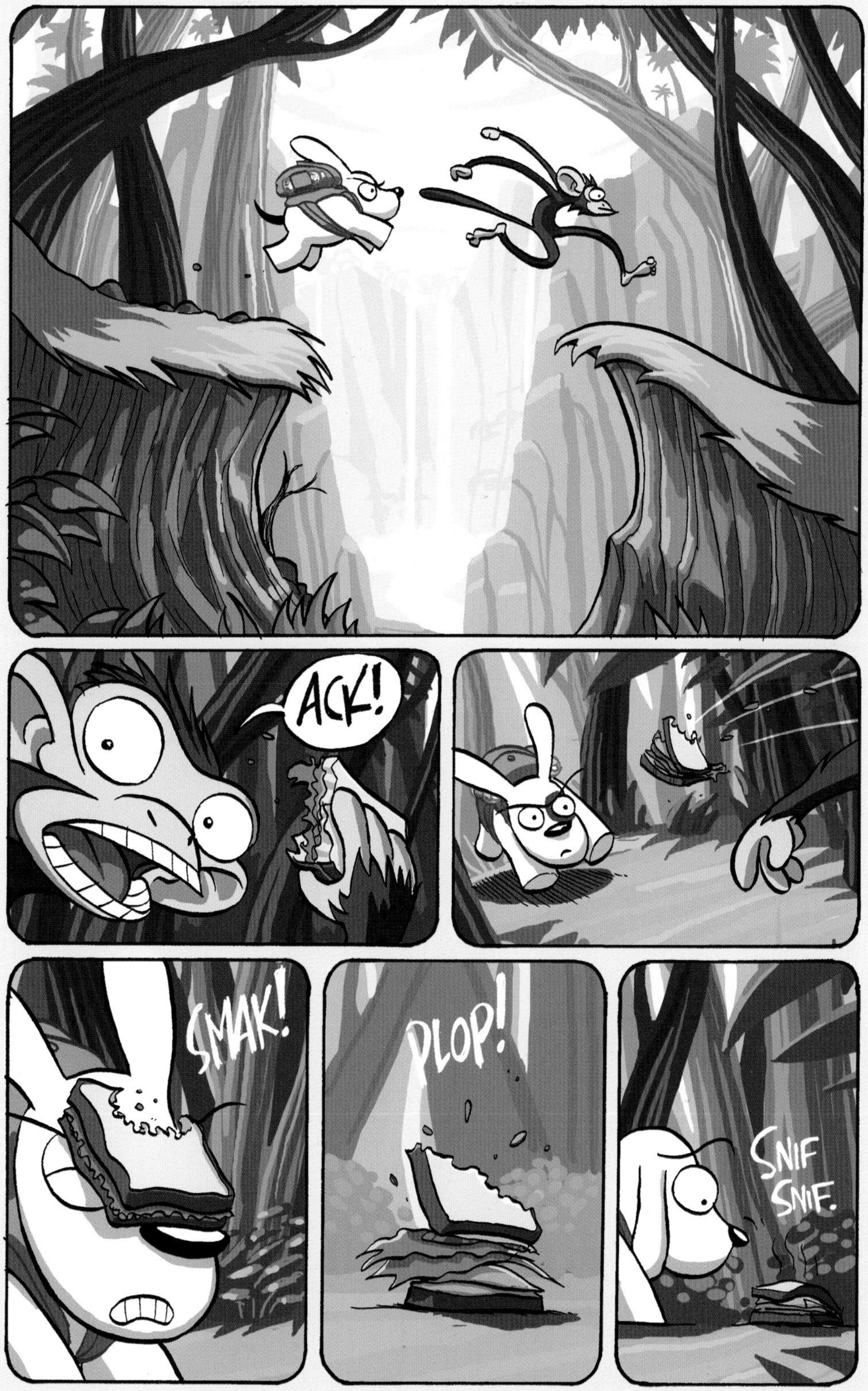
ACK!
SMAK!
PLOP!
SNIF SNIF.

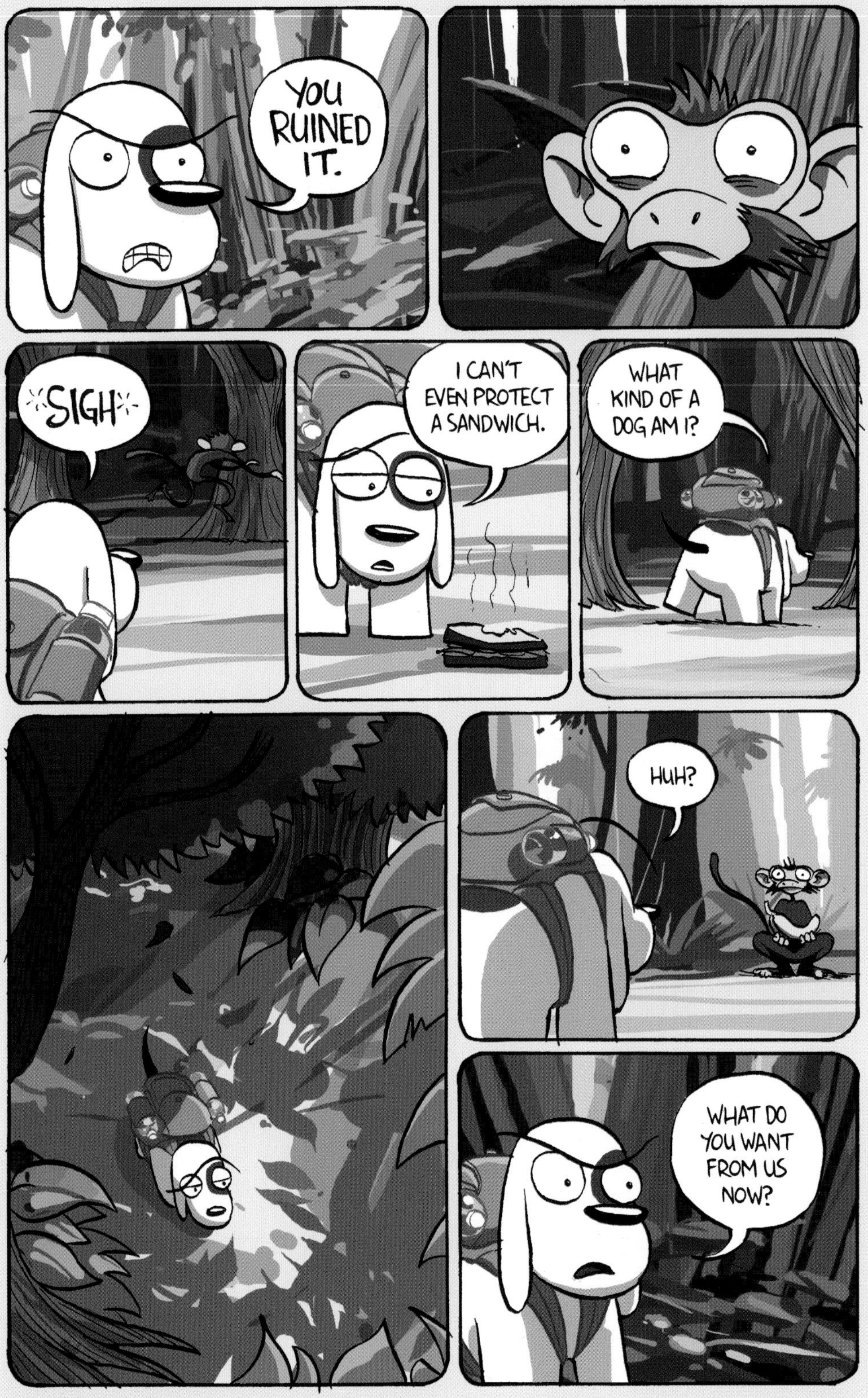
YOU RUINED IT.
SIGH
I CAN'T EVEN PROTECT A SANDWICH.
WHAT KIND OF A DOG AM I?
HUH?
WHAT DO YOU WANT FROM US NOW?

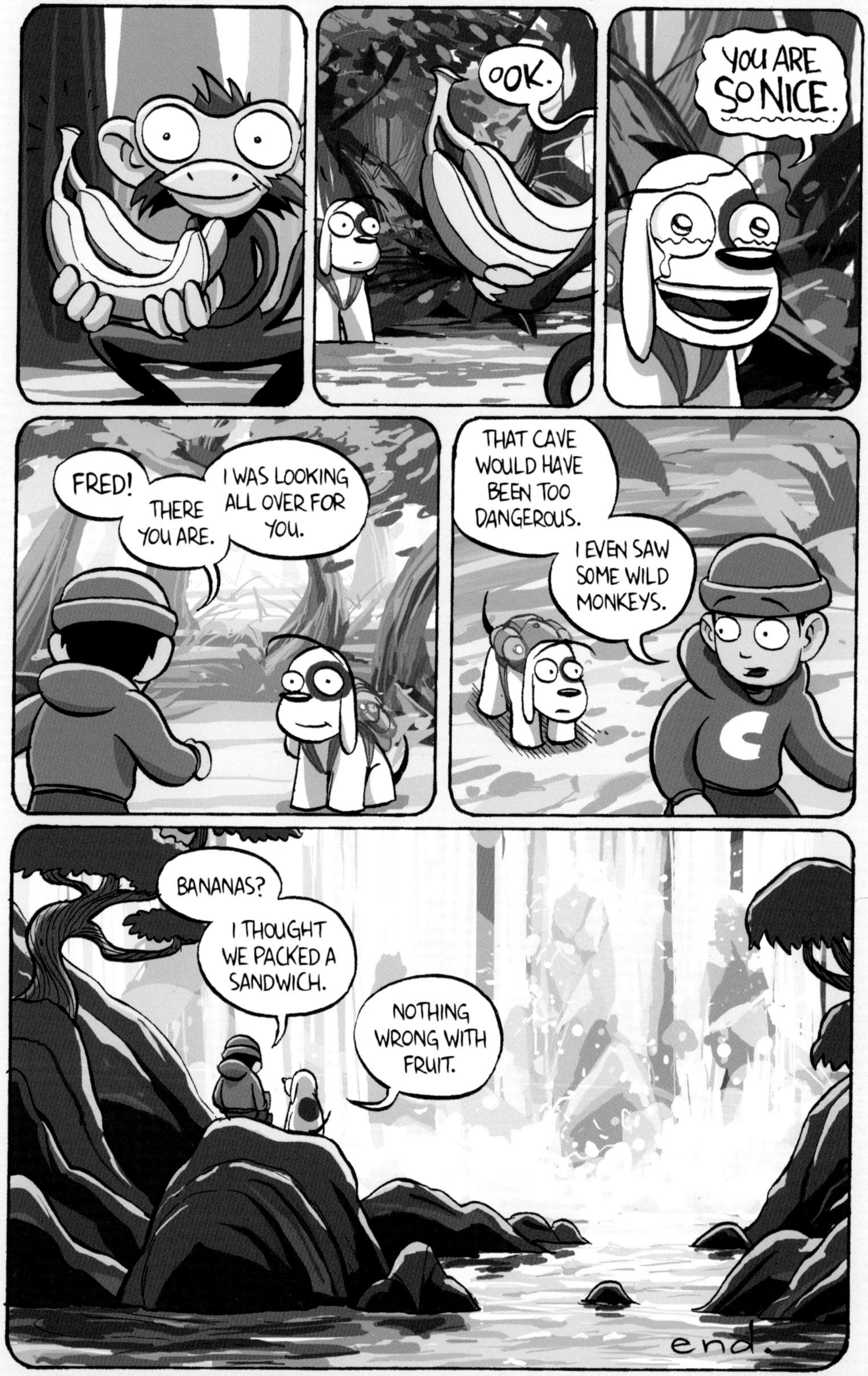
OOK.
YOU ARE SO NICE.
FRED!
THERE YOU ARE.
I WAS LOOKING ALL OVER FOR YOU.
THAT CAVE WOULD HAVE BEEN TOO DANGEROUS.
I EVEN SAW SOME WILD MONKEYS.
BANANAS?
I THOUGHT WE PACKED A SANDWICH.
NOTHING WRONG WITH FRUIT.
end.

Here I am getting ready to draw.

BEHIND THE SCENES

In this step-by-step process section, I'll show you how I actually go about creating a *Copper* comic. The steps include:

Turning an idea into a sketch

Penciling a page based on the sketch

Inking the penciled page

Cleaning up the image

Scanning the inked page into a computer

Digitally coloring the page

The way I draw *Copper* is far different from the way I draw most of my other comics. That's because *Copper*, a complete, single-page comic, is different from my longer comic stories in the Flight or Flight Explorer anthologies or my graphic novels *Amulet* and *Daisy Kutter*. Since these comic stories are very long, I needed to find ways to quicken the pace of drawing and producing them. So I adjusted my style to suit the need for speed. I used shortcuts such as inking with a pencil instead of a pen, or scanning my sketches and using them as the pencils by printing them out very large. Anything I could do to save me time.

When I work on each *Copper* comic, however, I slow down and take my time. I use simpler methods such as limiting the use of color gradation, space, and digital color layers (*Copper* is done predominantly with simple, flat colors). I believe that limitations can be very effective in fostering creativity, and these simpler methods force me to do more with less.

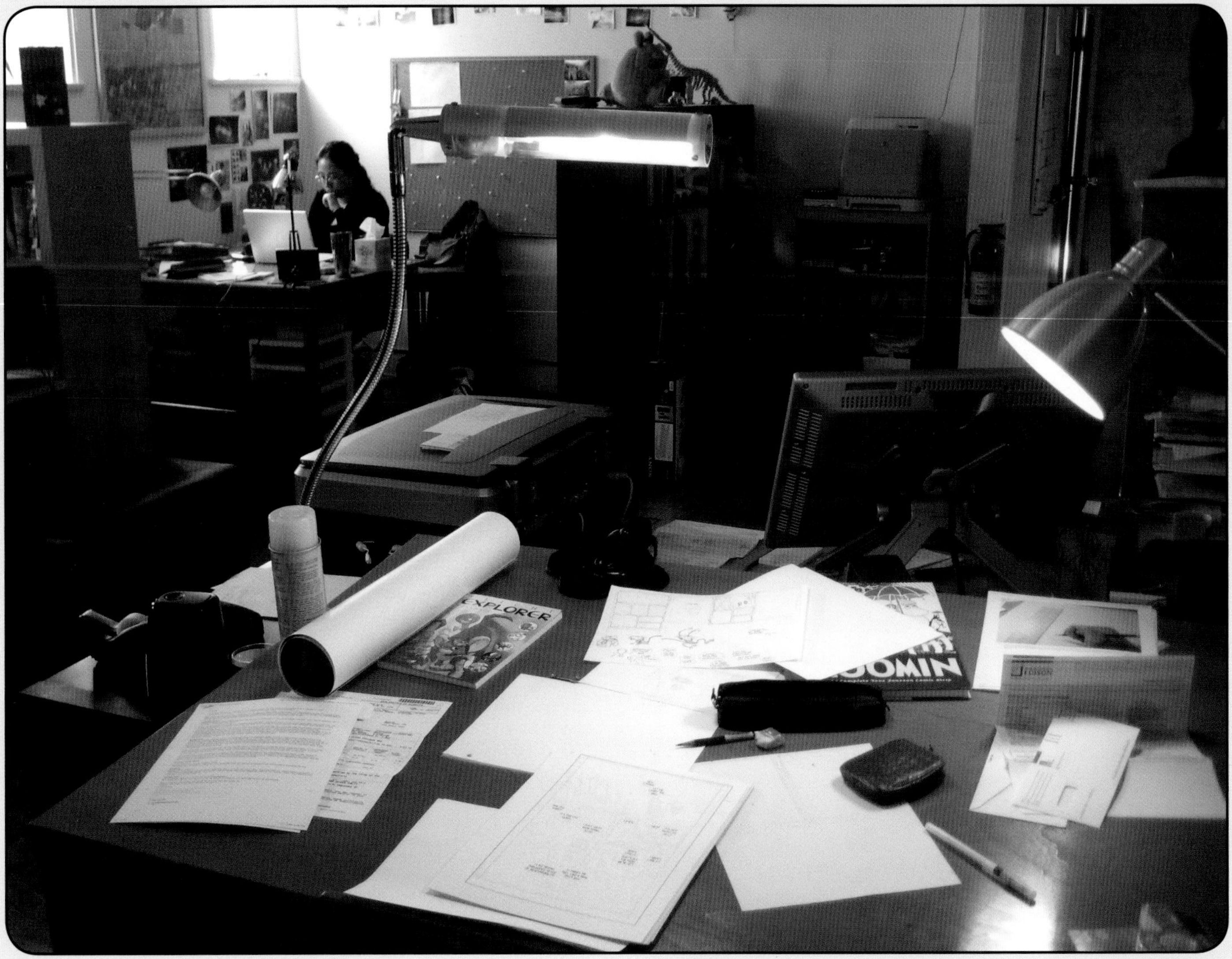
EXPLORER

This is the view from my desk. My wife, Amy, is working on her own books.

THE DRAWING BOARD

My desk is usually covered with books, movies, music, papers, pencils, and all sorts of junk. I like keeping most of my office very clean, but my desk is one place where I let loose. I love creative messes. Seeing all kinds of information around me gets my creativity flowing.

copper
JUST STAY CLOSE TO ME.
AND JUST REMEMBER TO NOT GO OUT IN THE OPEN.
IT'S REALLY HARD TO MOVE IN HERE.
YOU'LL GET USED TO IT.
GET OUT OF THERE.
UH OH.
I THINK THEY SEE ME.
THIS PLACE IS ACTUALLY BEAUTIFUL.
COPPER!
YOU'RE OUT IN THE OPEN!
WE'RE SPOTTED!
OH MAN,
ONE FALSE MOVE AND--
--COPPER?
I THINK I'M GONNA CALL IT A NIGHT, FRED.
DON'T STAY UP TOO LATE, OKAY?
JUST ONE MORE GAME.

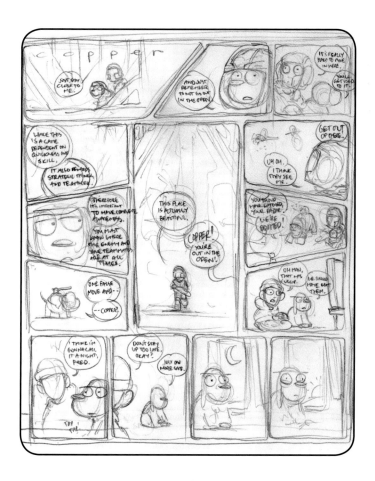

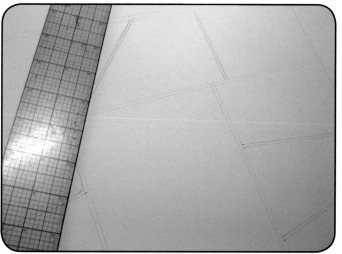

THUMBNAILS

Turning an Idea into a Story

I start by drawing a thumbnail of the *Copper* strip on a sheet of regular white paper. A thumbnail is a rough sketch version of the final comic page. In this case, I wanted to draw Copper and Fred inside of a video game, so I drew thumbnails around this simple idea. This thumbnail will be my guide as I lay out the *Copper* panels.

PANELS

Preparing the Canvas

My drawings for *Copper* are really BIG. This pad of Bristol paper is 19 by 24 inches. With a blue pencil, I draw lines to create a 15-by-15-inch square in the middle of the paper. This is the size of the final *Copper* strip. Inside this square box, I draw a line about a quarter-inch from the edge to establish the outermost panel borders.

Using my very rough thumbnail as a reference, I lay out all the panels I'll need to tell the story. These panels are not drafted to exact measurements. I just use a ruler and draw the panels to approximate sizes to save myself some time.

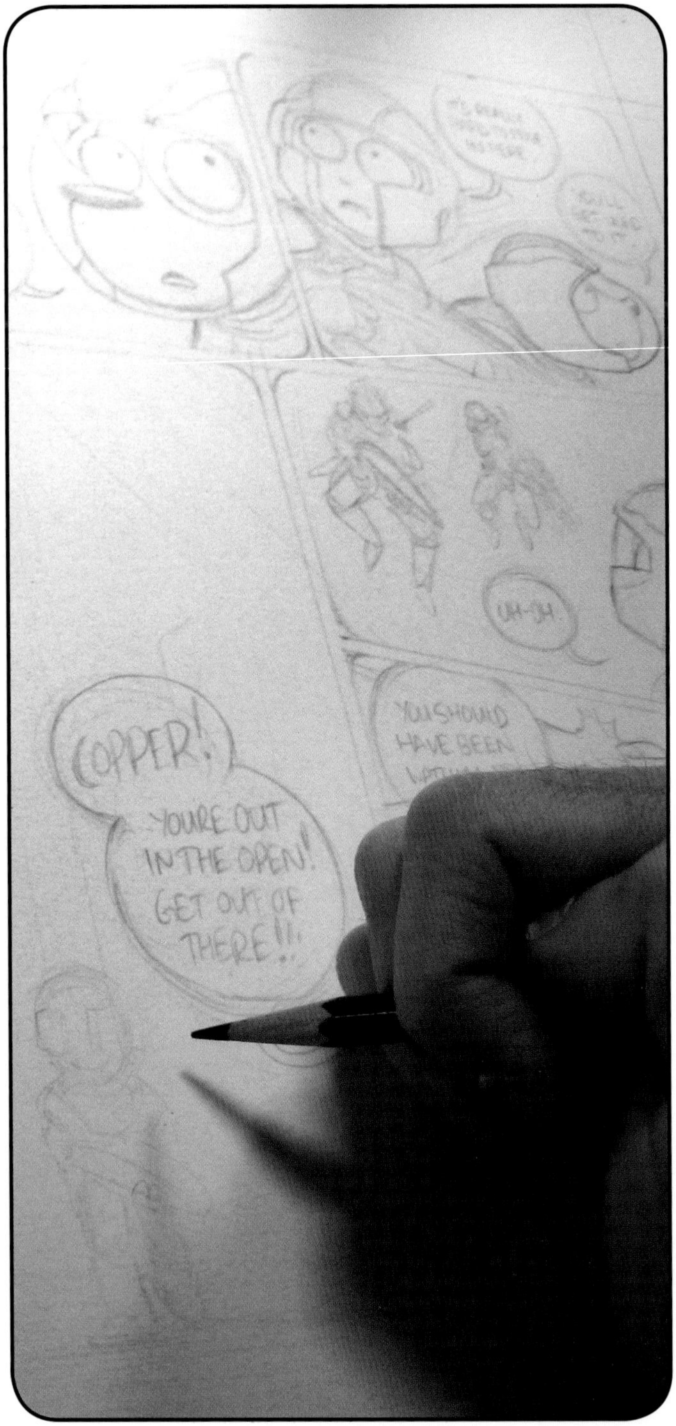
UH-OH.
COPPER!
YOURE OUT IN THE OPEN! GET OUT OF THERE!!

PENCILING

Laying the Foundation

Now we're ready to start penciling! I begin by scribbling rough versions of the images I want, and then go back to carve out all the details and solidify the shapes. I draw with a Prismacolor Col-Erase blue pencil. I find this pencil easy to use and the resulting lines easy to read. The blue color makes the lines invisible to a photocopier and can also be easily removed when scanned into a computer. Plus, it's erasable, so I don't have to worry about making mistakes.

In order to minimize the number of mistakes I make in my drawings, I use a lot of construction lines in my penciling. Construction lines are basic shapes drawn in a sketchy fashion; they're the basis for your final character and environment drawings. Construction lines are really helpful if you don't draw good shapes naturally, which I don't. I have to work hard for the image every time. In fact, whenever I sit down to work on a comic, especially *Copper*, I feel like I have to teach myself to draw all over again!

When I'm about halfway finished with the pencils, I also round the corners of the panels. For some reason, corner rounding gives me a sense of accomplishment and helps get me excited about finishing the rest of the strip.

It's all about inspiring – or tricking – yourself into getting things done. . . .

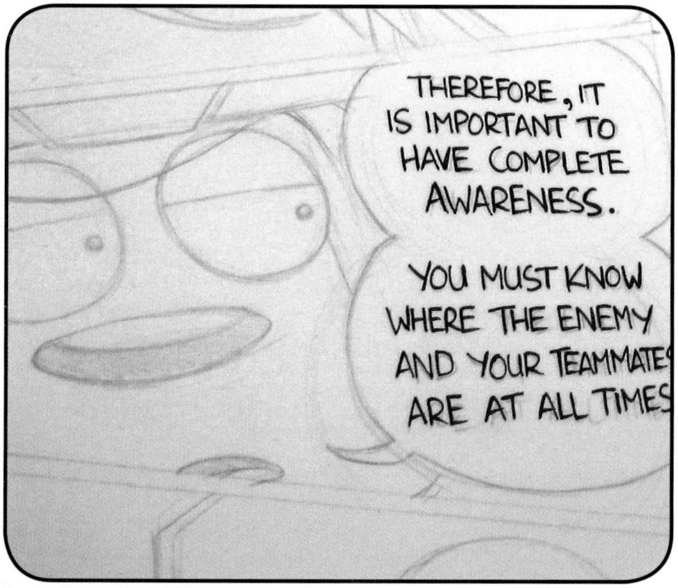
THEREFORE, IT IS IMPORTANT TO HAVE COMPLETE AWARENESS.
YOU MUST KNOW WHERE THE ENEMY AND YOUR TEAMMATES ARE AT ALL TIMES

LETTERING

Putting Words in Their Mouths

The pencils are finished, the dialogue is tightened up, and I've finessed any difficult-to-manage shapes in the fine details. So I grab a 0.3 Staedtler pigment liner pen and begin lettering the comic.

I prefer to hand letter my pages because I like to have control over the composition of every image in the drawing stage. (Since dialogue takes up so much room in a panel, I treat the letters like images.) I also like hand lettering because it gives me more organic control over the volume and flow of the characters' dialogue. Along with their expressions and movements, dialogue is the major indicator of any character's "acting" on the page, so I try to liven up any scene with fun text whenever I can.

The *Copper* comics in this book, with the exception of "Lunch Pack," are hand lettered. I use a digital font made from my handwriting for longer projects such as *Amulet*.

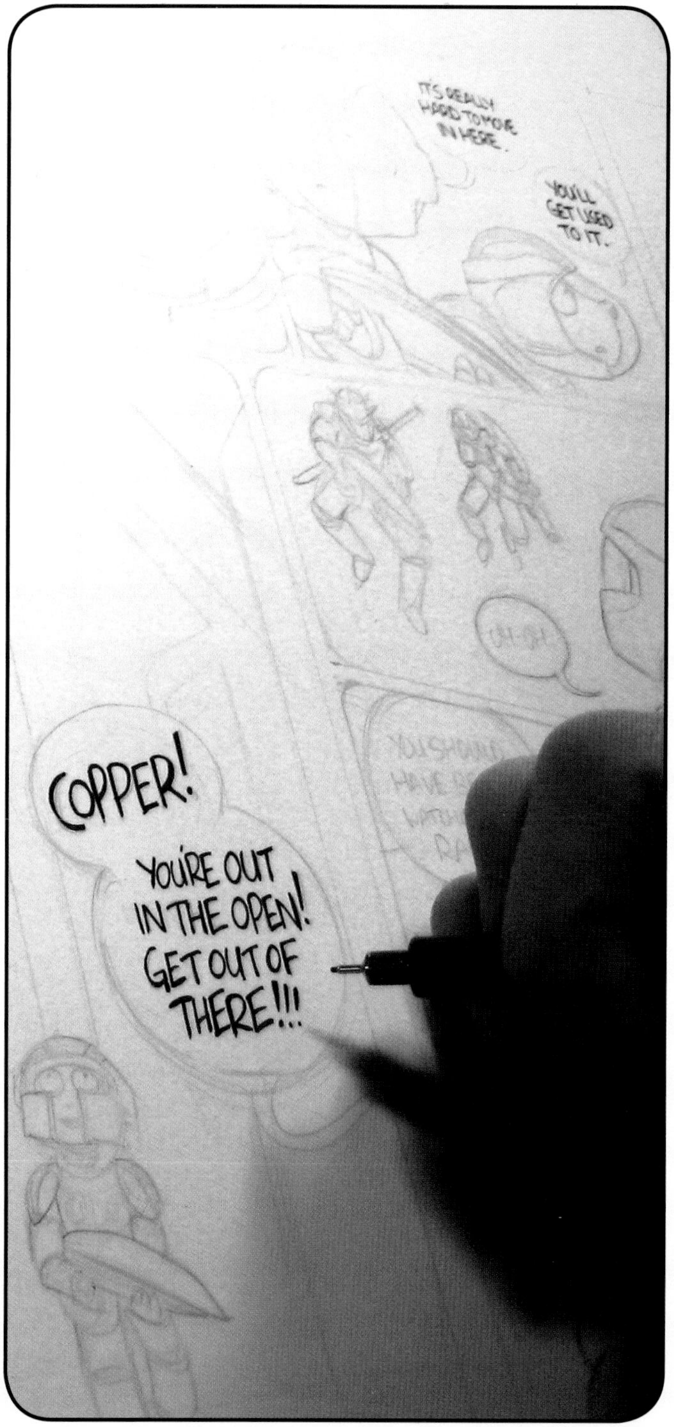
YOU'LL GET USED TO IT.
COPPER!
YOU'RE OUT IN THE OPEN! GET OUT OF THERE!!!

INKING

The Old-fashioned Way

Now it's time to break out the trusty old Hunt No. 102 Crow Quill dip pen. This is one of those old-fashioned pens that you actually dip into an inkwell. If there is a pen out there with better natural line variation, I have yet to see it. The ink is Higgins Black Magic India Ink by Sanford.

The dip pen is a difficult tool to master. I started using one back when I was about 12 years old, when I discovered that it was the pen comics professionals used to ink their comics. At first, I began using it wrong! I was applying the ink from the pen with the spoon-side facing up. I kept scratching the paper and ended up with thin lines.

The correct way to use a dip pen is spoon-side down, with the ink on it facing the paper. I know this seems dangerous, but don't worry. If used correctly, the ink will flow through the pen tip and not simply spill off and spoil your page.

After many years of breaking pen nibs, spilling ink, and ruining drawings, I've finally become comfortable with this old-fashioned tool, and I'm really quite fond of it. If you plan to use a nib pen, be sure to start early!

I make my way down the page, moving from left to right as I ink. I don't necessarily follow the panels in reading order. I go whichever way guarantees I won't run my drawing hand over any wet ink. With a dip pen, the ink dries very slowly. Only a few years ago, this page would have been covered in Wite-Out correction fluid to patch up all the smears left by my hand. Today, I'm much more adept because I've inked so many drawings, and now I rarely smudge the ink.

AND REMEMBER NOT TO GO OUT IN THE OPEN.
THEREFORE, IT IS IMPORTANT TO HAVE COMPLETE

COPPER! YOU'RE OUT IN THE OPEN! GET OUT OF THERE!!!
YOU SHOULD HAVE BEEN WATCHING YOUR RADAR!
NOW WE'RE DOOMED!
WAIT, THAT ONE DIDN'T COUNT.

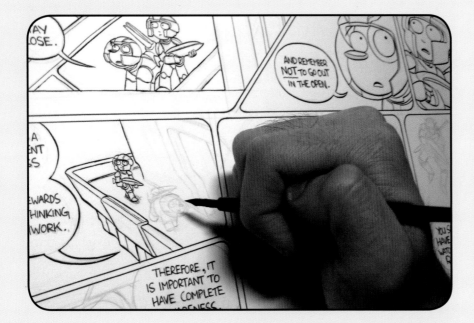

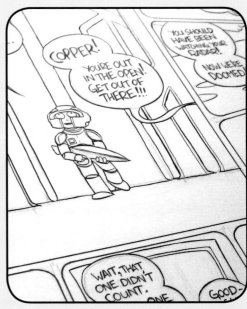

GOING DIGITAL
Technology as a Paintbrush

Once I put the old-school pen and ink away, things get a little advanced. You may not need all of this technology to create your own fine comic strip, but these digital tools do a lot to help me bring a professional level of finish to my comics. Coloring using the computer allows for tons of flexibility in the editing process and nearly all final files used for print production are digital nowadays.

For the digital part of the *Copper* process, I use a:

Computer
Scanner
Drawing Tablet
Adobe Photoshop

My computer is hooked up to a tablet screen and also a regular drawing tablet. A tablet is a tool that allows the user to draw on the computer. While the tablet screen allows me to draw directly on the screen, the regular tablet allows me to draw without my hand getting in the way of my view. Both tablets have their advantages, and I enjoy using both for different projects. However, the regular tablet can be purchased for a modest price (some cost less than a hundred dollars), while the screen is very expensive. I recommend using a simple, cheap tablet to begin with. I got my first by trading away a video game system!

Adobe Photoshop is the computer software I use to color all of my comics. It is an incredibly powerful piece of software that most professionals use to create and touch up images.

Here we begin the digital part of the process by scanning the comic into the computer. I currently use a large-format scanner to scan my comics. This is a luxury I was not able to afford until recently. For most of my career, I used small, cheap scanners purchased at the local electronics store. I used to have to scan the *Copper* comics in six separate parts and then piece them together in the computer. Now, I only need to stitch together two pieces! This saves me a lot of time. However, the cheaper, smaller scanners and a little extra patience will do the job just fine. I scan the comic at 300 DPI or higher to make sure I have enough information to make the files read clearly when printed. "DPI" stands for "dots per inch" and represents the density of the information being scanned. The higher the DPI is, the sharper the image will look.

COLORING

The Magic of Digital Paint

This is the comic after it has been scanned into the computer and pieced together to form one image. It is now a Photoshop file and I can begin to work on it digitally.

Using the Hue/Saturation and Level adjusts, I can cancel out the blue lines and the paper texture, cleaning the image and leaving me with only the black lines to work with.

The linework is left on its own layer, set to multiply (which allows you to see through the white portions of the page), and I will begin painting on separate layers underneath the linework.

I start by selecting the panels and coloring them with a neutral value. An example of a neutral value is the color gray, since it is lighter than black and darker than white. It is helpful to begin with this neutral color and add to it rather than to just drop different colors onto the white page. This allows for the color palette of the entire piece to remain balanced and cohesive. Painters call this applying a "key" color to the image. In this case, I chose a tan color to work from. The dialogue bubbles are kept white, so they are easy to read.

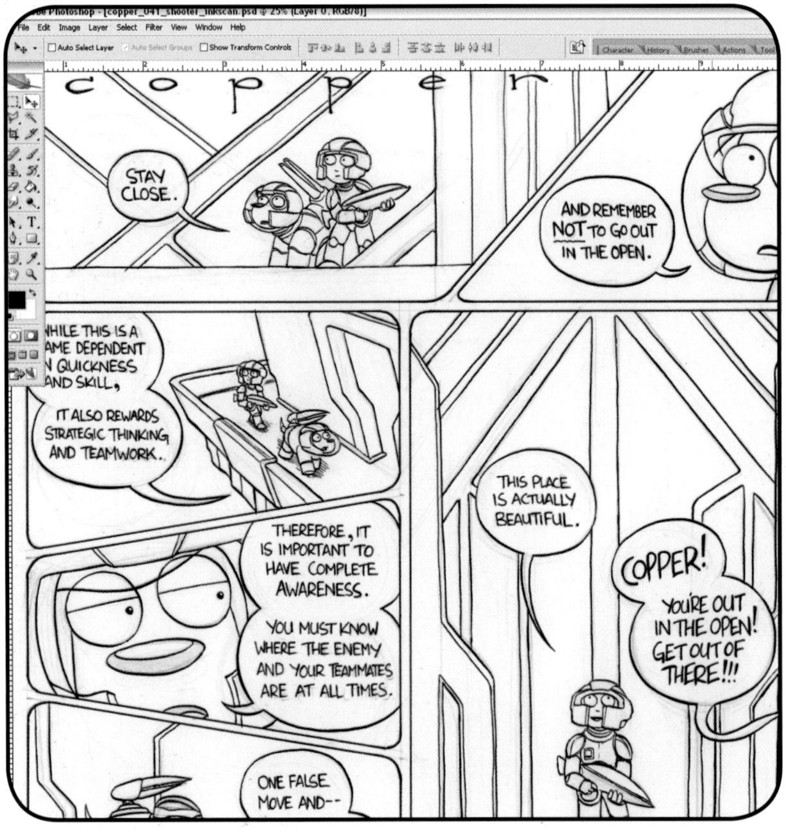
c o p p e r
STAY CLOSE.
AND REMEMBER NOT TO GO OUT IN THE OPEN.
HILE THIS IS A AME DEPENDENT N QUICKNESS AND SKILL,
IT ALSO REWARDS STRATEGIC THINKING AND TEAMWORK.
THIS PLACE IS ACTUALLY BEAUTIFUL.
THEREFORE, IT IS IMPORTANT TO HAVE COMPLETE AWARENESS.
YOU MUST KNOW WHERE THE ENEMY AND YOUR TEAMMATES ARE AT ALL TIMES.
COPPER!
YOU'RE OUT IN THE OPEN! GET OUT OF THERE!!!
ONE FALSE MOVE AND--

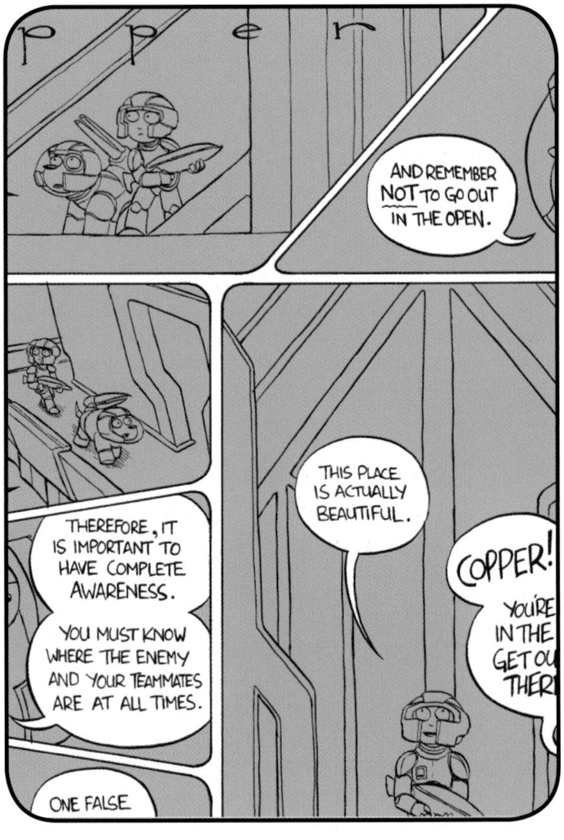
p p e r
AND REMEMBER NOT TO GO OUT IN THE OPEN.
THIS PLACE IS ACTUALLY BEAUTIFUL.
THEREFORE, IT IS IMPORTANT TO HAVE COMPLETE AWARENESS.
YOU MUST KNOW WHERE THE ENEMY AND YOUR TEAMMATES ARE AT ALL TIMES.
COPPER!
ONE FALSE

The next step is to color the characters and objects, setting them on separate layers for easy adjustment. While Copper and Fred have a designated set of colors, everything else around them is fair game for adjustment. The only rule is to make sure all the colors look good together. Easier said than done.

The characters and objects are painted with simple colors first, and on their own layers. These will provide the base for the comic's final color palette.

Since I am using only flat colors, I can easily select the individual colors and change them using tools like the Hue/Saturation adjust. I spend a lot of time messing around with the colors to get the comic to look just right. This process is kind of like choosing clothes to wear for the day. Sometimes it can take forever!

Here I have shifted the background panels to cooler colors using the Hue/Saturation adjust. I found that these cooler colors better fit the blue of the characters' armor. The green color is a mix of the tan color established above and the cooler blues of the armor. Having an understanding of how colors mix together is very helpful at this point, and one of the great things about working in digital media is the ability to test out various color combinations to see what happens. Before working on the computer, I never formally learned to paint or use color, but now I feel I have a good grasp of colors and basic painting techniques.

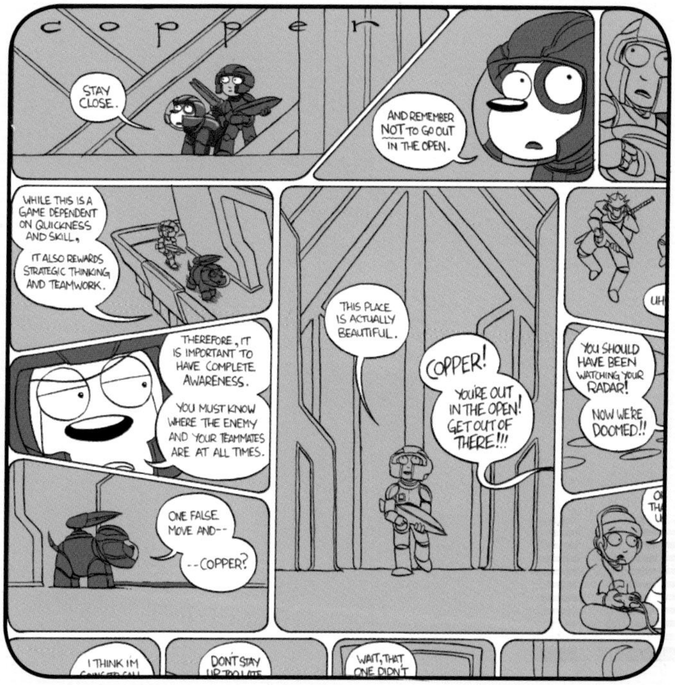
copper
STAY CLOSE.
AND REMEMBER NOT TO GO OUT IN THE OPEN.
WHILE THIS IS A GAME DEPENDENT ON QUICKNESS AND SKILL,
IT ALSO REWARDS STRATEGIC THINKING AND TEAMWORK.
THEREFORE, IT IS IMPORTANT TO HAVE COMPLETE AWARENESS.
YOU MUST KNOW WHERE THE ENEMY AND YOUR TEAMMATES ARE AT ALL TIMES.
ONE FALSE MOVE AND--
--COPPER?
THIS PLACE IS ACTUALLY BEAUTIFUL.
COPPER!
YOU'RE OUT IN THE OPEN! GET OUT OF THERE!!!
YOU SHOULD HAVE BEEN WATCHING YOUR RADAR!
NOW WE'RE DOOMED!!

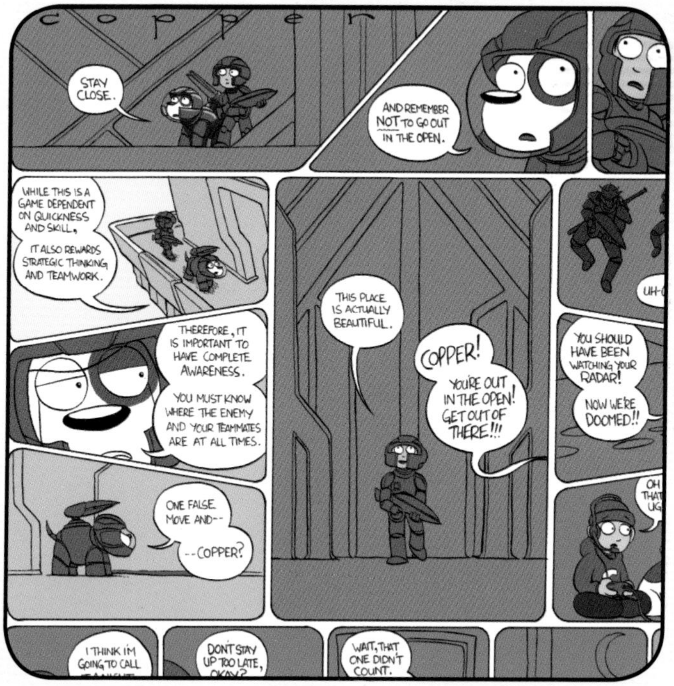
copper
STAY CLOSE.
AND REMEMBER NOT TO GO OUT IN THE OPEN.
WHILE THIS IS A GAME DEPENDENT ON QUICKNESS AND SKILL,
IT ALSO REWARDS STRATEGIC THINKING AND TEAMWORK.
THEREFORE, IT IS IMPORTANT TO HAVE COMPLETE AWARENESS.
YOU MUST KNOW WHERE THE ENEMY AND YOUR TEAMMATES ARE AT ALL TIMES.
ONE FALSE MOVE AND--
--COPPER?
THIS PLACE IS ACTUALLY BEAUTIFUL.
COPPER!
YOU'RE OUT IN THE OPEN! GET OUT OF THERE!!!
YOU SHOULD HAVE BEEN WATCHING YOUR RADAR!
NOW WE'RE DOOMED!!
WAIT, THAT ONE DIDN'T COUNT.

copper
STAY CLOSE.
AND REMEMBER NOT TO GO OUT IN THE OPEN.
WHILE THIS IS A GAME DEPENDENT ON QUICKNESS AND SKILL,
IT ALSO REWARDS STRATEGIC THINKING AND TEAMWORK.
THEREFORE, IT IS IMPORTANT TO HAVE COMPLETE AWARENESS.
YOU MUST KNOW WHERE THE ENEMY AND YOUR TEAMMATES ARE AT ALL TIMES.
ONE FALSE MOVE AND--
--COPPER?
THIS PLACE IS ACTUALLY BEAUTIFUL.
COPPER!
YOU'RE OUT IN THE OPEN! GET OUT OF THERE!!!
YOU SHOULD HAVE BEEN WATCHING YOUR RADAR!
NOW WE'RE DOOMED!!
DON'T STAY UP TOO LATE, OKAY?
WAIT, THAT ONE DIDN'T COUNT.

copper
STAY CLOSE.
AND REMEMBER NOT TO GO OUT IN THE OPEN.
IT ALSO REWARDS STRATEGIC THINKING AND TEAMWORK.
THEREFORE, IT IS IMPORTANT TO HAVE COMPLETE AWARENESS.
YOU MUST KNOW WHERE THE ENEMY AND YOUR TEAMMATES ARE AT ALL TIMES.
ONE FALSE MOVE AND--
--COPPER?
THIS PLACE IS ACTUALLY BEAUTIFUL.
COPPER!
YOU'RE OUT IN THE OPEN! GET OUT OF THERE!!!
UH-OH.
YOU SHOULD HAVE BEEN WATCHING YOUR RADAR!
NOW WE'RE DOOMED!!
WAIT, THAT ONE DIDN'T COUNT.

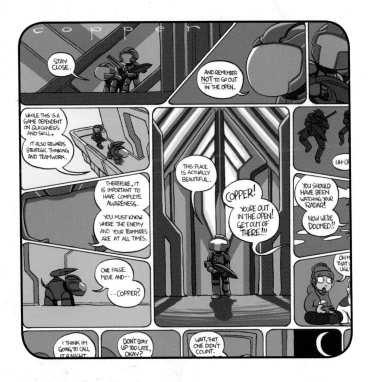

In most cases, I focus on one panel at the beginning, and get the colors just right for that panel. That way, I can use this fully colored panel as a guide for the rest of the comic. Once a color is selected for a particular item, like the armor, I can just apply that same color to the armor in each of the rest of the panels and save myself a lot of time.

On this comic strip, I decided to use effects layers. By applying a solid orange color on the characters' faces on a separate layer and turning the layer transparent, I create the illusion of a clear mask on the helmet. An effect layer is also applied to the background to create the illusion of shadows. This can be seen in the darker greenish hues on the backgrounds of the version below. Tricks like these can add depth to the images.

In the later stages of the coloring process, I add highlights to the characters and backgrounds to indicate the lighting in the scene. Putting a lighter blue on the tops of the helmets and armor really helps give the comic a sense of space.

While it may seem easy to do, the coloring process actually takes quite a while. This is a good chance for me to listen to music or an audiobook while I work, and I usually have a lot of fun during the process.

Here is the finished product. If I did my job correctly, the reader will not be thinking too much about the making of *Copper* and will simply enjoy this story.

I hope this step-by-step was helpful and informative for all you budding cartoonists. We can never have enough good cartoonists in the world, since everybody loves cartoons, don't they? Good luck on your fantastic creations and thanks for reading this book!

Acknowledgments

I'd like to thank my wife, Amy, and my assistants, Anthony Wu, Jason Caffoe, and Stuart Livingston, for helping me put together this book. Anthony and Jason did a wonderful job coloring the "Lunch Pack" story, and Stuart helped flatten some of the single-page comics. Amy helped with the organization and formatting of files, and has provided love and support throughout my career in comics.

Thanks, you guys. I couldn't possibly have done this without you!

OTHER GRAPHIC NOVELS BY KAZU KIBUISHI

AMULET
KAZU KIBUISHI
BOOK ONE
THE STONEKEEPER

AMULET
KAZU KIBUISHI
BOOK TWO
THE STONEKEEPER'S CURSE

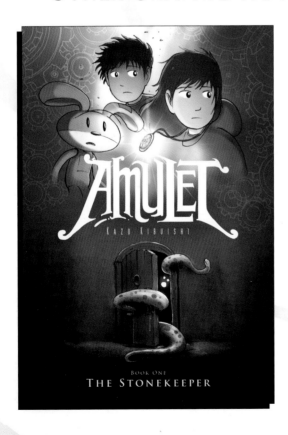

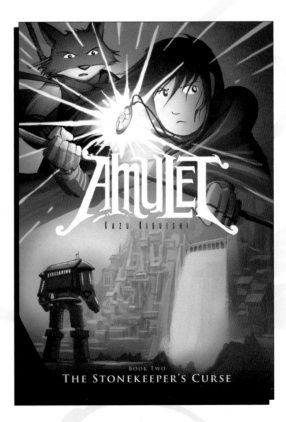